'Help me, Ferg!' Mick screamed, yanking at his arm as if he wanted to tear it from its socket.

Fergus ignored the plea. Instead, he turned his back on his partner and concentrated on escaping from the trench. The cries mounted in pitch and agony, but Fergus kept his eyes averted. He had seen enough in one quick look. Another glance at the ravaged body of his partner would turn him to stone. He searched frantically for finger-holds that were not in the soft soil. He did not turn again until the animal sounds stopped in mid-shriek. The sight brought him to his knees . . .

Now it was Fergus's time to scream. The will to live brought him once more to his feet. His hands clawed at the top of the hole, finding no purchase but bringing down sprays of dirt that found his gasping mouth. He screamed and leapt, screamed and leapt. Between the screams, behind him, came the rattling sound of dry bones.

And then there was an unholy silence . . .

Also by Brent Monahan in
New English Library paperback

The Book of Common Dread
The Blood of the Covenant

About the author

Brent Monahan lives in Yardley, Pennsylvania, USA, with his wife and two children. He is the author of several acclaimed novels of horror. With Michael Maryk, he co-authored *DeathBite*, which was adapted for film.

The Uprising

Brent Monahan

NEW ENGLISH LIBRARY
Hodder and Stoughton

First published in Great Britain in 1996
by Hodder and Stoughton
A division of Hodder Headline PLC

A New English Library paperback

10 9 8 7 6 5 4 3 2 1

British Library Cataloguing in Publication Data
A CIP catalogue record for this title is available from the British Library

ISBN 0 340 67168 8

Printed and bound in Great Britain by
Cox & Wyman Ltd, Reading, Berkshire

Hodder and Stoughton
A division of Hodder Headline PLC
338 Euston Road
London NW1 3BH

This book is for Bonnie—
*and for the cousins
in Carrick.*

The hand of the Lord was upon me, and he brought me out by the Spirit of the Lord, and set me down in the midst of the valley; it was full of bones.

And he led me round among them; and behold, there were very many upon the valley; and lo, they were very dry. And he said to me, "Son of man, can these bones live?" And I answered, "O Lord God, thou knowest." Again he said to me "Prophesy to these bones, and say to them, O dry bones, hear the word of the Lord. Thus says the Lord God to these bones: Behold, I will cause breath to enter you, and you shall live. And I will lay sinews upon you, and will cause flesh to come upon you, and cover you with skin, and put breath in you, and you shall live; and you shall know that I am the Lord."

So I prophesied as I was commanded; and as I prophesied, there was a noise, and behold, a rattling; and the bones came together, bone to bone. And as I looked, there were sinews on them, and flesh had come upon them, and skin had covered them, but there was no breath in them.

Then he said to me, "Prophesy to the breath, prophesy, son of man, and say to the breath, Thus says the Lord God: Come from the four winds, O breath, and breathe upon these slain, that they may live." So I prophesied as he commanded me, and the breath came into them, and they lived, and stood upon their feet, an exceedingly great host.

Ezekiel 37

1

Late June 1988

Roundabouts are murder.

Traffic circles everywhere are deadly inventions. Keenan MacBreed knew; in his thirty-two years he had driven highways over much of the world. But the Irish roundabouts were especially treacherous to him because he was an American and less than a week back in Ireland. He had hardly reaccustomed himself to driving on the left side of the road much less negotiating a busy traffic circle in clockwise fashion.

So it was that Keenan missed the main highway south out of Belfast. A lorry had loomed up on his left, and he had been too busy avoiding it to notice the highway sign. Before he knew, he was out of the roundabout and heading southwest toward Lisburn. Vexed, Keenan screwed up the corner of his mouth and admitted to himself that it hadn't been just the roundabout. He lived in Boston, where rotaries—the New Englanders' name for traffic circles— were traveled by the most aggressive drivers in the States. If one could navigate among the descendents of revolutionary hotheads, an Irish traffic circle should be simple.

The truth was that Keenan wanted out of Belfast in a hurry and he was driving too fast. His business in the Emerald Isle was in the Republic and not in Northern Ireland. Not where Catholics and Protestants had been killing each other for more than three hundred years— where the innocent suffered from bullet and bomb almost as often as the combatant.

Two kilometers down the road, in a suburb of Belfast called Dunmurry, Keenan·pulled the college's Range Rover off the road and onto the cinder berm. He snatched the roadmap from atop the metal box that was the cause of his trek up to Belfast. The box protected delicate carbon dating equipment that could not, it seemed, be repaired in any part of southern Ireland. Someone else had driven the ailing instrument up to Belfast a week before he had arrived from the States. Keenan would be the one using it all summer at Trinity college, so he was obliged to fetch the damned thing.

Keenan snapped open the map and dug the horn-rimmed reading glasses out of his jacket pocket. On the floor behind the driver's seat lay a brown Stetson fedora with an "Indiana Jones" trademark inside the crown. That was as close as Keenan came to the romantic image of an archeologist. No cracked-leather bomber jacket. No bull whip. No wire-rimmed eyeglasses. No scars. No raffish good looks. He stood an inch over six foot and carried himself lanky. His appearance was average and thoroughly Irish. Average build, though a bit more muscle than most. Not the emerald green eyes and flame red hair advertised by Aer Lingus and the Irish Tourist Board but the cool blue eyes and dark brown hair common to most on the island. Average shaped head, neither too broad nor too long—what archeologist Keenan MacBreed would describe as mesocephalic. But the stuff inside the head was far better than average and had enabled him to learn more about ancient Ireland and its people than any other living man.

The map indicated that the main highway could be

intercepted just southwest of Lisburn. Keenan refolded it and put the Range Rover in gear. As he steered back onto the road he looked around at little Dunmurry. It wasn't much different from Belfast. Gray. Stolid. Depressed. The only vibrant color decorated the wall of one roadside building—it was a political mural, showing a father and son reading a newspaper. The newspaper was *An Phoblacht,* proclaimed by the mural as the official organ of the Republican movement. Behind father and son stood the shadow of grandfather or some other ancestor, at the ready with a rifle. The red, yellow and green paints had little gradation and the artwork had a cartoon quality, but the message was eloquent nonetheless.

Surely it was a trick of perception, Keenan reflected, but all colors seemed to pale in Northern Ireland. The buildings on both parts of the island were mostly stone—elemental grays, browns and whites. But in Northern Ireland, the soot of a hundred and fifty years of heavy industry seemed to cloak them in ash. The grayness of poverty covered the people as well. More than a hundred years of booming industry had finally ended. Shipbuilding, the lifeblood of Belfast, had slowed dramatically and what world orders remained were being stolen away by the Japanese. Linen, the other major industry, had also largely evaporated. Keenan knew that almost 60 per cent of the Catholic men of Belfast were unemployed. He had seen the evidence on every street corner, where sullen eyes sought outlets for idle frustration. The whole of Northern Ireland was a pressure cooker with an old, tight lid on it.

The ordeal of entering Northern Ireland had also grayed Keenan's outlook. A mile before the border, yellow road signs warned motorists not to stop under any conditions. Keenan imagined himself being flagged down by a harmless-looking hitchhiker, pulling over to give him a lift and suddenly being surrounded by two or three toughs with guns. The college's Rover and his credentials would be

3

commandeered so that they could smuggle arms or explosives into the North, and he would be left in a nearby ditch, unconscious or dead.

At the border Keenan's foreboding had increased. The British soldiers who guarded it were not merely boys in khaki uniforms but likenesses of Falkland War combatants —battle-wary and heavily armed. A full squad paced along the back-up of vehicles, studying the cars and drivers prior to the formal inspection. Just beyond the border, the traffic was funneled into a large structure. More soldiers moved among the cars, poking their heads in suspiciously, firing off questions and demanding identification. Barriers and ramps prevented any car from dodging out of line and breaking for the open.

Once inside Northern Ireland, Keenan had been forced to stop twice. Both times, those who scrutinized him were not British soldiers but members of the less threatening Royal Ulster Constabulary. The shotguns and automatic rifles they carried, however, were enough to keep Keenan's nerves coiled tight. He did not hold himself a coward for wanting away from "The Troubles" as quickly as possible.

The Troubles, Keenan reflected despondently. The quintessential Irish euphemism. Only the Irish, a race so famous for their control of language, could devise such a benign name to describe such a horror. Not "The Troubles;" "The Horror," Keenan thought. The first three hundred years of occupation had been bad enough. But in the past nineteen years, since British soldiers were imported to restore order to the riot-shattered streets of Northern Ireland, the bloodshed had been appalling. Keenan remembered the 2,600 dead since August 14, 1969. Most of them civilians, both Protestant and Catholic. And 30,000 more wounded, many maimed for life. But this was only the bloody face of the monster they called "The Troubles." The vital heart inside the dark beast was despair, a despair nourished by the knowledge that an entire generation had been born and raised to accept hatred, violence and sudden death as an

4

immutable fact of life in Northern Ireland. Hope was dead, expunged from their collective vocabulary of emotions. Keenan could not imagine a greater horror.

As he entered the outskirts of Lisburn, Keenan began seeing the evidence of some large-scale activity. Cars were parked along both sides of the main road and in every alley. People walked toward him in small throngs, with uncharacteristically broad smiles on their faces. The day added to their cheer, Keenan supposed, because it was sunnier and warmer than the usual late-June afternoon. Then he spotted a sign tacked up on a pole. Lisburn Fun Run, it said. The traffic ahead of his Range Rover slowed to a crawl, even though the Fun Run seemed to be coming to a close.

Toward the center of town, the traffic was being directed into a detour. Keenan was willing to wait a while rather than go off course again and get himself thoroughly lost. A policeman stood in the middle of the road, directing the creeping traffic. Keenan cranked the driver's window down another turn and leaned out.

"Excuse me, guard." The policeman raised his eyebrows at the American accent. "Can you tell me how much longer until this road is reopened?"

"Only a few minutes, sir," the policeman replied. "The final race is just finishing up." His arm indicated a space where a car was pulling out. "You could wait there."

Keenan nodded his thanks. He pulled into the parking place, turned off his engine and settled back in his seat. The last runners staggered and weaved toward the finish line, and well-wishers closed in from the sidewalks, pacing easily beside them, offering drinks and towels. A group of young men in running togs approached, flanked by several British soldiers. The runners had obviously finished some time before and looked well recovered. It was also obvious to Keenan that the group members were fast friends and that the runners were soldiers out of uniform. One of their number caught Keenan's stare and gave him a merry wink.

Then they were past the Range Rover. Keenan followed

the group in his rear view mirror, watched the six men in running gear pile into a blue van parked in an alleyway just behind him. Their uniformed buddies peeled off and jogged into the street.

"Come on, Sarge," Keenan heard one of the soldiers say to the traffic policeman. "It's all over. Let 'em through, ferchrissake!"

The policeman apparently agreed; he waved the cars straight on, then walked to the corner and pulled down the detour sign.

Keenan fired up the Range Rover. The driver of the blue van leaned on his horn and kept nosing the vehicle forward until he had cleared the way for himself. The van lurched ahead with a roar but was forced to stop for a traffic light a block ahead.

Keenan was still looking out his rear view mirror for an opening in the traffic when he heard the explosion. His head swung forward involuntarily at the tremendous roar. His eyes squeezed shut at the fireball in the middle of the road. When he had fought them back open a second later, the white ball had shrunk to a yellow-orange upward-licking tongue of flame not much larger than the van within its center. He fixed his stare on the blackened, twisted van, still rolling but now in an arc that took it across the road, up the sidewalk and to a jarring halt against a wrought-iron fence.

A sizzling hunk of metal fell from the sky onto the Range Rover's hood. Keenan started off the seat. Part of him wanted to slide down onto the protection of the Rover's floor; the dominant part kept him frozen in place, staring slack-jawed at the carnage in front of him. From out of the destroyed van's bright flame and greasy smoke emerged a lone figure, no longer a young man in running gear but like a blazing, tar-coated skeleton. It took half a dozen faltering steps and collapsed in the road, to run no more. No one came forward to help. The onlookers either stayed on the ground where they had thrown themselves, attended to the handful of injured fellow-observers or merely leaned against poles and buildings, maintaining airs of calm curiosity.

It was the last group that shocked and revolted Keenan, who locked his fingers around the Rover's steering wheel to stop their trembling. Not one or two but half a dozen people in his view regarded the mass cremation with fatalistic resignation. Closest to him stood a man in a wool jacket, his hands thrust deeply into its pockets. Did one hand still clutch the radio control to the bomb's detonator? Or was the terrorist the woman calmly wheeling away the baby carriage? Or had someone been waiting patiently behind a window facing the street? In guerrilla warfare such as this, fought even amid a Fun Run, who was safe? And wasn't that the point?

Keenan MacBreed wiped the tears from his eyes. He had driven fast that day but not fast enough. He had been forced to look into the bleeding face of The Horror. He fervently hoped that he would never be forced to look on it again. He hoped in vain.

2

August 9, 1988

"Rotten weather for turf diggers," observed Mick Dunphy. "Most tractors'll mire down afore they reach the bogs."

"But fine weather for gravediggers," Fergus MacMahon countered professionally, studying the same slate-blue clouds his partner watched. "Just enough rain to make the first foot easy spading."

Mick grunted his agreement, stabbing the butt of his cigarette out on the shed's stone foundation. He noticed that the tips of his boots were getting wet from the rain dripping off the roof. He pulled his feet in tighter toward the backs of his thighs. At the same time he inched his back up straighter against the cold wall. "Looks like it's about to stop."

Fergus patted Mick's knee. "No hurry. They're not goin' anywhere. In fact, the longer they stay in the ground, the more it'll please Father Flynn. And don't forget—Dublin pays us by the hour, not the body."

"Bless 'em all, whoever they may be," Mick intoned.

Fergus pointed to Mick's shirt pocket. "Pass me a coffin nail, will ya?"

8

Mick fetched the pack of Woodbines and tapped the bottom. A single cigarette popped into view. "Not to mention how healthy the valley is lately. A good livin' summer is a bad dyin' summer."

"True," agreed Fergus. "It's a long stretch 'til flu season." He yawned grandly, exposing the dark gaps between his teeth. The missing teeth, a weatherbeaten complexion and the salt-and-peppering of his stubbled beard made him appear considerably older than his forty-eight years. At forty-four, Mick had no dental gaps, but his veined cheeks and a bulbous drinker's nose, however, aged his looks as well.

"Can you believe the fuss Father Flynn and the others put up over bones so old?" Fergus remarked.

Mick answered with an ambiguous grunt.

"I mean, it's not as if anyone has a father or even a grandfather up here," Fergus went on. "These are *old!*"

"Any older and we'd find the jawbone of Samson's ass," Mick declared, as if he were performing for a large audience.

"Or maybe the bone of Samson's own ass," Fergus quipped.

Mick grunted again. "Bones. I'll bet they don't get this worked up movin' a graveyard in Sweden or Denmark. Lutherans are pragmatic, y'know. It's the Catholics who always get excited about bones."

"Used to worship them in the Middle Ages," Fergus added knowingly, after blowing smoke into the drizzle. "Paraded them around with pieces of The True Cross and the thorns from The Crown."

"What do you mean, *used* to worship them?" Mick retorted. "I know for a fact that—"

Fergus rose to his feet. "Tell us later. It's clearing up. Back to the holes, Dunphy!"

"Speaking of holes," Mick said, following after his partner. "How many Kerry men does it take to wash a downstairs window?"

"Tell me."

"Four. One to wash the window, one to hold the ladder—"

"And two to dig the hole for the ladder," Fergus interrupted.

Mick scowled. "You heard it."

"I didn't," Fergus declared. "You just said 'speaking of holes.' How thick do you think I am?"

"You're a gravedigger, aren't ya?" Mick proclaimed. "Get in yer machine and let's go!"

Fergus fired up the backhoe and began deftly working the controls. The cemetery around the machine was a cratered wreck. MacMahon and Dunphy had never dug up an entire graveyard before and, for want of a better plan, had begun digging up sites around the central passageway and working their way inward. They were almost to the center. Most of the stones lay horizontal on the ground. Precious few headstones and crosses rose above the sod and those that did listed precariously in all directions, mossy gray with age and all but unreadable from the many decades of erosion. Before the gravediggers had begun, the ancient cemetery had looked more like a stony pasture. Now there was hardly a square yard where the emerald grasses had not been buried or at least sullied by upturned earth. Half the excavations they had not yet bothered to fill in.

The ground shook with the digging machine's vitality. Mick watched its repetitive movements from a distance, leaning on his shovel, waiting to do the delicate work the machine could not manage.

Fergus pushed his right arm forward, moving the digger's bucket down, so that its steel teeth could bite hard into the rich, brown soil. The bucket scraped against something wooden and hollow-sounding. Fergus raised the arm up and out of the way.

Mick hopped down into the hole and put his muscular arms to the shovel.

Fergus throttled the machine engine down so he could be heard. "How deep is it?"

"Maybe three feet," Mick answered. "Shallow one."

"I wonder why," Fergus mused, aloud. "Three feet's common in a lot of old graveyards, but not this one. Not so far. All the others were down proper deep."

The spadefuls of rich earth began to fly out of the hole, followed by a brief stillness, and then the sound of Mick's voice. "Put the chains on. I think this box will hold."

The coffin was not sturdy but it held together for the short trip to the flatbed wagon that would take it to its new resting place down the road in Carrick.

When Fergus had brought the machine again to the center of the graveyard, Mick was digging in the hole.

"Another one below?" Fergus inquired.

"If it is, it's stone," Mick replied. To make his point, he tapped the shovel straight down. The hard ring of steel on rock resounded.

"Just a boulder, then," Fergus said. "There's why they only put him down three feet. Too big a rock to move."

"I don't think so," Mick said, leaning his shovel against the shoulder of the hole and getting down on his knees. "It's only a foot wide, but . . ."

"But what?" Fergus asked, standing on the machine to get a better view. "Is it a rock or isn't it?"

"Holy God!" Mick exclaimed.

"What is it?" Fergus asked.

"Come here, Ferg, look at this!"

Fergus jumped into the hole, careful not to stand between the sun and the place where Mick dusted away soil with his bare hands. "A tombstone?" Fergus guessed.

"More than that," Mick replied. His voice was husky with awe. "But I'll hold my tongue until I'm proved."

Without another word, Fergus knelt beside Mick and helped scoop the soil away. Several more minutes of digging confirmed Mick's suspicion. Under the two gravediggers lay one of the most ancient and sacred symbols of Irish Catholic faith: a high cross.

They soon found the place where the cross arms bisected the shaft, then worked out to the circle that surrounded the crosspiece. In silence they brushed away more and more of the soil, exposing the ornate, abstract incisions covering the entire surface.

"'Tis huge!" Fergus exclaimed. "Must be twelve feet." He picked up the shovel to prove his surmise.

"But why is it flat in the ground?" Mick wanted to know.

"Must have fallen over."

"Then why didn't they put it back up?" Mick pursued. "Did ye ever hear of a high cross found flat on the ground? And, if it fell, how come it didn't crack?"

"'Cause it fell on grass," Fergus sighed.

"If you're right, then you'll find a base," Mick insisted, his voice betraying his skepticism.

"Just hold yer horses," Fergus said. Within a minute he had found the bottom of the high cross. But ten minutes more digging failed to reveal the massive base necessary to root a high cross to the ground.

"See?" Mick said.

Fergus squinted hard at his partner. "What are you tellin' me; they never stood this one up but just left it lyin' on the ground?"

Mick drummed his filthy fingers against his forehead in thought. "Tell you what," he exclaimed. "Let's lift it! If they *did* mean to lay it in the sod then they wouldn't have bothered to carve the other side. True?"

"Dig a tunnel under both ends," Fergus directed, clambering up from the hole. "I'll get the chains."

Twenty minutes later and ten minutes past the time MacMahon and Dunphy quit work each day—come hell or high water table—the gravediggers had the chains wrapped loosely around the giant cross.

"You know, we shouldn't be moving this on our own,"

Mick told Fergus, solemnly. "This is a rare find, and something we—"

"Yeah, right," Fergus cut in, acidly. "First the town fathers will be up here. Then the county officials. Then the people from Dublin. And in the end they'll still have us lift it. Five pounds says there's carving on the back side. Offer good today only."

Mick shrugged. "All right. Lift it."

"And the wager?" Fergus persisted.

Mick spit in his hand and offered it to his partner. Fergus shook it, climbed into the digging machine and set the arm into motion.

The chains went taut. Despite the engine's throbbing strength it looked for a moment as if the cross would remain locked to the earth. Then, with a deep, sucking sound it came up. For a second, the machine's rear wheels lifted. Then they settled back into the sod. Fergus guided the machine backward slowly. The huge stone cross swayed slightly above the hole.

Mick peered under the sandstone mass. "You owe me a fiver," he declared. "Smooth as a baby's behind."

Fergus swore under his breath, then swung the cross to the side of the hole and let it come to rest. He shut off the machine and hopped down. "This here is a great mystery we've found," he declared.

"Too much for the likes of us," Mick said, wiping his hands on his coveralls. "Quittin' time."

Fergus grabbed the shovel and jumped into the hole.

"What do you think yer doin'?" Mick asked.

"I say it stood," Fergus said, stiff-jawed. "There's a base under here somewhere, and you're gonna stay! I have five pounds on this."

"Just buy me a pint t'night an' we'll call it even," Mick said, anxious to be getting home.

"Five minutes," Fergus coaxed, while the shovel swung and dirt flew.

Mick sighed and leaned against the digging machine, burrowing into his pocket for his watch.

The shovel clanged against something hard. Mick came off of the backhoe. "Stone?"

Fergus bent and picked up a rectangular, gray shape. It was dull and pitted. "I think it's lead," Fergus pronounced. "And there's writing on it. Come here!"

Mick joined his partner in the hole, the center of which was now six feet deep. Fergus passed him the rectangle.

"CAVE SŌRC," Mick read wiping hard across the surface. "What is this? Cave source? There's no caves up here."

"Beats me," Fergus answered. "This little writing under it . . . what's that say?"

"I can't read it. Greek to me."

"You think there could be a cave under here?" Fergus murmured, mostly to himself. "And wouldn't that make you an' me famous! A cave under a high cross." He picked up the shovel again.

"For pity sake, Ferg!" Mick moaned. "Let's go."

"Three more minutes," Fergus said, digging.

Mick swung his watch in Fergus's face. "Three minutes exactly an' I'm goin'. It's a long walk into town."

Two minutes passed, with only the grunts of the digger, the bite of the shovel and the thump of falling dirt clods marking the moments. Mick put his watch away and walked up to the shallow end of the hole. Again the shovel rang metallically. Mick turned.

"Holy Mother of God!" Fergus breathed out. He set the shovel on the shoulder of the mound and dropped to his knees.

"What now?" Mick asked.

"Gold. Something made out of gold!" Fergus's voice quivered with excitement. "Mick," he directed softly, "get that little spade and the broom!"

By the time Mick had returned with the tools, Fergus had clawed away more of the soil, exposing not just a curving

surface of gold metal but a dull cream length of bone as well.
The broom swept back and forth, back and forth.

"It's a bracelet," Mick judged. "That's the forearm
comin' up to it and wrist bones inside."

"Christian," Fergus added. "See the cross etched into it?"

"It's so big!" Mick exclaimed. "There must be five, six
ounces of gold there."

"And there's more," Fergus said, whisking furiously.
"Look! Chain links."

All thoughts of quitting time were abandoned. Half an
hour later they had found four gold bracelets, two pairs held
together by golden links. Inside each of the bracelets rested a
skeleton wrist.

Fergus and Mick stood on opposite ends of the hole,
staring hard at the bracelets and the bones. Three complete
skeletons lay exposed to the late-afternoon sky.

"It's like they're handcuffs," Fergus pronounced. "The
two on the outside have the one on the inside prisoner
between them."

Mick's eyes swept back and forth along the length of the
mass grave. The three skeletons reminded him of a time as a
child when he had watched his older sister fold a sheet of
paper into thirds and cut out the shape of a doll. Grinning at
her superior knowledge, she had opened up the paper to
reveal the trio of dolls, miraculously joined together at the
hands. Then, with her tongue protruding through taut lips as
if to impart extra guidance to her pencil, his sister had
drawn features on the faces. The large circles of the eyes,
which she carefully blacked in, matched the loam-filled eye
sockets staring back at Mick. The difference was that his
sister had drawn three pairs of bulging, black eyes on her
dolls—Mick could only see two pairs of sockets on the three
skeletons.

"Why is the middle one lyin' face down?" Mick asked, his
voice little more than a whisper.

"Beats me," Fergus answered, his gaze directed to the

posterior skull bones of the skeleton in the center. "The weirdest thing I ever saw."

"How old do you reckon they are?" Mick asked.

"Well, how long ago did they stop makin' high crosses?"

"I don't know."

"Old," Fergus proclaimed. "Damned old."

"You think we'll get a reward for findin' this?" asked Mick.

Fergus laughed. "A letter of thanks and our pictures in *The Nationalist.*" Then the laugh disappeared from his rugose face. "Unless we take matters in our own hands."

"Meaning?"

"Meaning we leave everything just like it is now ... except for the bracelets." He gave Mick a challenging stare.

"Are you jokin'?" Mick countered.

"There's maybe twenty ounces of gold lying there, Dunphy. Ten for you and ten for me. Ten ounces we won't even have to pay taxes on." Fergus stepped closer to his partner. "Only you and me know what we found. Once we take 'em, who's to accuse us of anything?"

"That's true," Mick acceded.

"It's the down payment on that Audi you saw for sale in Kilkenny. Picture it in yer drive, Dunphy, old man." Above Fergus's gap-toothed smile, his eyes conveyed a look of cunning conspiracy.

"You take 'em off," Mick said, in a rush.

Fergus laughed again. "Glad to. Glad to." In a twinkling, the gravedigger had slipped the bracelets free of the bones and handed one pair to Dunphy.

"Now what?" Mick asked.

"We stash the gold, then we tell the *Gardaí* our astonishing news. Everything just as it happened, except we leave out the bracelets."

Mick grimaced as he shoved the golden bracelets into his jacket pocket. "We can't leave this open. Some kids could come along—"

"That's what the cemetery-keeper's for," Fergus interrupted. "What's her name?"

"Mary Liddy."

"You go up and tell old Mary Liddy that we made a fantastic find and she must watch it until we return with the *Gardaí.*" Fergus leapt out of the hole with an energy Mick had not seen in ten years. "Meanwhile, I'll hook the wagon up to the truck. We'll have to get those boxes down to St. Columba's before dark." Fergus offered his partner a hand up. When Mick stood again on green grass, Fergus slapped him hard on the shoulder. "We found the leprechaun's crock of gold!" He chortled with glee as he jaunted toward the coffin wagon.

Mick took a last glance into the hole. He had looked upon hundreds of human remains in his day, in all states of decomposition. None of it had ever fazed him. He had always possessed a slaughterhouse mind-set when it came to mortality. This once, however, he shuddered. He caught himself, checked to be sure Fergus had not seen his moment of weakness, then he turned his back on the hole and trudged up the gentle incline toward the cemetery caretaker's cottage.

Mary Liddy looked down into the hole and made the sign of the cross.

"You don't have to do anything, Mary," Fergus half shouted, trying at the same time to be soothing. "Just sit here and make sure nobody touches anything until we get back. Do you understand?"

"Sure I understand," Mary answered. Annoyance came clearly through her desiccated old voice. She looked up at the new gathering of clouds in the southeast. "Will you be back before dark?"

"Of course we will," Fergus assured. "Here, take my coat, in case it gets cold."

Mary accepted the coat without thanks. After the men

reassured her yet again that they would be right back, they piled in the truck and set it bouncing down the roadway toward Carrick-on-Suir.

Mary dropped the coat on the dirt pile next to the high cross and sat her old bones down on it. She shook her head wearily at the memory of how the gravediggers had talked to her. Like she was slow-witted. She knew that in the last few months she had picked up the epithet Crazy Mary. Just because she had stopped answering every time someone said something solicitous to her. She was feeble, but not feeble-minded.

Mary squinted at the sun, dying over the shoulder of Slievenamon Peak. She was dying, too, but not fast enough. Ever since her man, Tom, had passed on, life had not been worth living. The relatives were all in America, and money was tight. The pittance of a caretaker's fee for the cemetery would end when all the bodies had been reburied at St. Columba's. Her fingers were arthritic, her hearing was going, her strength was gone. She lacked enough muscle tone to keep the wind inside. She lived more and more in the memories of her past, because the future held nothing but increasing depravations and senescence. Suicide was out of the question, since she was a devout Catholic, but she prayed twice a day for God to take her. In His infinite wisdom He had sustained her on and on.

Mary wondered if this miraculous find in the burial ground could somehow help her communicate her wish to the Creator. She got down on her knees, kissed her thumb, touched it to the ancient stone, then made the sign of the Cross on her head and chest. She squeezed her eyes shut and began murmuring 'Mary's Crown.' First came the Our Father and then, after a rapid breath, what she intended to be the first of ten Hail Marys.

"Hail, Mary, full of grace. The Lord is with thee. Blessed art thou amongst women, and blessed is the fruit of thy w—"

Mary's lips froze in mid-pucker. She had heard a loud,

rattling noise from down in the hole. Despite her feebleness, Mary started from her knees. She wobbled a moment over the high cross, touched it to steady herself, then came up as straight as she could. She stood stock still and listened. The noise had stopped. Mary crossed herself three times in rapid succession. The grave was now silent. Mary moved away from the pit and looked to the nearby road. Any other time, it seemed, a car or lorry passed every minute. But now the road was as still as the burial ground around her.

Mary ventured cautiously toward the grave. It took her a full minute to draw close enough to look down into it. Nothing stirred. She told herself that the gravediggers had cut through a burrowing creature's hole and that it had finally ventured out to see what havoc had been wreaked. Mary saw neither animal nor animal hole. But the noise hadn't been made by fur or claw anyway. It was knocking, rattling. Maybe like ten pins falling onto dirt? Her tongue circled her cracked lips. She looked down at her trembling hands and clasped them together.

Suddenly Mary laughed, amused by the irrationality of her own fear. What was the worst thing that could happen to her? Hadn't she just been praying for death? It seemed that survival instincts died hard. She stared down at the three half-buried skeletons. If the high cross was sacred, how much more sacred must be the people buried beneath it, she thought. Down there was where she should be praying for death. Maybe the souls of these ancients lingered nearby, ready to intercede on her behalf.

Slowly and carefully, Mary made her way down into the hole. She sidled along the first skeleton and stopped in the dead center of the grave. She crossed herself one last time, then kneeled and touched the heel bone of the venerable middle skeleton. Mary stared at the three bundles of bones, lying so still in the sod, all three skulls turned face up, three pairs of eye sockets staring up into the darkening sky.

* * *

The dusty Ford with GARDA stenciled on its side pulled into the cemetery and groaned to a halt. Before Sergeant Dick Meagher could turn off the engine, Fergus and Mick had piled out and were trudging toward the most recently opened grave.

"Wait a bit!" Meagher called out. The pair stopped together, but neither acted as if they had heard the policeman.

"What's she doin'?" Meagher heard Fergus ask. Meagher strained his eyes to peer into the twilight. A figure was at work down the slope in the middle of the ancient Lamoge graveyard. No one answered Fergus's question and, in the ensuing moment of silence, Meagher heard the faint noise of a shovel attacking the earth.

First Fergus, then Mick looked back at Sergeant Meagher for direction. He strode forward purposefully.

"Is it Mary Liddy?" he inquired.

"'Tis," Fergus replied. "Now I know why they call her Crazy Mary. She has our shovel, and she's diggin' for all she's worth."

Meagher started forward. He knew Crazy Mary Liddy only by reputation, not sight. What he saw as he approached was a woman in her seventies, wearing a plain black dress and plain brown shawl, her iron-colored hair disheveled from the intense labor of her digging. She stood some two feet deep in a fresh hole.

"Mary Liddy!" Meagher called out.

Mary turned with a start. She had obviously not heard their approach. Then her look shifted past Meagher and the gravediggers to the *Garda* car, and her eyes grew wide with surprise.

"What's she—" Mick began.

Mary threw down the shovel and, with a speed that shocked all three men into momentary immobility, ran down the hill.

"Should we catch her?" Fergus asked the sergeant.

"Yes. Just don't hurt her," Meagher advised. The gravediggers gave chase like trained hounds pursuing a fox, and the policeman followed as quickly as his stout legs and generous belly would allow.

Mick caught the old woman as she was scaling the stone cemetery wall, grabbing her by the ankles as the rest of her was disappearing out of reach. Mary let out a howl of outrage and kicked back. Mick fell on his rear end, but by then Fergus had gotten hold of Mary's middle and was hauling her toward the ground.

An auto horn blared from the cemetery entrance. Meagher looked back and saw another *Garda* car pulling up onto the lawn. A green, people-packed Volvo rumbled behind it.

Mary rolled over, yelling and flailing. Fergus and Mick struggled to subdue the old woman.

Dick Meagher kept back several paces, expecting at any second that Mary would come to her senses and lie still. Instead, Fergus let out an anguished yelp, and suddenly Mary was up and running, heading right for the sergeant, bowling him over with her momentum, tumbling herself, coming back up on her feet and retracing her steps in a new bid for freedom.

By the time Mary had again reached the center of the graveyard, six men and two women were converging on her from three directions. Mary gave one last look-round for an avenue of escape, realized the futility of renewed effort, and promptly set her bottom down against the top of a grave marker. Her head lowered with exhaustion, her small chest heaved for air, her arms hung limply at her side.

"Now what-the-Devil was that all about, Mary Liddy?" Sergeant Meagher demanded, weaving around the unclosed grave holes.

Mary's head jerked up, one ear cocked toward the policeman, as if he had uttered the worst obscenity at her. Her eyebrows knit. Then her head straightened and she studied the people surrounding her, one by one.

"She should be arrested!" Fergus cried out with venom.

21

He thrust his hand in front of Dick Meagher's face. "See what she done to my thumb? Opened it right to the bone."

His thumb was indeed a sorry sight. The flesh on the underside was neatly split open.

Meagher grimaced. "At least it's not bleedin' bad," he offered. "But that will take some stitches. How did she do it?"

"Christ, but it hurts!" Fergus swore, shaking his wounded hand up and down vigorously. "I don't know, Dick. There was arms and legs everywhere. I think she bit me."

Meagher shot him a look of doubt.

"I think you cut it on a stone," Mick pronounced. His attention was turned to the place where Mary had been laboring. "She was diggin' dead center in the cemetery. What for?"

"Mary?" Meagher cued.

Mary looked at the hole she had made, and at the shovel leaning out of the hole. She seemed drained of energy.

"I think she's snapped," one of the women in the crowd announced. Meagher scowled at her. There were always a couple of townfolk who kept their radios tuned to the police band. You could count on them to arrive either right behind or sometimes even before the *Gardaí*.

"Why don't you back off, Ella," Meagher suggested, "and let us take care of this?"

"She needs hospital," Ella persisted. "Anybody can see that."

"*I* need the blessed hospital!" Fergus moaned.

"Right," said Meagher, finally catching his breath again. He crooked his finger at the driver of the other *Garda* vehicle. "Rory, you and Mick see about putting a barrier around what was found. I'll be taking Mary and Fergus into Clonmel for medical help."

Fergus glared at Mary. "And don't be thinkin' of any more violence or I'll forget I'm a gentleman this time and bash ya!"

Mary did not look intimidated. She continued to study the faces and clothing of all present.

"So, what did you find?" one of the men from the gawker's group asked Mick.

Dick Meagher glanced to his left. Resting on the ground not twenty feet from him was a perfect high cross. He was too busy to examine the three skeletons Mick and Fergus had reported, lying in a row, the middle one face down. Both Fergus MacMahon and Crazy Mary Liddy needed his immediate attention. One thing was sure, the excitement wouldn't end tonight. The ruckus would go on for weeks, making his life hell on earth. He had hoped the debate over moving this cemetery would be buried along with the reinterred. But a sacred high cross was powerful fuel to rekindle the theological blaze. Well, he wouldn't and couldn't handle this alone. The first thing tomorrow morning he would give Dublin a call.

3

August 15, 1988

Lá breá bog the Irish called it—a fine, soft day. The sun shone brightly as it glided from one cloud formation to another, turning the rough pastures and bogs from forest to emerald green, then to peacock and moss. Keenan MacBreed glanced left and right off the highway and knew he was looking at the lushest pastureland in all of Europe. Central Ireland was a huge bowl, hemmed in by mountains on all sides except for fifty miles of eastern beach. The mountains captured the mild breezes of the Atlantic and wrung the moisture from them to nurture the world-famous grasses and shamrocks.

Keenan had been behind the wheel of the Range Rover for two hours, and the ranges of Tipperary now rolled around him. The car's speakers reverberated with the sounds of the Clancy Brothers and Tommy Makem singing "As I Roved Out." Keenan had many other tapes to choose from, but this day called for Irish music. After all, how often was a centuries-old high cross unearthed?

Highway R 697 climbed a hill and made a gentle turn. At

the end of the turn a dozen or so vehicles crept along. In front of them, a herder drove his slow-moving sheep. There were no angry blarings of horns or dust-churning about-faces at the slowdown. Such behavior was expected in America or even in Dublin, but in the hinterlands of Eire the shepherd and his animals were still a valued way of life and not considered an annoying inconvenience. Keenan shifted the Range Rover into low gear and settled back in his seat, fully content with what he was doing and the pace at which he was doing it.

To the Irishmen who knew him, Keenan MacBreed was one of their rich American cousins, the grandson of emigrants who had fled the poverty and oppressions of the Auld Sod to make their fortune in the New World. Their dream was not idle. His grandfather had arrived in America with few skills but had quickly learned the building trade. Nearly as quickly he had learned the politics of the building trade, at least in the Roman Catholic quarter of Boston. The proper deference and contributions to the cardinal guaranteed his family the roof tarring contracts of every church, rectory, convent and Catholic school in the diocese. The same business connections led to the absorption of a brick and stonemason's company. Soon after Keenan's father, Patrick Aloysius MacBreed, entered the family business, he expanded it into property dealings. Again, connections, deference and bribes guaranteed success.

Keenan grew up in Beverly, about fifteen miles north of the tenements of the average Boston Irish and conspicuously close to the exclusive Anglo-Saxon bastion, Pride's Crossing. The family sat nearly as high as a Massachusetts Irish family could. Keenan's older brother, Patrick Aloysius, Jr., played football for Notre Dame and later studied business at De Paul, so that the MacBreeds could be free once and for all of "those damned Protestant bankers." Keenan's sister was raised to be the sort of lady who would attract the son of another wealthy Irish clan. So long as that clan's yearly earnings were in the middle six figures Maureen could pretty much choose for herself; the only absolutes were that the boy be Irish and devoutly Roman Catholic.

Pat, Jr. was all his father and grandfather expected, making Keenan a superfluous commodity and leaving him to fulfill the aspirations of his mother. Keenan faced the traditional fate of the second son. Pat, Jr. would inherit the family's worldly estates and trades; Keenan was expected to provide for their otherworldly concerns. He became the youngest altar boy at Our Lady of Perpetual Sorrow. Parochial school indoctrination was not enough for him; Mary Catherine spent an hour every afternoon drilling Keenan in the prayers, the Ten Commandments, the Stations of the Cross and the lives of the saints. She crammed the dogma of her faith into her son's head, all in preparation for his inevitable priesthood.

But the Church and Mary Catherine MacBreed failed. The harsh lessons of the outside world and the day-to-day examples set by his family convinced Keenan that the cosmos did not operate as the Church declared it did. Quietly, in the unassailable fortress of his own mind, Keenan decided that God (if He existed at all) did not watch the fall of every sparrow, did not in fact number every hair of his head. God (if He existed at all) had set the world spinning, had worked his chemical, physical, electrical magic, had populated the planet with life and had moved on to bigger and better creations.

Wars, famines, plagues, unfairly dealt diseases and deaths combined to convince Keenan that God, if He caused or even allowed these things to happen, must be evil as well as good. Before he was a teenager, Keenan rejected the Church's argument that such things were either the residue of original sin or served as trials of faith. God was either at the other end of the universe or else had never been there in the first place. This God certainly needed no priests.

The MacBreed family never missed Mass on Sunday, but that pious attendance didn't stop Keenan's father from swearing at the other faithful who got in his way when he drove out of the parking lot. Nor did religious conviction stop him from cheating his customers, or from defaming every other nationality but the Irish. Mass didn't stop his mother from spending twenty times what she donated to charities on her wardrobe or looking down her nose at anyone who didn't have the kind of money the MacBreeds had. When Keenan studied his parents he thought of a passage from his favorite book: "Under all wrong-doing lies personal vanity or the feeling that we are endowed by privileges beyond our fellows." Keenan was not about to waste his time being a surpliced shepherd when the fold was filled with sheep like the MacBreeds.

But Keenan's parents were also loving and good to him, and he was an obedient son. For ten years he agonized over how to avoid the priesthood and still find a profession that would make his mother and father proud.

The answer lay in the same favorite book. If it was Irish it was good, and so the MacBreeds filled their ostentatious library with every volume that spoke well of Ireland. One called *Irish Fairy Tales* was filled with wondrous accounts, beautifully illustrated by Arthur Rackham. Keenan had marveled over the stories, read and reread them in fifth and sixth grades. But it was not until he had learned in high school about such things as archeology and anthropology that he regarded the book in a new light. These stories were not newly invented to entertain children; they were in fact the voices of his long-gone ancestors and highly respected in academia as the oldest vernacular tales of Europe. When Keenan studied at Boston College he learned that, because of these familiar legends, the ancient language of Ireland was better known than any other ur-language in Europe. In his junior year at college he realized that Irish archeology could make him a hero in the MacBreed clan.

Through research in his senior year, Keenan discovered that there were only two universities in North America that granted graduate degrees in Celtic Studies: Harvard and St.

Francis Xavier in Nova Scotia. The department that had the greater Q-Celtic expertise was the university in his own back yard. Keenan fixed his interest purely on the Irish-Scottish Goidelic language and not on the P-Celtic of Britain, Wales and the rest of Celtic Europe. Once at Harvard, Keenan learned that his chosen area of expertise was so specialized that funding for its pursuit was impossible to obtain. This further endeared him to the MacBreed clan, since they could, in one fell financial gesture, glorify Ireland and their ancestry and make a claim of scholarly support that none of their friends or enemies could hope to match. So it was that Keenan saved himself from the Church and became instead an archeologist.

Down the road, one of the more rambunctious sheep had strayed from the flock and gotten itself hung up trying to leap a wiry hedge. Its back legs churned frantically to no effect. The herder turned at the anxious, bleating noises and stopped the flock's plodding progress so he could help the stray sheep.

Keenan set the gear shift in park and stretched toward the back seat for a pair of books, prizes he had discovered the day before in a second-hand bookshop in Dublin. The volumes, *The Rise of the Celts* and *The Greatness and Decline of the Celts,* were original English-translation editions, dating back to 1934. The author was the Frenchman Henri Hubert, one of the first to write authoritatively on the history and character of the Celtic race. These books were so important that Keenan's professors had referred to them simply as *The Rise* and *The Decline.*

Keenan chose *The Decline* and began reading the foreword. His eyes swept across one passage, then he paused and reread it slowly. "A society," it said, "may have every kind of aptitude for forming a nation but fail to be a nation if it is not definitely organized as a state." The sentence summarized the opinions of quite a few Celtic scholars, Keenan MacBreed included. He recalled the words of Camille Julian, who wrote that "Celtic unity was in the domain of poets rather than of statesmen." The stock out of which the modern Irish people developed was a fierce, self-sufficient people. Their passions ran to music, art and poetry; their loyalties were to the individual spirit and the immediate family. They had little use for politics. Left to themselves, they might have continued as clans and petty kingdoms forever. Unfortunately, the scions of a legendary pair named Romulus and Remus made that tribal existence untenable.

Keenan's lips pursed as he read the passage. Quite plainly, Hubert was saying that the Irish carried the seeds of their own destruction. Worse, there was nothing to be done about it, since the seeds had already grown to calamitous bloom. He was glad that his studies covered the time of *The Rise*. The real Good Old Days. He closed the book and replaced it gently on the back seat.

Up ahead the shepherd was finally driving his flock through a gate into a craggy pasture at the side of the road. Keenan studied the breathtaking countryside, intent on burying negative thoughts. Despite the beauty of the landscape, it was not an easy exercise. For all the glory of its surface, Ireland's bedrock lacked the minerals and fuels that had made other European countries great and the strategic position to build its might on trade. Because man had arrived too late and lived too simply here, Keenan doubted he would ever make an earth-shaking archeological or anthropological discovery in this country on the outermost rim of the European continent.

Keenan knew he was the only one who cared about this last fact. To him, however, it was no small matter. Because of Ireland's late settlement, he would never have a reputation like Leakey or Schliemann. Then again, since there were so few scholars of ancient Irish culture, he did not have to claw for a specialty in some esoteric subfield. He could dabble in all his loves: archeology, cultural anthropology and linguistics. And since there seemed to be nothing spectacular buried under Irish sod, he would not have to compete with hordes of archeologists every summer. Except for a few native compatriots from Trinity college and Galway college, he had the place to himself. The Republic of Ireland welcomed the self-financed Dr. MacBreed on his annual expeditions. Naturally, the greatest finds went to the "home teams," but Keenan was free to search for finds on his own and was assigned the more innocuous digs whenever an excavation or highway-widening revealed something interesting. His musing put him back in a good mood. This was Keenan's fifth summer in Ireland. He felt in his bones that time was on his side.

Once the sheep cleared out, the traffic resumed at a good pace. At Windgap Keenan decided not to turn due east and head for the unearthed cemetery with its high cross. It would be better to get the whole story from his friend, Sergeant Dick Meagher first. Keenan had met the policeman the summer before, when the announcement of the cemetery's "shifting" had caused a clamor not heard in County Tipperary South Riding since their own Sean Kelly became a world cycling champion. It had been Meagher's duty to maintain the peace, especially at the open council meetings that discussed the move. On the north side of the cemetery stood a billboard with a huge black dot on it. This was the Republic's way of letting motorists know that this place on the road had been the site of vehicular death. Between 1957 and 1985, the hairpin turn around the cemetery had caused three fatal accidents. Then, a year ago, the cemetery's stone wall claimed two more lives in one spectacular, fiery crash. The time for governmental action had clearly arrived.

If the burial ground had been recently or currently in use it would have been impossible to prevail against families with loved ones there interred. A vocal number of conservatives were nonetheless outraged at the thought of disturbing good Catholic remains. To calm the objectors two outside authorities had been invited to Carrick-on-Suir. The first was an official of the Department of the Environment, who assured the citizens that the remains would be treated by the government with the utmost respect and immediately returned to consecrated ground. He reminded everyone exactly how treacherous the turn around the cemetery was and how many lives might be saved in the future by straightening the roadway.

Then Keenan addressed the crowd, explaining that the relocation would afford new opportunities for historians and allow the people of southeast Tipperary to learn about their ancestors from as far back as 1000 A.D. He assured the citizens that relocations of Catholic burial grounds were common the world over. His speech was well received. Afterward Dick Meagher invited him to "throw back a pint or two" at a favorite pub and use the spare bedroom in his bachelor digs. Keenan had liked the older man on first introduction and had accepted.

Winking blue lights drew Keenan's eyes to his rear view mirror. His heartbeat accelerated. He had no idea if the *Garda* car had just leapt out of hiding or had been following him for some time. Lost in thought, he also had no idea if he had been speeding.

Keenan pulled off the highway and began concocting a plausible story. He heard the police car door slam and watched in his side mirror, but the policeman did not come into view.

"Where's the fire, Yank?" a familiar voice asked gruffly, through the open passenger's window.

Keenan whirled around to his left, scowling. "You have nothing better to do than lie in wait for tourists, Sergeant Meager?" he asked, deliberately mispronouncing the policeman's name, as it looked in print.

"Afraid I'll *mar* your driving record?" Meagher countered, punning with the correct sound of his name. "And I'll thank ya to refrain from such ill-*breed* remarks, Mac!" He smiled broadly, elevating his rough Father Christmas cheeks.

31

"How are you, Dick?" Keenan inquired, leaning across the passenger's seat and offering his hand.

"Not bad, not bad, Keenan. Things were quiet in town, so I thought I'd sit out here and wait for the Trinity Range Rover."

"And here it is," said Keenan. "With one anxious professor champing at the bit to see this high cross of yours."

"Let's use this lovely weather, then," suggested Meagher, "and do just that. I'll lead the way."

Meagher drove up a pair of dirt roads and bounced out onto Regional Road R 697, almost directly in front of the cemetery. As he entered the burial ground he leaned heavily on his car horn. Keenan saw the cause of his anger. Four boys, about ten years old, were playing in the holes. As they ran, they continued to pitch the last of their dirt bomb arsenals at each other.

Meagher clambered out of his car, shaking his head. "If it's not the gawking adults it's the teenagers out to scare each other at midnight. And if it's not them it's the boys playing World War I trenches."

"I'm sure you'll be glad when this is all dug up," Keenan offered.

"They won't be satisfied until one of them falls in and breaks his neck," the sergeant complained, slamming his car door. "Come on, I'll show you."

The center of the cemetery was fenced in with heavy-duty chicken wire sloppily secured to metal posts. As Keenan approached he noted that one section of the wire was pulled up and mangled.

"Ach, now look and see what they done!" Meagher grumbled on.

Keenan sighed softly at the fence. "Don't you think you need something more secure around it?" he suggested.

"Out of whose budget?" Meagher asked, fishing into his pocket for a key.

Keenan held his tongue as he waited. He would be sick if the cross was damaged. Other ancient works of art sat out in the elements all over Ireland, taking far more abuse from nature than from people. Meagher pulled back the make-shift gate and gestured for the archeologist to enter. Keenan swung his rucksack off his hip and lowered it to his side as he moved forward.

The high cross lay undamaged on the ground, washed cleaner by a week of intermittent rain. Keenan had wanted to see it sooner, but he was forced to complete an opened dig before relocating himself to southeast Tipperary. He noted at once that it was a particularly massive example, like the Cross of SS. Patrick and Columba, at Kells in County Meath.

"It's marvelous, ain't it?" the sergeant exclaimed.

"It is," agreed the archeologist.

"How old, would you say?"

Keenan kneeled and touched the old stone, feeling its rough texture and coldness. "Very. Late eighth to early ninth century. This is the area where high crosses were first made, you know."

Meagher raised his eyebrows in appreciation of the news. "How can you fix its age so quickly?" he wanted to know.

"The stonework," Keenan answered. A natural teacher, Keenan was always eager for an opportunity to talk about his favorite subjects. "This is a curious mixture of two periods. The transepts and the circle are covered with what we call nonfigurative interlacings and spirals. The high crosses without human figures are the most ancient. The earliest of any kind of local stone cross are late seventh century. We think ones like this are copies of metal crosses."

Keenan duck walked up along the cross, until he could set his hand on its very center. "There's been a bit of detail erosion from water and soil acids, but you can still see that these raised dots here are ornamental studs. And over here are cylindrical angle mouldings. Both clearly copies of metalworkers' art. The reason they switched to stone was because the Vikings were constantly raiding and carrying off anything that was made of metal."

"A stone this big wasn't worth anything to 'em," Dick said.

"Exactly."

"This is a mixture because of the carved figures?" Meagher surmised.

"Right." The professor moved to the bottom of the cross. "Figures of people didn't become a major element in high crosses until about a hundred years later. This may turn out to be an important transition piece."

"Looks like the one on the top side has a hood around its face," the sergeant observed.

"It might be a cowl," Keenan agreed. The facial carving was typical of the period, a wide-eyed, thin-lipped, androgynous rendering placed there for allegory and not portraiture.

"And heaven's opening up for him," Meagher went on.

Clouds swirled above the figure, and one stony feather of air curled down toward its head.

"Two figures holding up crosses on the sides," Meagher went on, while Keenan was content to admire the artistry in silence. "You say high crosses started around here first. Why?" asked Meagher. "And why so many of them?"

"Good question," Keenan replied. The guard was right about the high number. Nowhere else in Ireland did high crosses rise in such profusion. To date, no one had learned why.

"It has no base to it," Meagher pointed out.

"And that's another curiosity," Keenan said, touching the very bottom of the cross, feeling the intricate framework of Celtic lacework curves.

"But it wasn't meant to stand," Meagher declared. "There's no carving on the back side."

"So I was told. Very strange." Keenan dug into his rucksack and pulled out a Hasselblad loaded with color film and a Konica with black and white. "Let's see what's in the hole."

"Bones," said Meagher, trenchantly.

Keenan laughed. "You're right, Sergeant. Here they are,

big as death." He noted the guard's discomfort. In the professor's experience, very few people—policemen included—could look at human bones without some anxiety. Keenan guessed the main reason was the implicit message of human mortality. To him, bones were just history. He'd seen skulls, femurs, sternums by the hundreds, teeth by the thousands. Most of the time he would have traded a wagonload of them for one complete ancient weapon.

When Keenan had taken several pictures of the high cross, Meagher said, "I think there was a wooden cross under the stone one. The damned gravediggers made a mess of it, but there's little pieces like this all over. Some's still lyin' there, along the same line the stone cross took. See, between the skeletons there?"

Keenan set down his cameras, then fished in his sack for a pair of white scale sticks and a camel's-hair brush. "That could be significant," he affirmed. "I'll set up a screen frame later and sift through the dirt pile." Meagher had gingerly climbed down into the ditch, and the younger man followed.

"This is what I mean," the guard said, pointing to striated brown material that was just distinguishable from the rich loam. Almost anywhere else in the world, Keenan reflected to himself, the wood would have completely eroded hundreds of years before. But the cool climate and the Irish earth's natural acids greatly slowed the decay of living things.

"You're right, Dick," Keenan agreed, setting down a scale stick and grabbing his Konica. "So, this cross predated the high cross. Probably seventh century."

The sergeant whistled. "And, from the looks of it, just as big. Two huge crosses laid in the ground. For what?"

Keenan made no immediate reply as he probed around the northernmost skeleton. A minute later, he said, "I might have the answer to the riddle." He held up a small stone cross, about the length of his middle finger. A hole had been drilled through the top of the staff. "A necklace. I think we have three holy men here."

"That's what the carvings are trying to tell us. You think maybe they're saints?" Meagher asked, awed.

"Maybe. One of the base stones at Ahenny has seven holy men."

"The seven brothers who became priests," the policeman echoed. "Maybe that's why they buried them all in a row like they were holding hands. Did Vikings get 'em?"

Keenan moved to the center skeleton. "Hard to say. No wounds to the first one's bones. Maybe an epidemic." The central skeleton was embedded deeper in the earth. Keenan carefully brushed away at the hipbones.

"Why's that one face down?" Meagher wanted to know.

"Good question," muttered the archeologist. Five minutes later, he exclaimed. "Well, scratch the holy men theory. This one is a woman."

"How can you tell?"

"Shape of the hipbones." Keenan's eyebrows furrowed. He stopped working.

"What is it?" Meagher asked.

"This skeleton's a different age than the others."

"How different?"

"Centuries. Look, Dick! Even with all the dirt on it you can see how much denser and whiter it is. The percolating water hasn't had time to leach out much of the mineral content. In fact, it looks as if this dirt has been purposely rubbed into the bones to try to make them look older."

"Now, how could that be? The cross was on top. . . ." The policeman glanced at the part of the fence that had been yanked up.

Keenan grabbed his cameras and took several shots of the skeletons. He handed the cameras to Meagher and kneeled over the middle skeleton and examined the skull. "I think we've had a practical joke played on us. Someone other than your gravediggers has unearthed a skeleton and replaced the original."

"Damn, Keenan, I'm sorry," Dick said, staring out across the cemetery. "I should have—"

"Uh-oh," Keenan said, in a tone that instantly silenced the policeman. He had drawn the skull from the earth and turned it over. One hand cradled the occipital bone, the other had the mandible unhinged. "When was the last person buried here?"

"It had to be eighty years ago."

Keenan made a sharp *tsking* sound.

"What, ferchrissake?" Meagher groaned.

Keenan held up the skull for inspection, letting the jawbone hang down, exposing teeth with shiny silver fillings. "I'm no forensic specialist, Dick, but I know they didn't do this kind of work eighty years ago. From these fillings and the overall condition, I'd be surprised if this skull is buried more than five years."

"Ah, Blessed Mother!" Meagher exhaled, leaning back wearily against the ditch wall.

Keenan set the skull up on the edge of the hole and stared at it. "It's probably from another cemetery nearby. Just a joke in very bad taste."

"Or else a woman someone killed five years ago and suddenly figured out where to dump."

Keenan smiled grimly, squatting again over the bones. "I don't think so, but it should be fairly easy to figure out who this is if she's local. This gal was getting on in years. Arthritis in her hands. Some osteoporosis. Just check back ten years on all the women over fifty who died. Make it forty to be absolutely safe. Get their dental charts and compare them to Smiley here."

Meagher kicked the dirt. "Shit! I don't have enough to do! That must be two hundred women. Three hundred if I draw my circle wide enough."

"What else can I tell you?" Keenan offered, studying the pattern of fillings and extractions.

Meagher stared hard at the rest of the middle skeleton. "That was the exact one we found right after the gravediggers come for us. I'd bet my life on it!" He dug into his pocket and extracted an instant camera photograph. "Here!

37

One of my boys took this with a flash not half an hour after we arrived. See how the position is exactly the same?"

Keenan checked back and forth between photo and subject. "I agree with you. Which means this corpse was placed here sometime between when the grave was opened and you took this photo. You think your gravediggers would be stupid enough to pull this prank?"

Meagher shook his head. "They know they'd both lose their jobs."

"I'd still talk with them," Keenan advised. "If it wasn't them, then it had to have happened between the time they left to get you and the time you arrived."

The dark scowl on Meagher's countenance brightened. "Maybe it was Mary Liddy."

"Who?"

"The cemetery-keeper. She's a natural."

Keenan had heard the term *natural* before. It was an Irish euphemism for insanity. A more common term was *innocent;* Irish tradition held that such people were inspired and saw the world in a unique manner that ordinary men should not judge.

"She's the one Mick and Fergus left to guard the hole when they came to fetch me," Meagher went on. "When we came up here we found her with a shovel in her hands. She tried to run away when she saw us."

"She sounds like a definite suspect," Keenan remarked. He positioned his scale markers.

"She's over in Clonmel, in psychiatric hospital. I'd like you to come with me, if you've a mind," Meagher said.

"Be glad to," Keenan answered. "If you'll help me sift dirt until the light gets poor."

"No, there's no reason you can't talk to her," the physician said. "But if you're looking to talk *with* her I think you'll be disappointed."

Somewhere in the bowels of the hospital someone was

ranting. Keenan watched a nurse hurry past them down the corridor in the direction of the disturbance.

"Why is that, doctor?" the sergeant asked.

The doctor tapped his pen repeatedly against his clipboard. "Very strange case," he answered. "For a woman her age she seems to be in reasonable health. External examination of her head showed no marks, no reason for trauma. X-rays revealed no tumors, no sign of stroke. Also no signs of chemical insult. And yet something radical has recently happened to her brain. It's as if, the day she was brought in here, her entire memory was erased. Wiped clean."

"Amnesia?" Meagher probed.

"Technically, yes," the doctor replied. "Clinically, I must say no."

"Why?" Keenan asked.

"For one thing, amnesia lasting more than a few hours is quite rare. For another, amnesia that prevents a person from speaking is even more unusual. Mary Liddy had forgotten how to speak."

Suddenly, the ranting stopped. All three men glanced in the direction of the silence, then looked back at each other. "But she's all right now?" Meagher pursued.

The doctor stopped tapping. "Not really. She's speaking, but very simply and with difficulty. It's almost as if she were a foreigner learning the language from scratch. Or a child, actually. In fact, she's been using the children's books and tapes. She's in the pediatric section now. No children stay the night here, and we let her use the playroom in the evening. Come, have a look at her." The doctor led the way along the corridor.

"She's called Crazy Mary," the sergeant revealed. "Has she ever been here before?"

"No," the doctor replied. "Nor at Waterford. I checked."

"If she's physically sound, doctor, what do you think caused this?" Keenan asked.

"Extreme psychic trauma. We don't know from what. Her mind is evidently protecting itself from the cause."

"Which means she won't remember anything about the skeleton, I'll wager," Meagher fumed.

The doctor stopped at an open doorway and pointed. "Here she is."

Mary Liddy sat on the floor with her back against the wall, clutching a large throw pillow with her thin, loose-skinned arms. She seemed unaware of the men's presence, transfixed by the images on the television. The program was an American Western.

"She's partly deaf," the doctor cautioned. "Oh, and one more thing—she may be starting to remember. She asked me yesterday why there were so many holes in the ground where she was caught."

"And what did you say?" Meagher asked.

"I told her the truth—that the whole cemetery was being moved, to make the road straight." The doctor indicated his confusion by turning his palms up. "I'm not sure she understands what a cemetery is."

"Let's go in," Keenan suggested.

The three men entered the room. Mary continued to stare at the television screen.

"Mary!" the physician said, loudly. "You have visitors."

The old woman glanced in the men's direction. She obviously knew the sergeant. Her gaze lingered on the new figure of Keenan MacBreed. Keenan offered his most winning smile. Mary returned her attention to the television.

Dick Meagher squatted down beside the old woman. "Mary, do you remember my name?"

"You are Meagher," she replied, with space between each word. Her eyes never left the black-and-white screen.

"That's right. Now, after the two men, the gravediggers, left you alone in the cemetery, did anyone else come in?"

Mary ignored him.

"Did someone move one of the skeletons in the hole?"

Mary laughed. Keenan looked up. On the television screen, an Indian had just lifted the scalp of a cavalryman. Keenan looked at the old woman. Her even white teeth showed between lips drawn back in what seemed to be positive mirth over the Indian's success.

"Mary, you are not being nice," the doctor declared.

Mary lifted one hoary eyebrow and trained her attention on the doctor. "I am sorry. Do they make more holes in the cemetery?" she asked, carefully.

The doctor glanced at his two visitors for an answer.

"No," Keenan answered. "Not until I've finished working there."

"Who are you?" Mary wanted to know.

"This is a very wise man," Meagher said, talking not only loudly but in a detached pattern that closely matched the woman's. "He has come to look at the cross and the bones."

Mary seemed mildly interested in the news. Her eyes focused sharply on Keenan. The archeologist blinked in surprise. Until that moment he had always thought "flashing eyes" was just an expression. Certainly, he never thought he would see the eyes of an old woman flash. But that was exactly what was happening. An energy, a vitality far beyond what the old woman should possess emanated from her pupils. It emitted a force that normally only anger could kindle, but the look was not one of anger. Keenan found himself rocking back, giving whatever it was a respectful distance.

"Wise man?" Mary asked. "What is wise?"

"The sergeant thinks I'm smart," Keenan offered. "Good brains." He tapped his head several times. The woman nodded and reset her attention on the television.

"Mary . . ." Meagher began again. "What were you doing with the shovel? What were you digging for?"

The old woman laughed, again showing both rows of white teeth. Keenan looked up at the screen. Two cavalrymen were talking—as unfunny a scene as he could imagine.

"You think this is funny?" Keenan asked.

"Yes. It is funny. Very funny," Mary replied, her eyes still fixed on the television.

"Why?" Keenan asked. "Mary? Mary?"

"We won't get anything out of her," Meagher sighed. "Thank you, doctor."

On the way back to the police car, Dick mused, "A sad case. I wonder if she'll ever get her mind back."

"Had you ever spoken with her before you took her in?" Keenan asked.

"No. Why?"

"I've been all over Ireland, but I've never heard an accent quite like hers. It's Irish, yet . . ."

Meagher hitched the belt back over his large belly. "I wasn't listenin' that close. I've got more than accents to worry about. Let's go talk with the gravediggers."

Fergus MacMahon lived in a whitewashed cottage on the western verge of Carrick-on-Suir. The front yard looked as if he plied his trade there as well; it was all heaps of dirt with only the occasional shock of grass poking up. In the middle of the "lawn" stood a miniature house, made of stream-rounded pebbles, shards of bottle glass and seashells, all cemented together. To the side of the bungalow stood a rickety garage with doors that lay sagging on their hinges. A light glowed in the front window, through the lace curtains.

The sergeant planted his feet wide apart, in an official manner, and knocked on the door. Half a minute later a woman stood in the doorway, a dish towel in her hands.

"Sergeant! Is anything wrong?" the ginger-haired, middle-aged woman asked.

"Not to worry, Mrs. MacMahon," Dick soothed. "Myself and Dr. MacBreed just stopped by to ask the boss some questions about the old Lamoge burial ground."

"He's just watching the tellie," the wife said, rubbing her hands on the towel. "Come in, won't you?"

Fergus MacMahon sat in an old easy chair with his stockinged feet propped up on an equally old hassock. The television's color was out of adjustment, showing a soccer field that was too green and players with orange skin. On the wall behind the television were framed lithographs of Pope

John Paul and John F. Kennedy. "Come in, lads," Fergus bid, without bothering to rise. "Can we get you a drop, to ward off the damp?"

The policeman and archeologist declined. Meagher introduced MacBreed, and Keenan graciously endured the usual insincere praisings of his profession.

"How's the thumb?" Meagher asked Fergus, rescuing Keenan.

"Almost like new," MacMahon said, holding up the injured digit for inspection. "I was worried it would infect, but instead it closed right up."

"You're lucky," Meagher granted. "Fergus, we're after a bit of information. When you lifted the high cross out of the grave, how did you find the skeletons?"

Fergus's face clouded with confusion. "Just a bit under it, if that's what ya mean."

"I mean how were they lying?"

"Well, all in a row, arms out, almost touchin'. The two on the outside face up, the one in the middle face down."

Meagher shifted his weight, rocking closer to MacMahon. "And did you touch anything?"

A defensive aura emanated from the gravedigger; just as quickly he cloaked it in a too-broad smile. "Touch?"

"Yes," Meagher said, emphatically. "Move something."

"Nothin' but the cross. Why would ya be askin'?"

"One of the skeletons seems to have been switched."

Fergus laughed, overloudly. "Now, why would someone do that?"

"I hope merely to be funny. You or Mick know of any old woman's skeleton missing, somebody who died within the last five years?"

Fergus ran his tongue around his lips. "No. All I know is Mick an' me were doin' our jobs. Soon as we found the cross and them three skeletons we come right into town and fetched you. If there was funny business done it was probably that Crazy Mary Liddy. Go ask her!" Fergus' rising ire brought him erect in his chair. Keenan noted that the antimacassar was deeply soiled. So were MacMahon's fingernails, on the hand now waggling at the guard. "Mick and me should be gettin' medals for what we found, instead of bein' accused."

"No one's accusing you, Fergus," Dick said, evenly. "But we have to get to the bottom of this, and your help will be appreciated."

Fergus relaxed. "Well, sure. Of course. Whatever we can do. I'll see what I can dig up."

Keenan burst out laughing. Fergus glanced at him, realized what he had said and joined in. Meagher kept his face expressionless as he consulted his watch. "Tell Mick I'll want him to drop by the station tomorrow morning." Meagher lifted a warning forefinger. "Only you, me and Professor MacBreed know about this skeleton switch. Once you tell Mick that's as far as it goes. This is problem enough without raising the hackles of Father Flynn and his friends."

The gravedigger invoked the name of Jesus to prove that his lips were sealed. Outside the house and heading toward the car, the sergeant said, "He acted guilty as hell."

The car door creaked as Keenan swung it open. "But that doesn't make sense, for all kinds of reasons." He got into the police car and smelled again the deeply embedded reek of tobacco smoke. "You'll figure it out in time, Dick. Speaking of time, I need to get over to the Bessborough before the reception desk closes."

"And after that a pint or two?" Dick said, hopefully.

"Tomorrow," Keenan promised. "Tomorrow and the night after. My work here will take a lot of time . . . and effort."

4

August 16, 1988

The day was as full as the professor expected. The formula for archeological fieldwork is a thousand measures of tedium to produce one piece of treasure, and no one knew it better than Keenan MacBreed. For the first time in his career, however, he abandoned his careful millimeter by millimeter sifting and spaded roughly around and into the grave site. The cause of his unusual behavior was a premonition of discovery, a sense that this plot of Irish sod might yield him a shred of academic glory. Yet for all his perspiring efforts, by the middle of the afternoon he had found nothing more than a second crucifix necklace, beside the third skeleton. Whenever he rested he would sit on the edge of the hole and stare down at the trio of remains and reflect on the curious pattern in which they had been interred.

The ancient skeleton on the south side of the hole showed a sharp rib break near the sternum, just above the heart, as if perhaps it had been pierced by a sword. That, at least, was the suggestion of Rory MacCullen, the outspoken policeman Dick Meagher had sent up to strengthen the fence around the site. In the hour and a half that he labored there,

45

MacCullen formulated a full-blown theory of how a monastery of monks had been chased into the hills by Vikings sailing up the Suir River, caught at this very spot and massacred. He professed to be something of an amateur historian himself and would not be surprised at all if finally MacBreed came to the same conclusion. Never once did the young *Garda*, who prided his powers of observation so highly, show any suspicion that the middle skeleton was any younger than its companions. Nor did the sprinkling of curiosity-seekers who stopped by.

Toward three o'clock a student arrived, to transport one of the old femur bones back to Trinity college for carbon dating. Shortly after, the weather shifted and brought in a downpour that sent policeman, onlookers and archeologist to their cars.

Instead of driving straight back to Carrick, Keenan made the turn for Clonmel and took an unhurried journey through the lush, rolling countryside, watching the colts cantering beside their mothers, glancing at the ruins of round towers in the distance, and at old manor houses badly in need of restoration.

The road sign at Clonmel's limit held both the Anglicized version of the town's name and the Gaelic—Cluain Meala. Cluan-mealla was the ancient Irish name, meaning "plain of honey." This was where the legendary Tuatha de Danann people first settled upon landing in Ireland. The story was that they released bees and followed them to the most fertile meadows in the land. Looking at the lush countryside, Keenan could see how the legend had arisen.

Keenan navigated to the same parking space Dick had taken the previous night. Before entering the hospital he found a candy shop and bought a box of chocolate-covered cherries. The Irish language in all its forms—Old Irish, Middle Irish, Gaelic, Hiberno-English and its several discrete regional dialects—fascinated him. He hoped the candy would provide the leverage to loosen old Mary's tongue, so he could fix her unusual accent.

The children had already left for the day, and Mary had once more taken her place in front of the television set. The movie on this time was one that Keenan had seen called *The Day After*—a made-for-television Hollywood product that was quite shocking in its depiction of the aftermath of total nuclear war. The scene looked calm and normal; the movie had evidently just begun.

"Mary?" Keenan said, angling into her line of sight from a good distance, so not to alarm her.

Mary gave Keenan a quick look, then leveled her attention at the candy box in his hand and the tape recorder slung over his shoulder.

"How are you today?"

"I am fine today," Mary replied, precisely.

"Do you remember me?"

"Yes."

"I brought you a present."

Mary took the box and stared at its colorful cover.

"It's candy. May I help you?" Keenan gently lifted the cover, exposing the candy.

Mary picked a piece out of its cup, held it aloft and eyed it. Keenan studied her eyes. He decided that their potent energy held cunning. He had never dealt with the mentally disturbed before. He wondered if this was the look of madness.

"Food?" Mary asked.

"Yes. Cherries with chocolate around them. They're my favorite. See?" Keenan picked up a piece, popped it in his mouth, chewed deliberately and smiled. "Mmmm!" he enthused with exaggeration, hoping no one would peek into the room at that moment.

Mary sampled her piece. She did not smile, but she took a second and then, rapidly, a third.

"I think I made the right choice," Keenan said. He looked down at the tape recorder, to be sure the tape was turning.

"What is this t'ing?" Mary asked. The accent was there, still elusive to the Goidelic language expert. The difference was more than the habit quite a few Irish people had of pronouncing hard *th's* as *t's*. Her tongue, lip and facial muscles seemed trained to another linguistic system.

Keenan answered Mary's question by winding the machine back several feet and playing their last words. Mary seemed more impressed with the recorder than with the candy. "I want to listen to you speak," he told her.

"Why?" she asked.

"Because you sound different from me. I've never heard anyone speak like you."

Mary laughed. Chocolate besmeared her white teeth. Then her face grew solemn. "You dig in the eart'."

"Yes." Keenan pressed the machine's record button. "Why?"

"I look for things. Things put there a long time ago."

A nervous tick fleetingly crinkled Mary's eyelid. "You t'ink I am a long time ago?"

Keenan smiled. "No. You're no May flower, but you're certainly not the kind of woman I dig." The humor, as he expected, was totally lost on her.

"So," she persisted, "why do you listen at me speak?"

Keenan glanced at the recorder's window, assuring himself that the tape was engaged. Mary was leading the conversation in weird directions, perhaps following the logic of the disturbed. But Keenan didn't care what was said as long as he could capture its accents, meter and inflections. Half his brain listened hard to the sounds while the other struggled for an answer to keep the dialogue going.

"I do a lot of things. I'm a . . ." He wanted to test her knowledge of Gaelic, and a word for "jack-of-all-trades professor" failed him. *"Ollam,"* he said, knowing the instant it was out of his mouth that his consciousness had searched down the wrong branch of his mind and fetched the right word but out of Old Irish.

The word struck the old woman like a static charge. Her body twitched, her eyes grew wide. The box of candy slipped out of her hands, spilling pieces onto the wooden floor. She

48

did not seem to notice. Her flashing eyes fixed hard on Keenan.

"Tu-dam?" Keenan asked, even though he knew it would be highly improbable for the woman to know Old Irish. And yet, her eyes grew even wider.

Then, suddenly, it was as if Mary Liddy had drawn a steel curtain down between herself and Keenan. She stared trancelike at the television. Keenan tried several more phrases, in Old Irish, in Gaelic and in English. She responded to none, did not so much as blink. The interview was over. As Keenan left the room he took one last look. Mary had picked the remaining chocolates off her lap and replaced them with her big throw pillow.

The drive back to Carrick was a quick one. Keenan realized with a start that he had driven more than ten miles without noticing the road. He knew the reason—Mary Liddy. He had put the recorded tape in the Range Rover's player and let it play twice. The sounds were subtly different from any Irish accent he had heard. *Modern* Irish accent. Except for the clues of rhyme and inflection from ancient texts, who really knew what Middle Irish truly sounded like? Irish from four hundred years before. Or Old Irish, from a thousand years back in time's mist. Did it have Mary's lilt?

Carrick-on-Suir appeared, pushing Mary Liddy in the back of Keenan's mind. Keenan watched the old town as he drove into it—it was one of his favorites. Carrick had not been touched by the plastic and neon of the larger cities. The buildings were of natural materials, and only the central cluster rose three stories high, so that the several church steeples and the town's clock tower dominated the Carrick landscape. The sleepy town lay solidly rooted in the past. As the place where the Suir River's tidal shift ended, it had long been an important commercial landing. The Earl of Ormond's manor house, dating from the fourteenth century, still stood. From the photographs Keenan had seen, the center of Carrick had changed little in the past sixty years. But it also thrived. Unlike the big cities, the names on the

shops—Fox's, J. Babington, Coghlan's, Treacy's, Meany's
—were the names of the people who owned and worked in
them. Though it only boasted one movie house, the feature
films changed twice a week, and the theater served double
duty as home of an operatic society known throughout the
British Isles (or so Dick Meagher had proudly told him).

An ancient stone bridge connected Carrick with Carrick-
beg, or Little Carrick, on the south bank. Straddling the Suir
River and nestled between low, lushly forested mountain
ranges, they presented a picture of good Irish life as stereo-
typically perfect as Keenan could imagine.

Keenan drove the Range Rover onto Main Street and
parked as close to the Bessborough Arms as he could. It was
the only hotel inside the town, but, as Sergeant Meagher had
promised, it provided excellent accommodations. Keenan
took his supper in the hotel and trudged upstairs to rest. It
had been a long day already, and he had agreed to do the
pubs with Sergeant Meagher, which was *not* a passive
activity.

The television was tuned to Radio Telefis Eirann. Keenan
was dividing his attention between the broadcast and *The
Nationalist* when he heard a knock on his door. He glanced
at his watch; Dick was not due for another fifteen minutes.
He tucked in his shirt and pulled the door open.

The woman standing in the hall was simply the most
beautiful Keenan had ever seen. She stood about five-foot-
six, dressed in a skirt and blouse that showed her curving
proportions off to good advantage. She had an oval face of
porcelain skin, finely dusted with freckles that bridged a
retroussé nose. The lamp light over Keenan's shoulder
reflected in her crystal green eyes. Thick, titian-colored hair
crowned her head, which was slightly cocked on a long,
slender neck. Her elegantly bowed lips curled up with
amusement at Keenan's rapt stare.

"Mr. MacBreed?" she asked. The perfect image was
blemished. Her teeth were uneven and nicotine yellow. She

exhaled the strong scent of tobacco, suggesting a habit not to Keenan's liking.

"Yes," Keenan managed, still happily drinking in the woman's image. She looked to be in her late twenties.

"I'm the official greeting committee," she said. "Welcome to Carrick."

"Thank you," he replied, surprised both that the town would bother to welcome him officially and that they would do it a day after he had arrived.

"May I come in?" she asked, her smile growing broader.

Keenan stepped aside, not bothering to question his good fortune.

"How was your trip?" the woman asked, her back to him as she surveyed the room. She carried a small portfolio in her left hand, which Keenan noticed as he took in the lines of her buttocks.

"Fine," he said, content to let her direct the conversation.

"And how is the colonel?"

"Excuse me?" Keenan asked.

The woman turned. The smile rapidly disappeared from her face. "What's my name?" she demanded.

"I'm sure I don't know," Keenan admitted, deflating. He knew his luck wasn't this good. "Was someone supposed to tell me you . . ."

The woman glanced around the room in confusion. Then she made straight for the open doorway. "There's been a mistake."

"But I *am* Keenan MacBreed," Keenan heard himself saying, inwardly wincing at the anxious sound of it. He followed her through the doorway and out into the hall. "I'm an archeologist. From . . ."

Once out of the room the woman hurried down the stairs and out of view.

". . . America." Keenan sighed. He stood a moment looking where the woman had disappeared. Then he turned off the light and looked out the window.

The woman trotted across Main Street to a red Ford Granada. To Keenan's surprise, she climbed in the passenger's side; she had not been alone. A few seconds later, the car roared to life and sped away.

Keenan locked up his room and went downstairs. The desk clerk was engaged on the telephone. As soon as he hung up, Keenan asked, "Do you have a reservation for another Mr. MacBreed?"

"No, sir. Should I?"

"I'm sure I don't know," Keenan came back, aware of the slightly peevish sound of his voice. "Did you talk to the woman who just walked through the foyer?"

"Yes, sir."

"What did you say?"

"She asked me if Mr. MacBreed had checked in. I told her yes and that I believed you were upstairs." The clerk looked a little sheepish. "Would you prefer that I telephone you for visitors?"

"No, that's not necessary," Keenan said. He glanced out the main door. "I think."

The door was abruptly filled by Sergeant Meagher's considerable girth. "Ready to go, I see."

"I'm not so sure," Keenan replied.

"Why? What's the trouble?" asked the policeman.

"Dick, you probably know everyone in Carrick, at least by face."

"I suppose."

Behind Meagher, a red car passed by on Main Street. Keenan strained to make out its shape and saw that it was smaller than a Granada. He returned his attention to Meagher. "Do you know a beautiful woman, about this high, well built, green eyes, auburn hair, mid to late twenties?"

"Sounds as if I'd like to, but I'm afraid I don't. What's this all about?"

Keenan let out an exasperated breath. "The strangest thing just happened to me. In fact, strange things have been happening ever since I arrived yesterday. I feel like I've climbed through Alice's looking glass."

"You're not the only one," Dick harmonized. He rubbed his rough chin with his fingers. "Well, this calls for a quiet pub, where we can sort out the events of the past two days."

"Sounds good to me," Keenan agreed.

"We'll go out to Delaney's. There's a fiddle player tonight. We'll take my car."

Keenan walked beside the sergeant to New Street. On the way, they passed three pubs already in full swing. With a population just over five thousand, Carrick supported almost forty pubs. Television, the movies, organized sports and all the other entertainments of modern life had not put much of a dent into Irish pub-going. The pub remained the center of socializing for the average man and woman. Pubs were more than places to drink; they formed extensions of the nuclear family that enlivened and supported day-to-day existence. They extended to almost all celebrations, including weddings, baptisms, funerals and sporting events. Not the impersonal saloon businesses of the New World, most pubs were literally part of the owners' homes, communal recreation rooms. All but the smallest sported dance space. Each one had a definite personality, often molded around the type of music played, which was as important to the pub-goers as the alcohol.

Delaney's was not crowded. Keenan ordered his Bushmills; Dick did not have to ask for his Guinness Extra Stout. On the way to the pub and while they waited for their drinks, Keenan had related his strange encounter with the beautiful woman.

"Mistaken identity," Meagher concluded. "What else could it be?"

"What indeed?" Keenan said. "Except that MacBreed's not that common a name, even in Ireland. And the desk clerk did not expect another Mr. MacBreed."

"Well," Meagher said, "we may never know the reason, but it has to be explainable somehow."

Keenan took a deep draw of his whiskey. "I'm willing to accept that for one mystery. But I'm an investigator of mysteries by profession, Dick. I can't just accept *everything* that's been happening without finding answers."

"I'm with you, Keenan," Meagher agreed. "I assume you're including this business with the skeleton."

"Of course. You have any news?"

Meagher suppressed a belch. The fiddle's melody filled in the pause. Keenan recognized the tune—"Arthur Mc-Bride." It had to do with British army officers trying to tempt Irish lads with coin and liquor to fight a British war on French soil. Keenan had never learned which war the lyricist had written about, but he assumed it was World War I.

Meagher took his fist down from his mouth. "No news. And in this case that doesn't mean good news. I dragged my carcass all over this corner of Ireland. Got to every registry office in a ten-mile radius. Nothing." He dug into his jacket pocket and extracted a photocopy of a dental chart. "Here. You might as well have a map of Mrs. Smiley's mouth. There are no reports in Clonmel, Kilkenny or Waterford of an open grave, a missing skeleton or a missing old lady."

"In other words," interpreted Keenan, "no one but us cares that we have this skeleton."

"And we do care, don't we?" Meagher said, and tipped back his mug of stout.

"I take it there was no report of old bones appearing either."

"Of course not."

"So," said Keenan, "that's two unsolved mysteries. And I have a third." He told Meagher of his second visit to Mary Liddy, of his accident of speaking Old Irish to her and her reaction.

"*Ollam* is the ancient word for wise man," Keenan explained. "Part poet, part astrologer, magician, physician, lawyer."

"Patting yourself on the back, were you?"

"Unintentionally. I wanted a Gaelic word. But once she reacted I said to her, in Old Irish, 'You understand.' I *think* that's what I said. I've never spoken it, only read it, of course. And I swear she did understand."

"Sergeant Meagher!" a male voice boomed. Keenan turned and saw a well-dressed man holding an empty whiskey glass.

Dick introduced the man, a merry-faced estate agent named Tuohey.

"Welcome home to the Auld Sod, Professor MacBreed," Tuohey greeted. To Keenan's relief he omitted the usual interview, intent instead on passing along a joke.

"You see there was this Protestant minister in Belfast," Tuohey began. "He was driving along, but he wasn't watching where he was going. So he drove right into the boot of a priest's car. Now, while the priest and the minister are surveying the damage along comes a Belfast cop. He takes one look at the cars, then says to the minister, 'So, Reverend, how fast was the priest backing up when he hit you?' "

Meagher smiled. "I'll add that to my repertoire, William, thank you."

Discouraged by the cool reception, Tuohey excused himself and edged into another group.

"A lovely lad, but a poor delivery," Meagher criticized. "Now, where were we?"

"I was about to ask you how Mary Liddy could know Old Irish?"

"Just because she lived in the rough doesn't mean that she didn't do some reading at one time."

"Old Irish!" Keenan shot back, incredulously.

"People have strange hobbies," Meagher offered. "Look, I know I'm reaching, but what else could it be?"

Keenan tilted his head, raised one eyebrow and stared into his glass. "Have you ever heard of Bridie Murphy?"

Meagher laughed. *"That's* your idea of solving a mystery? Another Irish woman reincarnated?"

"There have been some pretty compelling cases in its favor," Keenan defended.

"So, you're saying she remembered the words from a past life?"

Keenan shrugged. "Maybe when her present memory vanished, the old one was able to come forward . . . fill in the void. That's where the accent comes from."

Meagher rose ponderously. "And how should we explain a new skeleton under a thousand-year-old cross? Put there by extraterrestrials?" Before Keenan could reply, he added, "What does the Good Book say? All the worry in the world won't add a second to your life nor solve anything. Give me yer glass, MacBreed. We'll both attack our mysteries tomorrow—scientifically. Tonight, let's drink!"

5

August 17, 1988

"And what did Professor MacBreed have to say after that?" Father Flynn delved.

"He told us to keep diggin'," reported Fergus, "but to stop the minute we struck something out of the ordinary."

Father Flynn sucked in his cheeks and looked around the cemetery. The archeologist had put Mick and Fergus to work excavating a thirty-foot-wide pit around the site of the high cross. They had obviously been doing his bidding all morning and afternoon, for a dozen outer holes still lay open. Flynn's right hand grasped his left wrist, a gesture of pious strength that had become one of his numerous affectations. He pulled up his left hand, winging out his elbows, demonstrating his high dudgeon.

"And is he paying you two for the hours you're doing his work?" the priest demanded.

Fergus glanced at Mick, then back to the priest. "I don't think so. But the government is, and the whole cemetery has to be dug up anyway."

"Not the whole cemetery," corrected Father Flynn. "Just the burial sites."

Mick cleared his throat for the priest's attention. "Ah . . . the bodies under the cross proved that we don't know where all the sites are."

"All I know," returned Flynn, "is that there are three coffins in St. Columba's basement, with the earthly remains of souls inside disturbed from what should have been their final resting place. I insist that you put them back into sacred ground before you continue with this adventure."

Fergus leaned against the mechanical digger in defeat. "All right, Father. We'll do it tomorrow."

Father Flynn snorted in triumph. "You and I shall be doing business long after the professor has moved on. If he wants this cemetery scoured for artifacts, let him bring in people from Dublin." The walk up to his car was punctuated by a series of mutterings as a final declaration of his ire.

"Righteous bastard," Fergus pronounced under his breath.

"Let him blow," Mick said, hefting his shovel. "We've got the last laugh."

"Dick Meagher hasn't been after you anymore, has he?" Fergus inquired.

"No. You?"

"No."

"Even if they suspect gold was down here, they can't prove it," Mick said. "We're safe, as long as we lie low. You've got yer gold safely buried, haven't ya?"

"Absolutely," Fergus agreed, solemnly.

"Wait one year, then melt it down and sell it. Right?"

"Right."

The priest's car rumbled away down the hill. The noises from its muffler sounded a bit like the noises made by its owner.

Fergus looked at the sun, heading down a cloud-strewn sky. "Let's do one more row and call it quits for today."

Mick nodded his agreement. Fergus guided the digger down the slope and began a trench that he intended to work inward toward the huge central hole which had held the high cross and the three skeletons. While he worked, Mick tied two coffins they had uncovered that afternoon to their wagon. As Mick snapped the lock around the last chain, the machine's engine throttled down.

"Mick! Come here!" Fergus called out excitedly. "I think we've found another one!"

Bustling shovel work revealed a second high cross, again without cap or base.

"You think there's gold under this one?" Mick asked, the sun's yellow glint reflecting in his pupils.

"Only one way to find out," Fergus said, climbing into the digger's cab. This time, the treatment of the stone monument was less than gentle. Within five minutes it was hoisted out of the way and dropped to the sod.

"I'll be damned!" Mick cried out.

"What is it?"

"Three pairs of skeleton feet, bottoms up. Just under the cross, running down in a row."

"They buried these three headfirst?" Fergus said, rising from his seat for a look.

Mick bent and picked up a rectangle of thin, gray material. "See for yerself, Ferg. And here's another one of them signs, CAVE SÓRCÓRES."

"Forget about that!" Fergus commanded. "How are we goin' to dig out the gold if they're on their heads?"

"If we disturb 'em," Mick thought aloud, "MacBreed and Meagher will suspect us for sure. But if we dig a parallel hole on the outside edge, say we dug that one first and *then* discovered the cross . . ." He tossed the plaque aside.

"Lovely idea," Fergus praised. He set the machine to maximum speed and rapidly dug a seven-foot hole. As soon as the shovel cleared, Mick jumped down and began work. Fergus turned off the digger and followed.

"I bet there's yet another high cross in this boneyard," Fergus wagered, as he chewed at the dirt wall with his spade.

"Yer a greedy bastard," Mick said, without venom. "What you mean is a third set of gold handcuffs. Keep diggin', lad, 'cause we haven't found set two yet."

"Well, here's a skull . . . still nicely attached to its neck." Fergus shivered. "Christ, it's gettin' chilly."

"It is," agreed Mick. "Thank God we're in a sweat. Ah! Here's fingers!"

Prodded by the cold, the gravediggers' efforts redoubled. All along their lengths, parts of the three skeletons, including hands and wrists, gleamed whitely in the dying sunlight.

"No handcuffs!" Mick complained, his voice edgy.

"Dig deeper!" Fergus directed, his teeth chattering from the cold. "They're in here. They've got to be."

"I'm ready to pack it in," Mick said. "I know this is supposed to be a cold job, but I'm freezin'! And this is August."

"I think I've got a jacket in the truck," Fergus said. "You keep diggin' and I'll get it fer ya." He moved to the end of the hole, stretched up his arms and attempted to boost himself up. "Ahh! We shouldn't have been in such a hurry, Mick. I forgot to make an incline out. Give us a hand up!"

Behind Fergus, Mick wailed. Mortal fear ripped the air. The cry shook Fergus to his core, but he forced himself to turn.

"Help me, Ferg!" Mick screamed, yanking at his arm as if he wanted to tear it from its socket.

Fergus ignored the plea. Instead, he turned his back on his partner and concentrated on escaping from the trench. The cries mounted in pitch and agony, but Fergus kept his eyes averted; he had seen enough in one quick look. Another glance at the ravaged body of his partner might turn him to stone. He searched frantically for finger holds that were not in the soft soil. He did not turn again until the animal sounds stopped in midshriek. When he turned his head, the sight brought him to his knees. His short-circuiting brain faintly registered that the opposite end of the trench had a shallower bottom, but there was nothing on earth that would move him in that direction.

Now it was Fergus's time to scream. The will to live brought him once more to his feet. His hands clawed at the top of the hole, finding no purchase but bringing down sprays of dirt that found his gasping mouth. He screamed and leapt, screamed and leapt. Between the screams, behind him, came the rattling sounds of dry bones.

And then there was an unholy silence. A silence soon replaced by a quiet, gurgling sound. This sound also died, and all that remained was the whine of the cold, plaintive wind.

Keenan set the fork and knife in a cross pattern on the plate and pushed it away. The utensils' position indicated that he was finished, but he had left half the food on the plate. He stared at the untouched portions of cabbage, spuds and steak. The problem was not the food; it was an unsatisfied mind that had killed his appetite.

The ancient grave beneath the Celtic cross had evidently been a single incident site. Probably not the burial ground for a bacterial or viral mass epidemic. As the young police-man had suggested, maybe there had been a Viking raid on a monastery. Just north of Carrick had been home to one of the oldest monasteries in Ireland. Say that three monks slaughtered by invaders had been buried by their fellows, under a wooden cross that commemorated their martyr-dom. Some time later, the grave was improved by the addition of a stone high cross. A simple and easily explica-ble incident and thus a mere footnote in any scholarly tome. Maybe only a note in an appendix. Keenan had had his disappointments before. He would have been able to walk away from the site without a second thought if it hadn't been for the missing third skeleton and the substituted modern woman's bones. And where was the missing third cruciform necklace? It was like buying a novel and finding the last chapter purposely torn out. Natural mysteries and missing artifacts he could deal with; a vandalized dig he found more than vexing.

And then there were the two living mysteries—the beautiful red-headed woman with the crooked, yellow teeth and the wizened, old woman with the strange accent. The old woman who spoke English as if she were a newly-arrived foreigner but who understood Old Irish, who didn't even recognize boxed candy or a tape recorder. Quite old and yet with the perfect, white teeth of someone young. She and the beautiful red-head should have exchanged mouths, Keenan thought.

Keenan's eyes brimmed with tears. He reached to the back of his neck, to stroke down the hairs that had suddenly stood straight up. His mouth hung agape.

"You've got to watch their horseradish, lad," the man sitting opposite Keenan advised. Keenan nodded his false appreciation. He set his napkin on the table, threw down a ten pound note and hurried up to his room.

Keenan placed his first call to Dick Meagher, asking him to stop by as soon as he could. The second call went to the psychiatric hospital in Clonmel.

"What do you mean she's gone!" Keenan complained to the doctor.

"I shouldn't be discussing this with you, Dr. MacBreed," the physician said calmly, "but I know you have some connection with Mary Liddy. As I already told you, we found no neurological damage whatsoever. In our estimation she is sound of mind and has sufficiently regained her faculties to merit release."

Keenan scowled at the words. "And did she ask to be released?" he inquired.

"Yes, indeed. She began asking three days ago."

"Who picked her up?" Keenan asked.

"She took the bus. I assume she would call someone when she reached Carrick."

"You assume too much," Keenan could not help saying.

"Has anything happened to her?" the doctor anxiously asked.

"No. You're safe, Doctor," Keenan answered, then quickly hung up. He knew he was venting his frustration at the psychiatrist, but he had no other outlet. The old woman with the simultaneously young and ancient white teeth was free.

Dick Meagher met Keenan as the archeologist was about to climb into the Range Rover. "I thought *I* was supposed to come to *you,*" Dick remarked.

Keenan did a quick appraisal of the policeman. He was a friend, but there were all kinds of people one called friends —acquaintances, social confederates, business colleagues, those more famous or wealthy than you who hardly knew you. Even the occasional relative. But the person to whom you could open your innermost thoughts, the darker or more eccentric notions, were few and far between. Keenan suspected that Dick Meagher could become one of those friends if they had the luxury of time together. They were not that close yet, but Keenan really needed to talk with someone. Meagher had the only reasonable ear in Carrick.

"Whatever," Keenan answered. He surveyed the street and saw a pub three doors down. "Is this place quiet enough to talk?"

"Unless you've got weak lungs," Meagher answered. They stepped inside and found the most isolated corner.

"How's the day's hunting been?" Dick asked, as they were sitting.

"Nothing new," Keenan informed. "Unfortunately, I spent most of it with the town fathers, trying to figure out what to do with the high cross and how the highway construction will be affected. How was your hunting?"

Meagher shook his head. "Half of me is a foxhound. I love the chase. The other half's a pragmatist, my friend. If nobody but you and I care about that bunch of bones—and believe me, that's the case—I say let it go."

"Are you a religious man, Dick?" Keenan asked.

The policeman fixed his watery eyes on the younger man. "I'm a good Catholic, if that's what you mean."

"In the United States we have these religious people we call fundamentalists," Keenan went on. "They believe that every word in the Bible comes directly from God and espouses absolute truth. Are you that kind of religious man?"

"What are you driving at?" Meagher asked, leveling his gaze on the professor's eyes.

Keenan suspected that Meagher had consciously steered their previous night's conversation away from reincarnation to more innocuous subjects. Apparently, the extraordinary upset the policeman. But Keenan plunged on. He had to release his bizarre suspicions or explode with them.

"You know the Book of Ezekiel?"

"Not word for word, but I've read it."

"The part where the Lord takes Ezekiel to a desert filled with bones and tells him to preach to them."

"And the bones rise up."

"Do you think it happened?"

"Anything is possible with the Lord," Meagher responded.

"Do you think it could happen now?"

"Today?"

"Yes."

Meagher scrunched up his face. "Are you codding me, Professor?"

"No," Keenan answered, dead serious in his expression.

"This isn't a riddle or joke?"

"No."

Meagher sighed. "I would say 'no.' Not because the Lord couldn't do it, but because He's given us science in place of miracles."

"But you think all those bones rose back then?" Keenan pursued. "Stood up into skeletons, took on flesh and blood and lived?"

"I believe—you can't call me on this—but I believe

Ezekiel may have been talking in metaphor. Doesn't it say right after that the bones represent Israel; the people are mere dead bones without the prophets giving them the Word of Life?"

"What if it wasn't metaphor?" Keenan asked.

Meagher's inner control snapped. His face reddened. "And what if you've been sniffing too much formaldehyde, Professor?"

Keenan persisted in spite of the retort. "The gravediggers say they found three sets of bones. The grave also indicates that there were three. Two skeletons are definitely ancient."

"And the third?"

"What if the third ancient skeleton is missing because it took the body of a living woman and left that woman's bones in the hole?"

Keenan had expected derisive laughter. Instead, he stared at a man who clearly thought he was crazy.

Meagher downed his drink in one gulp and rose. "I'm going to assume you *are* codding me, Dr. MacBreed. Otherwise, you should take a vacation from the past and all its fairy tales and come live in the real world until your head clears."

Keenan watched the heavyset policeman shamble out of the pub. Then he set his chin on his fists and stared down at his drink. He knew that his hope for a sympathetic hearing from Meagher had been unrealistic. The Bible passage was as realistic a parallel as he could draw; his own theory belonged more properly to Halloween. In truth how could he, a scientist, suspect a wholly unnatural thing with so little hard evidence? If Meagher had even bought halfway the theory, perhaps he would have had the courage to pursue it.

Keenan swirled the whiskey in his glass, watched it slosh and circle, slow and settle. For an instant, he stepped outside his skin and took a look at his image, hunched over the alcohol, feeling confused and sorry for himself. It conjured up the Edward Arlington Robinson poem, *Miniver Cheevy*, about the man who dreamed of glorious, long-past times, called his bad luck fate "and kept on drinking." A man too timorous to deal with life, who longed to retreat into the past. That was Keenan MacBreed. Hiding behind the walls of academia because the "real world" was so cruel and dangerous, choosing instead to live a safe, esoteric existence with the dead. Now the dead were no longer esoteric—the dead had arisen. Or so he suspected. All Keenan had to do was prove it. All by himself. He had told himself for twenty years that he had chosen his ivy tower profession solely to please his parents. That his passive behavior in potentially violent conflicts reflected his Christian ethic, and the episode of racing out of Belfast because of The Troubles evinced realistic caution and prudence. He was not a coward. If sufficiently pushed, he had vowed to himself, he could face up to anything.

Finally, Keenan had the opportunity to put to the test whatever courage he professed to have. If he discovered what he suspected was true, the world would need to completely rewrite its understanding of existence. If he was right, this was the opportunity any archeology professor would have sacrificed his tenure to experience. If. If.

Keenan opened his mouth and threw back the drink. "Bartender!" he called out with resolve, "a double whiskey!"

The stars strewn across the blue-black sky hardly twinkled in the cool air. Down low, a breeze lifted the sweet smell of grasses off the earth, making them rustle like the sound of a reaper at work.

A four-cylinder car engine strained up the road's grade; headlights glinted off the metal of the gravedigger's wagon, then swept on.

Out of the burial ground rose the shapes of Fergus MacMahon and Mick Dunphy, moving slowly and lugging a third shape between them. When they reached the road they stopped, lowered their burden to the ground and silently studied the stars. Words passed between them, strange utterances which only they understood. Fergus moved slowly and deliberately. Confused pauses punctuated his speech. At last he stood still and pointed upward, his forefinger tracing a prominent constellation. Mick touched Fergus on the shoulder and indicated with a nod of his head the cumulus clouds gathering in the distance. The pair retrieved their common burden and started down the shoulder of the road.

John O'Connor lived alone. He had followed a bygone Irish tradition and remained unmarried late into life. But before he could take a wife his parents became old and infirm. John had been an only son; no woman wanted to share the burdens of John's familial duties and the pitiful farm he was to inherit.

So John had remained a bachelor, pulling what subsistence he could out of the earth. He needed very little and got as much, content to entertain himself with his television and his own singing. He favored a song called "The Jolly Miller," about a character who lived on the River Dee and cared for nobody "if nobodee cares for me." He had no close neighbors, which did not bother him in the least.

Thus, he was surprised and annoyed to hear footsteps out in his front yard. He was sure his television light could be seen through the curtains, making it impossible to pretend he wasn't home. He poised in his chair, awaiting the inevitable knock.

It didn't come. The footsteps continued. They belonged to more than one person—they seemed to be milling around, unsure of their purpose.

John expelled his breath in mild exasperation and thrust himself out of his chair. His sixty-year-old bones creaked with the effort. He shook the stiffness out of his right leg as he approached the front door.

"Who's there?" he called out.

The footsteps stopped, but no one answered.

John stared at the door lock. Surely it couldn't be anyone out to do him harm. Whoever they were, they were not acting stealthily. John unlocked the door and swung it open.

"Now . . ." John began. His eyes narrowed, adjusting to the gloom. "I know you," he recovered, taking a step outside. "You're the two diggin' up the cemetery."

The two figures faced him full on, one looking slightly older than the other and slightly heavier as well, but both of the same height and both looking rugged and worn from seasons of outdoor work. On the ground between them lay a large piece of tarpaulin, folded over, with a good-size mass inside.

"What do you want?" O'Connor demanded.

The gravediggers looked at each other in silence, then down at the tarpaulin. John's eyes followed theirs. The feeble light from inside the house fell on something white and smooth poking out of the cloth.

"What's in there?" John asked, taking another step forward. "It's not a body, is it?"

As if in answer, the older of the two gravediggers reached down and grabbed a corner of the tarp. He gave it a tug, then let it fall flat. There lay the top half of a skeleton, in perfect anatomical formation, as if strung together by wire.

The sight repelled O'Connor but, at the same time, he was unable to look away. One boney arm lay bent across the ivory rib cage; the other stretched out under the skull, as if cushioning it. The empty eye orbits seemed to stare up directly at the farmer.

"Jay-sus!" breathed O'Connor, eyes bulging out of their sockets, drinking in the unnatural sight and letting it overwhelm his attention.

Mick's hand was inches away from the farmer's right arm when John noticed it. "What—" he began, jerking his arm back.

The gravedigger's movement was quicker. Like a python

gathering in its prey, Mick's hand slid into the farmer's, interlacing their fingers. O'Connor threw himself back, gasped, but the stranger was hard onto him, driving him into the wall of the house. O'Connor felt his left hand being searched out and entwined. Over Mick's shoulder he saw the second digger calmly pulling out the tarpaulin containing the intact skeleton.

John O'Connor's adrenalin kicked in. Giving a desperate scream, he pushed against his attacker with all his might. The sound of ripping cloth filled his ears, and he suddenly felt naked. But the stranger held on.

"Let me go, you bastard!" John yelled with all his might, directly into the expressionless face of the man who held him. Mick's lips peeled back from his teeth, into a grimace that looked like a macabre half-smile.

O'Connor's fear became outrage. He struggled to close his imprisoned hands around Mick's throat. In his effort to throttle his attacker, John's own thumbs came up directly in front of his eyes.

Mick grabbed the thumbs and squeezed. John watched his fat fingers grow bright red, then split like overcooked sausages. Droplets of blood sprayed across his face.

Then the pain began, and John screamed as he never had before, not just from the pain but in final, abject horror. He watched helplessly as his flesh, sinew and muscle neatly peeled off his phalanges like a glove being pulled apart at the seams.

The chance was fifty-fifty. Carrick supported only two dentist's offices, and unless Mary Liddy had gone out of her way for dental care, one of the two would have her records.

Keenan glanced left and right, as far as he could see into the darkness of the neighboring back yards. There was neither sound nor movement. He had selected this place because the other office had been part of that dentist's home, with a much greater chance of discovery.

Keenan picked up a white-washed, garden-edging rock and wrapped it in his handkerchief. He took a last look around, drew one more deep breath and hit the glass pane. If he was intent on proving his nerve and courage, breaking and entering was a good start.

The door glass shattered dully. Keenan set the rock back in place, picked the broken glass from the sash, reached through the opening and unbolted the lock. The office was small, with an old file cabinet directly behind the receptionist's desk. Keenan was greatly relieved to see the lock button protruding from the cabinet's body. He had no skill whatsoever at picking locks; once, in vainly trying to open his own campus office, he had snapped his American Express card.

Mary Liddy's records were properly filed in the second drawer. Keenan pulled out the contents and left the empty folder. With any luck, the real purpose of his break-in would never be discovered. If his suspicions were right, Mary would not be coming back for further dental care. He wiped the cabinet and doorknob clean of his fingerprints. He figured the act was needless, but the example set by dozens of adventure movies was too much to ignore.

Within five minutes, Keenan was in and out of the dentist's office. Another five minutes' brisk walking brought him back to his hotel room. With trembling hands he laid Mary Liddy's dental records alongside the chart of the mystery skull that Sergeant Meagher had given him. Tooth for tooth, gap for gap, they were identical. A drop of perspiration fell from Keenan's forehead onto the photocopy.

Keenan sat down at the tiny hotel room desk, withdrew a sheet of stationery from the drawer and wrote Dick Meagher a note. If he disappeared, he wanted Meagher to know precisely why. He knew now that he was dealing with something truly unworldly. Staring at the hard evidence in front of him, Keenan also knew that his being murdered was a distinct possibility.

THE UPRISING

Keenan folded his note in two and placed it on top of Meagher's photocopy and Mary Liddy's dental records. He walked to the window, puzzling out his next move. Below on the street, people strolled by, enjoying the night, talking, joking, listening to music, totally absorbed in the visible world. Keenan envied them their innocence.

"Come quick!" the hired hand cried, fixing his wide-eyed stare on the master of the farm. "There's a fire up the road. I think it's O'Connor's farm."

Liam Walsh rose quickly from the kitchen table and stabbed his feet into his work shoes. His wife, Sheila, let the plate she was holding slip safely into the dishwater. "Dear Lord, Kevin," she said, "let's pray you're wrong."

The farmer and his wife followed the young man out into the night. They stared at the yellow-orange glow that hugged the horizon to the north and the telltale rise of smoke darker than the night.

"That's Johnny O'Connor's farm," Liam declared, grimly. "You'd better get on the telephone," he told Sheila.

"What's that light coming down the road?" Sheila asked.

For several moments they stood transfixed, following the wavering ball of flame.

"It's three men," Kevin called out from his vantage point halfway between the stone cottage and the gate of the long front wall. His twenty-year-old eyes strained to gather more information. "I think one of them is O'Connor."

"Are they hurrying?" Sheila asked.

"No," reported the hired hand.

"That's peculiar," said Liam. "Maybe the fire's *not* at Johnny's place."

The three men emerged from the darkness, lit by the torch in John O'Connor's right hand. As they neared, the Walsh's Irish setter bounded toward them, growling loudly. The three men stopped short in the gateway.

"Red, come here!" Kevin called out.

"What's wrong with Red?" Sheila asked her husband, her voice tense. "He barks all the time, but he never growls."

The dog came within a length of the three men, springing, snarling, circling nervously around them.

"What's going on, Johnny?" Liam called out.

Ignoring Liam's words, the three men stared down at the threatening dog.

Kevin strode forward several steps. "Mr. O'Connor?"

"Red!" Liam shouted. The dog also ignored him.

Kevin retreated toward the cottage with long steps.

"This is very strange, Liam," his wife worried aloud.

"It is," agreed Kevin, coming up closer to them. "That's Mr. O'Connor all right, but somehow he's . . . taller." The young man's face showed his extreme bewilderment.

Red circled toward the center man and, as he neared, John O'Connor thrust out his torch, catching the dog full on with its flaming tip. The dog rolled backward in surprise, a patch of its hair aflame. Red yelped and rolled, kicking up dirt until the fire on its chest was extinguished. Then it bounded away into the night, wimpering loudly.

"Get the shotgun, Kevin!" Liam commanded. "Load it up!" The hand bounded by the older man into the cottage. Liam took a step forward.

"Don't go near them, Liam!" Sheila begged.

"It's my damned property!" Liam snapped, then, to the three men, "What do you want?"

In a line that widened with each step, the men moved forward.

"Stay where you are," Liam called out, glancing anxiously behind himself for Kevin's return. "You can talk from there." The men continued forward. "Sheila, get inside the house!" With his eyes fixed on the approaching men, he listened to the sounds of his wife obeying.

Finally, the figure of John O'Connor spoke to the man on his left. The words were unlike any Liam had ever heard.

"Stop!" Liam shouted. "Not one step closer!" Kevin

rushed up to his side, chambering a shell into the shotgun. "Give it to me!" Liam ordered, holding out his right hand, while his left went up, forefinger raised. "This is your last warning!"

The three men started forward menacingly. "Shoot, Mr. Walsh!" Kevin pleaded.

Liam put the shotgun to his shoulder and trained it directly at John O'Connor. O'Connor did not seem at all frightened.

Liam fired. The blast caught O'Connor in the leg. He buckled and fell. The other two stopped. Slowly, without uttering a sound, O'Connor stood. He started forward again, limping badly.

"My God!" Kevin gasped.

Liam recovered from the shock of the gravely wounded man recovering, shouldered the shotgun and pumped it. O'Connor had come within twenty feet. Liam's hands trembled so that he had trouble keeping his aim. The only ammunition he owned was rabbit load, and he knew that he would have to wait if he wanted to kill the man outright. But killing was not in Liam's character.

"Shoot!" Kevin shouted.

Liam flinched at the command. His trigger finger squeezed involuntarily at the same time that his shoulders and arms twitched. The shotgun blasted.

The evidence of Liam's poor aim was instantly visible. Most of the pellets tore into O'Connor's right shoulder, tearing his shirt and spraying blood. A few caught his neck and ear, ripping away bits of flesh. Still he moved forward, showing no sign of suffering or fear.

From both flanks the strangers rushed forward.

The farmer stood in semishock. "They're crazy!" he gasped.

"Come on!" Kevin yelled, yanking hard on Liam's arm. Liam allowed himself to be turned. The shotgun fell from his hand. Kevin pivoted, saw how close the three aggressors had come, and abandoned the weapon. The front door slammed shut with Kevin and Liam inside an instant before Mick threw himself against it.

John O'Connor limped up close to the cottage and lifted his torch.

The thatch flared up rapidly, the flames dancing along the angles of the roof and back down among the timbers.

Fergus picked up the shotgun and circled the cottage. When Liam opened the back door he was there, brandishing the weapon, forcing the farmer back inside. Wisps of smoke escaped through the open doorway.

"What do you want?" Sheila wailed.

The three men silently circled the house, John with his torch, Fergus with the shotgun and Mick with a pitchfork he had found leaning against a storage shed. The trio made sure they blocked every exit.

The back door opened again and Liam Walsh hurtled out, holding a wooden kitchen chair straight out in front of him. Mick thrust the pitchfork lightly into Walsh's side, then yanked it back. He reached out to grab the farmer's hand, but Liam struck him a glancing blow with the chair and stumbled backward into the thickening smoke and crackling noise. The door slammed shut. Sheila's series of screams dissolved into coughs.

Roaring his outrage, Kevin burst through the front door, then darted quickly to his left. One hand clutched a fireplace poker, the other a stool—he flailed both blindly. His puffy, tearing eyes were all but useless to him, and his heaving lungs failed him as well, forcing him almost double from the wracking spasms.

John moved in quickly, pushed the torch hard against Kevin's collar, then trailed the fire down his back. The young man's clothing burst into flame. Kevin felt the fire and collapsed to the ground. He rolled frantically, back and forth, kicking up clouds of dust that reflected the fierce glow of the cottage. His head lolled to one side. One leg twitched. Then he lay still.

John and Fergus came together over Kevin's prone form. Fergus set his booted foot on the middle of the hired hand's back and ground out a patch of flame that persisted. The air groaned out of Kevin's lungs. His chest fought in new air. John lowered his badly wounded body to the ground until he lay exactly parallel to Kevin's form. He looked up at Fergus expectantly.

Fergus's eyes measured the two figures on the ground. He looked at John and shook his head, then offered a hand so that the wounded man could stand again. Coin-size pools of blood stained the earth where John had lain. He limped away from the dying hired hand. Fergus raised the shotgun and chambered a shell, as he had seen the farmer do. He set the gun to his shoulder, curled his finger around the trigger, took careful aim at Kevin's head and fired.

Keenan worried about the lack of light as he drove toward Lamoge cemetery. Light was critical for him to find and confront the thing that hid inside Mary Liddy's flesh. He was convinced that it would either be at the cemetery already or would arrive soon. Although her bones had been discarded, images of her life in the twentieth century might have survived in Mary's brain—pictures of houses, roads, hills. The creature would therefore know how to get back to the caretaker's cottage. But even if no memory remained in the stolen brain, the being would still find its way back to the burial ground. Keenan was betting on it. Dick Meaghers first sight of her had been in the act of digging furiously, dead center in the graveyard. The being had stayed there after killing Mary. Something vital to it was under the emerald sod. As Keenan drove he allowed his imagination to run wild. Maybe the object was a magic wand, to complete the thing's power. Maybe it was an ancient tome of incantations, buried inside a tiny metal coffin. Or maybe a hoard of gold. The ancient Wicklow gold mines lay not far away.

Keenan worried that his oil lantern and krypton flashlight

would not blaze brightly enough into the dangerous night. As he weighed the problem, he caught a faint glow, hugging the mountain's shoulder. Soon, he realized the light came from two separate fires. Was the thing inside Mary Liddy at work again, murdering? The thought made him want to turn the Range Rover around and head for the fortresslike security of Trinity college. But the creature that called itself Mary was not a nameless terror to him. He had spoken to it, seen its logical mind and rational behavior. It had even betrayed itself in the hospital and still let him escape. Frail reassurance, but enough to make him bet his life that he could reason with it.

When Keenan neared the burning farm, he noticed a cluster of vehicles. Closest to the cottage were two small fire engines. They were almost quaint in comparison to the huge hook-and-ladders of Boston. Farther away sat four cars and a truck, vehicles owned by either the fire fighters or the gawkers who had gathered about. Nearest to the road stood Sergeant Meagher's familiar *Garda* car.

As he stepped out of the Rover, Keenan turned his attention away from the fire, swinging his powerful flashlight into the encroaching darkness, straining to spot the reflection of a pair of old woman's eyes. He saw nothing.

"Just the man I wanted to see," Sergeant Meagher said, coming up to Keenan, looking very weary.

"Not about this, surely," Keenan replied.

"Not directly. But you *are* part of the great mystery, of which this is the latest manifestation."

Keenan looked at the cottage, at the flames that were rapidly succumbing to the dousings of the hose and bucket brigade. He did not want the sergeant to read or misread any of his thoughts. "I don't . . ."

"Sergeant Meagher, I must insist—" A bespectacled man, waving a note pad and pen, bore down on the policeman.

"All right, all right," Meagher interrupted. "Give me three minutes, and I'm all yours."

The man seemed grudgingly satisfied, turned and waved an accosting pen at one of the fire fighters.

"He's the local reporter for *The Nationalist*," Meagher imparted. "It does me no good to get on his bad side." He hooked Keenan's elbow and guided him toward the farm's outer stone wall. "A little more than an hour ago I got a call from Mrs. MacMahon."

"The gravedigger's wife?"

"The same. She was worried because Fergus hadn't come home. It seems that no matter what else he does, he always begins his evening with her dinner. She called all of his usual haunts, but he'd shown at none of them. I tried to put her off. It rarely pays to worry sooner than twelve hours after people disappear. They invariably show up—especially the Fergus MacMahon type. But the missus then told me she was worried because he'd been acting strangely of late. So I stopped over.

"She took me back to their garage. Fergus had put a new lock on it and kept the key to himself. When the missus inquired after the banging he was making inside, he told her he was building her a surprise. She doubted it, because, other than employing his shovel, Fergus is not the handyman type."

Meagher dug his right hand into his jacket pocket and held it there. "Now, she wants me to bust the lock. Of course I tell her I can't, but I show her how to do it. And what do you suppose we find inside?"

"Not the missing skeleton," Keenan said, with true conviction.

"This." Meagher raised his hand and opened his palm. In it gleamed two circlets of gold with golden links dangling from them. He handed one to the archeologist.

Keenan stared in wonder at the treasure. The bracelet's center was deeply incised with a cross. The rest of the surface was covered with intricate Celtic scrollwork and filigree. "It's incredible!" Keenan breathed. He turned it over and hefted its weight, as if to be sure it was not an illusion.

"There were also several sheets of beaten gold leaf," Meagher reported. "Fergus musta been pounding some of the links is what the missus heard. It looks like manacles, but whoever was held by it coulda pulled almost pure gold links apart without much trouble."

"It must have been decorative," Keenan suggested, already fairly certain of what he held but not wanting Meagher to guess the truth.

"Are you sure?" Meagher came back. "Couldn't it have been meant to restrain one of the bodies, in some ritualistic way?"

Looking hard at the policeman, Keenan appraised his friend's powers of deduction. He realized he would have to be clever to deceive Meagher. "I suppose," the archeologist admitted.

Meagher dipped his head. "But, of course—as you said only a few hours ago—there were *three* skeletons. Well, if Fergus walked away with gold, you could bet Mick would demand the same. I assume there must be another pair just like this. I told Mrs. MacMahon we'd find her husband, then drove over to Mick Dunphy's as fast as I could. Well, he was missing, too. 'He's been actin' skittish of late' says the wife, but she couldn't help me find the manacles."

Meagher held out his hand and snapped his fingers for the treasure. As he put it away, he observed, "These will probably go to you eventually, but for now they're evidence."

"You know, perhaps your gravediggers broke the middle skeleton when they were removing the bracelets," Keenan suggested, curious to draw out the policeman's private thoughts. "They were afraid I'd wonder why they'd disturbed it, so they substituted another skeleton."

"From where?" Meagher shot back. "It certainly didn't come from Lamoge."

"Well, there's got to be a logical answer," said the archeologist.

"Does there?" the policeman countered. "And what about the bizarre things you've been spouting at me these past few days?"

Keenan focused over the policeman's shoulder at the ruined farm yard, anxious to avoid the assessing eyes. "But you practically took my head off," he answered. "Told me to get in touch with the real world again, remember?"

Meagher followed Keenan's gaze. He nodded his head in the direction of the cottage. "The real world. Such as this farm, right? We got a call from the woman of this place . . . whose remains are no doubt still inside. Mrs. Walsh was rather hysterical, but she did manage to describe the three men who were attacking them. The one was John O'Connor." Meagher swung around and indicated the dying glow up the road. "That was his farm there . . . totally destroyed. The other two men fit the descriptions of Mick Dunphy and Fergus MacMahon. We record every call that comes into the station. You can listen to it if you've a mind."

In the short time Keenan had known the policeman, he had come to believe that Meagher could keep a sense of humor and balance about any crisis, even something as stressful as moving a burial ground. But looking in his eyes now, Keenan saw outright dejection.

"You and I know that something strange happened to Mary Liddy," Dick went on, as he fetched a grimy handkerchief from his back trouser pocket and used it to mop his sweating, sooty brow. His voice dropped to an emphatic whisper. "Now it seems that something even stranger has come upon John O'Connor, Fergus MacMahon and Mick Dunphy. Much as I hate to admit it, Father Flynn was right; it was a mistake to open up that burial ground. Something evil's gotten out, and it's affecting everyone who comes up on this mountain. You have an opinion on what it is, and I—"

"Your three minutes are past," the reporter called out, advancing again.

Meagher sighed. "Yes, Donal, I'm yours." His eyes swung back to Keenan and narrowed into slits. "I don't know if they'll let me sleep tonight, but I'll be in the station house before noon. See that you're there, Professor." Meagher lumbered toward the blanket-covered corpse in front of the cottage. The reporter guarded his wake jealously.

Keenan climbed into the Range Rover, brought it to life, but waited until the sergeant had his back fully to the road before pulling away. He did not want Meagher to see him heading north, toward the cemetery. A half mile farther on, he passed the smoldering wreck of John O'Connor's cottage. The roof had collapsed into the stone walls, and the window openings and empty doorway glowed brightly like the eyes and mouth of a huge jack-o'-lantern. A *Garda* car stood between the cottage and the road.

Another mile north brought him to the Lamoge burial ground. He drove beyond it, around the dangerous turn in the road to the cemetery-keeper's cottage. The rugged driveway wound around the house, making it possible for Keenan to conceal the Rover. He stepped from the car, flashlight in hand. Sweeping the beam in a slow circle, he found no sign of life.

The cottage was stuffed with darkness. Its windows reflected the light Keenan directed at them, giving him no clue as to what lay inside. He moved to the low back door to test the knob, expecting that it would be locked. This time the door had no windowpanes that could be smashed in. It was solid but old. Keenan suspected that it would give to several hard shoulder rammings. He did not hesitate at the prospect. It had nothing to do with the success at the dentist's office; it had nothing to do with no one being within hearing range. It was simply that, after seeing the carnage and destruction in the farmhouses to the south, he was sure he had to pursue the mystery to whatever lengths were necessary.

THE UPRISING

To Keenan's surprise, the knob turned easily. His heart-beat sped up to a quick-march tempo. If he could get inside with no sign of entry, so could the thing masquerading as Mary Liddy.

Keenan entered as quietly as possible. The cottage was unprepossessing, containing little more than the bare necessities of life. The living, dining and cooking areas flowed across one large room. To his right lay an archway, which Keenan supposed led to a single bedroom and bath. The openness of the room left no place to hide, allowing him to breathe easier. He considered looking for a weapon, then rejected the idea. If burial in the ground for at least a thousand years had not killed the ancient, there was little hope a knife or cudgel could protect him. He would have to rely on his judgment of the being and his own wits.

Keenan glided noiselessly through the archway and into the bedroom. At first, he thought the place smelled like boxwood, then realized it was the faint odor of incontinence. His flashlight beam traced along the seat of an old rocker, its varnish dissolved by repeated soakings with urine. The tiny bathroom lay empty. Keenan got to his knees and dared to look under the bed. When he found only a legion of dust balls, his saliva began flowing once more.

A little path had been trampled down the back of the Liddy property into the cemetery. Keenan followed it, exclaiming nervously at each obstruction. An obstacle course of stones poked out of the earth, threatening to trip him and send flying the lantern in his left hand and the flashlight in his right. In Keenan's mind, if the eight died, so did he.

The cemetery had been Keenan's best hope for meeting the ancient again. The place had obviously held more than the bones now inside Mary—something "she" had not had the time to unearth. While he had been in Carrick meeting with local officials, the two gravediggers had continued their work. The exact center of the cemetery lay open, and beside the large trench lay a second high cross. Keenan made his way gingerly toward the excavation, well aware of the many open holes. The digging machine looked like an immobile yellow dinosaur.

Keenan examined the newly exposed high cross. At first glance it looked identical to the first one. He had spent enough hours staring at that exquisite object to know that the areas around the transepts and circle were near-perfect duplicates. But as he swung his light toward the bottom of the cross he saw the pronounced difference. Like the first, this cross had three figures near its base. Unlike the first, all three figures were identical. Identical skeletons. Someone with less knowledge than Keenan might have mistaken them for stick figures. He knew that the artists of that ancient time were far more talented; he also knew that these skeletons were not allegorical. Beneath each was an amorphous heap with barely discernible head, hands and feet.

Keenan picked his way to the first high cross, still lying where the digging machine had set it down. He knelt at the bottom and shone his flashlight up along its length from a low angle. He whistled softly at his discovery. Diffuse daylight obscured and flattened the weathered relief of the carving; light from a single source popped the high spots out. Now Keenan could see the faint swellings of breasts on the central figure. And the shape around the head, which Dick Meagher had guessed was a hood, became a crown of hair, with soft, undulating skeins and perhaps a pair of plaited strands. The figure of the creature now inside Mary Liddy, as imagined by an artisan from a hundred years after her burial. The men on either side held up crosses, as if to ward her off. What was that old adage? The Devil hath power to assume a pleasing shape?

Keenan returned to the second cross. As he swung his flashlight, its beam caught a gray, flat rectangle of metal. He picked it up and read it. CAVE SŌRCŌRES. Latin. Beware of the sorcerers. Or sorceresses. Definitely plural. Too bad Dunphy and MacMahon couldn't read Latin. "Mary" had not been digging for a wand, a book or gold; her goal was to free three beings like herself. Beings now in the bodies of John O'Connor, Mick Dunphy and Fergus MacMahon.

To the west Keenan saw the black shape of 2,400-foot-high Slievenamon Peak. The Old Irish name meant "Mountain of the Fair Women." Some said it was the "Mountain of the Fairy Women." Keenan had a chilling suspicion how the peak had gotten the name.

Keenan arced the flashlight once again in a slow circle, aware of his contradictory feelings. He was terrified of the undead thing inside Mary Liddy's flesh; yet he worried that he had not found her in the cottage or cemetery. Sergeant Meagher, in his current frame of mind, would certainly pick her up if he saw her walking north past the burned-out farm. What would "she" do if Meagher tried to hold her against her will?

Keenan sighed deeply. He was in the burial ground; he might as well use his time investigating. He approached the large central hole and shone his twin lights down. At the bottom of the pit lay two complete skeletons. The bones of MacMahon and Dunphy, no doubt. So where was John O'Connor?

Keenan put the oil lantern on the ground, sat on the edge of the hole and lowered himself. The darkness had lessened his sense of depth. Keenan was surprised at how deep the hole was. He immediately shone the light around, in search of an exit, but found no easy way out. He resolved to worry about the problem later. There was a mystery still unsolved. The beam of light showed him that the west wall had three deep indentations, running vertically. This trio of bones had evidently been buried at right angles to the normal burial position. His guess was that the sorcerers had taken Dunphy and MacMahon immediately and had carried the third set of bones to John O'Connor's farm, where the third ancient had stolen the farmer's flesh.

The bones were clean of flesh. There was no pool of blood; no telltale coppery smell. Just a grave site with two sets of bones in it. Keenan shivered, not only from looking at bones of men alive a few hours ago but also from the unnatural cold in the pit. Abruptly, he could not stand being in the grave. He turned to find a way up.

Mary Liddy looked down at him, the oil lantern throwing up light that cast demonic-looking shadows on her face. Keenan started; he had not heard the slightest sound of her approach. She regarded him calmly.

Keenan drew in a deep breath. "I've been waiting for you," he said. "Your friends are gone, as you can see."

Without reply, the old woman slowly kneeled, bringing her flashing eyes closer to his. Her left hand stretched forward.

Keenan licked his lips and glanced from side to side.

"Come up!" the old female voice ordered. She surveyed the hole and decided to kneel on both knees.

Keenan raised his hand to hers, doing his best to steady it against the fear that radiated from the depth of his being out to his fingers. She grasped it and tugged. He expected to be jerked up by fierce, supernatural strength. He was relieved to find that she had no more strength in her bones than the old woman's she had replaced. Two feeble pulls told Keenan that his weight would only yank her down into the hole with him.

"I'll find a way up," he told her. His flashlight beam found a niche in the wall where one of the skeletons had lain intombed. He struggled up and out. As he came to one knee, Mary was waiting for him, oil lantern in her right hand. Her left hand shot out and ripped his shirt open to the third button. Keenan shrank back, but the old woman held tight. Her face leaned down; her darting eyes searched the area of his throat. She seemed satisfied and suddenly let his shirt go. Keenan sat down hard.

"I'm a friend. *Chara,*" Keenan said, with emphasis.

The old woman did not seem particularly impressed. *"Cia cnámai i lecht?"*

Keenan glanced at the hole. "Those are the bones of the

two men who dug the hole. The ones who caught you. Do you understand?"

"*No-dam.*"

"Good." Keenan stood slowly. Suddenly, Keenan understood the reason for the woman's attack. He opened his shirt. "I wear no cross. I am not like the men who buried you."

Mary nodded. "Where are *mo charasai?*"

Keenan pointed south. *"Deisceart.* Did you not see them when you came here?"

In halting English, peppered with her native words, the woman told Keenan how she had gotten off the bus in Carrick and hitched a ride on the back of a farmer's wagon. When they traveled into the shadow of Slievanamon Peak, she realized she was going too far west and hopped off the wagon. She had walked almost five miles, the last two in near-total darkness. Keenan could read the weariness of the journey in her face and the stoop of her shoulders.

"I need to know more about you," Keenan said.

"Táim ag dul," Mary answered, moving south.

"No!" Keenan said, forcefully. "You can't go. Not by yourself. Men are waiting for you." Mary's eyebrow arched. Keenan raised his hands, palms up, hoping the gesture did not mean anything offensive to her. "I told them nothing. But your friends have been killing . . . killing more than the three bodies they need." Keenan paused significantly, hoping for response. In the past week, Mary had had ample opportunity to escape from the hospital and go on a killing rampage. She had done neither. She was not like the three ancients in the other grave. Perhaps the difference in the way they had been buried was significant.

"They kill because they believe these people are enemy," Mary proclaimed. "That is why I must go to them now."

"Well, you won't get very far walking down that road," Keenan pointed out. "The guards—you understand guards, *Gardaí?*"

"I understand."

"They want to talk with anyone who lives near this cemetery. I know where your friends are going . . . probably where they are. I will drive you there in my car."

"You are . . . *achtach,*" Mary said.

Keenan smiled. "No, I'm not brave. I am someone who has studied your people, your time. I want to understand you, help you and be your friend. You need a friend."

Mary assessed Keenan for a long moment. "Yes."

Keenan felt the huge knot of fear and tension partially unravel in his stomach. "You are a woman."

Mary laughed, showing her straight, white teeth. "Yes. A woman."

"Druith?"

"Druit'," she replied, correcting his pronunciation.

"Your name?"

"My name is Mary Liddy."

"Your Druid name," Keenan pursued.

"I am Mary Liddy," the woman insisted.

Keenan realized that Mary had been ready to abandon the burial ground. Almost certainly there were no more of her kind buried there, but he had to ask her nonetheless. "Are there only four of you? *Ceithri?"* he translated, as he held four fingers up.

"You ask many questions," Mary replied. "More than I."

"I'll answer any you like."

"You will answer t'ree for one I ask," Mary countered. "I can ask all of your people my questions."

"But you cannot trust them," Keenan returned. He raised his ten fingers. "And in all of this island there are not ten people who speak your language, not ten who know as much about *your* people as I do."

"I must go," Mary said, pushing past Keenan.

"Wait!" Keenan called out. "I promised to help you, and I will. But first you need warmer clothing and better shoes." Mary stopped. "Come back to Mary's cottage with me.

Then I'll drive you to where I think your friends are." Mary turned and waited for Keenan to lead the way.

Mary sniffed the air noisily several times before she entered the Liddy cottage. Its smell undoubtedly bothered her.

"Are you hungry?" Keenan ventured, walking inside.

"Yes," Mary answered, moving after him warily.

Keenan searched through the cabinet next to the stove. He stopped at the packet of porridge. "Stir about" had been a staple in the Irish diet even in the ancient's time. "I think you'll like this," Keenan said, as he lit the stove. Mary made no reply, but eased herself onto one of the kitchen chairs.

After Keenan had the porridge mixed and cooking, he turned and gave Mary his best smile.

"Who was the king of your region, Mary?" he asked, as casually as he could. "Who was your *rí túaithe?*"

"Caicher."

The name told Keenan nothing.

"Are you *ollam* in truth?" Mary asked.

They had a deal; she was entitled to her questions. *Ollam* was within a country mile of what he was. Getting into archeology and anthropology did not seem like a good idea. Besides, she had seemed awfully impressed by the word the last time they met.

"Yes. *Ollam,*" Keenan answered, poker-faced. He turned away and sought out a piece of paper and a pencil. He sketched a Viking long ship. "Do you remember ships like this?"

Mary shook her head.

Keenan thought of Mary's aversion to the cross. "What about Pádraig?"

Mary's figure tensed.

"Christos' fer?" Keenan asked.

The hatred in the flashing eyes was awesome. St. Patrick, Christ's man, was more than a legend to her.

Mary looked away, to the stove. She pointed to the steam escaping from the pot of boiling porridge. Keenan discreetly moved to her service. Mary ate the food hungrily, ladling the spoon into her mouth as soon as she was sure each bit was cool enough. For a while Keenan sat and watched her, using her left hand to feed herself. Then his glance chanced on her legs. They were bruised and crisscrossed with cuts from many falls during her dark journey to the cemetery. The hem of her skirt hung tattered in several places.

Without comment, Keenan took the remaining hot water, poured it into a bowl, found a dish towel and kneeled at Mary's feet. She eyed him in silence, the spoon halfway between her mouth and the bowl. She allowed him to wash away the dirt and blood. When he had finished and stood, he found her look softened, less wary.

"You should wash your face," Keenan suggested, moving through the archway and lighting the bathroom. In the bedroom's old wardrobe he found a pair of woman's long cotton pants, a sweater and walking shoes. No sound came from the bathroom. The door stood open. He walked in, holding the clothes and shoes.

Mary stood in front of the mirror, transfixed by her image. A tear drifted slowly down her wrinkled cheek. The dewlap flesh of her throat worked up and down. Keenan set the clothing on the rim of the bathtub and left, closing the door softly behind him.

"The name of your tuath?"

"Tuait'e de Donn," replied Mary. The clan of the brown haired.

"Was your hair *donn?"* Keenan asked, glancing from the highway and wondering if the ancient woman knew just how slow five miles an hour was for an automobile. Even at that crawl, they would reach their destination in less than two minutes.

"No," Mary answered. *"Ród."* Red-haired. Her left hand thrust across the steering wheel. "What is this?"

"To make the light brighter," Keenan answered, hurriedly. He was not about to explain the washer, wipers and turn signals also contained on the stalk. Time was too precious, and Mary, while relaxing her edict of three questions for every one of his, was just as intent on learning as he was. His few questions had cost him a *quid pro quo* tutorial on the use of the Range Rover. He flashed the high beams to demonstrate.

"The Christians buried you because you were a Druidess, an enemy."

"Yes. Do you know cowboys?"

Keenan laughed. "No, I don't." A truck's lights swept up the road. Keenan accelerated to ten miles an hour.

"Indians?" Mary asked.

"No. Sorry. No Indians either." The truck, a food purveyor, passed. Keenan eased off the accelerator. "How old were you when they buried you?"

Mary held up both hands, flexed her fingers twice and added two more.

"Twenty-two," Keenan translated. "Were you in any other bodies?"

"No. I took this woman's body because I believed her an enemy and because I had not one other to take."

"I understand," Keenan said, neutrally.

"Mary Liddy wanted to die," the ancient revealed, matter-of-factly.

Keenan's foot lifted from the pedal. "How do you know that?"

Mary made a sound in her throat, as if trying to coax the words up. "Like the tapes I listen to. Before you hear the strong words or music sometime, you hear it quiet. Most of her memory gone wit' *s'anam,* but some stays in her *cenn.*"

Keenan marveled at the Druidess' perceptive analogy. If the word *anam* meant *soul* in Old Irish, as it did in Middle Irish, he was sure she meant that most of Mary's memory had departed with her soul and yet the chemical imprints of her life experiences lingered faintly inside her head, etched in her brain. As the magnetic signal on recording tape sometimes bled through to the next winding or remained behind after an imperfect erasing. The lingering imprints could have been how Mary had oriented herself to a modern, alien world so quickly, how she had assimilated basic English in less than a week.

The revelation had Keenan so stunned that he almost missed the boreen, a narrow dirt road which was little more than two ruts in the grass. He pressed hard on his brakes and steered off the road. Fortunately, the Walsh farmhouse was the last one until highways R697 and R697A met. At that point, the land rose steeply on both sides, and some of Ireland's only dense forest grew. Keenan was fairly sure that the three other creatures would avoid the highways after the killings and that the black night, the star-masking clouds and the dense vegetation would stop them until first light. He had calculated that they could have gotten no farther than the place where he had turned off. After seeing the destruction at the two farmhouses, he was not anxious to be overly accurate in trailing them.

"They are here?" Mary asked.

"Nearby," Keenan answered, stopping the Rover and killing the engine and lights. "We won't be able to find them until morning. Here." He reached into a case behind Mary's seat and pulled out two Irish ordinance maps. He placed the Tipperary map at right angles on his own lap and spread the East Cork-Waterford map sideways in front of Mary. "We're here. This is the cemetery."

Mary scowled briefly at the cemetery's symbol. Her annoyance at the cross figure did not last long; it was obvious that she was fascinated by the maps. "Where is Carrick?" she asked.

"Here. And here's Clonmel. Where you were in hospital."

"This yellow?"

Keenan explained the colors of the various elevations, then the differences in types of roads and other symbols. It gave him pleasure to introduce Mary to an alien invention.

The forefinger of her right hand drifted south-southwest, through Carrick, across the Suir River, through Carrick-beg and into the Comeragh Mountains. She seemed content to study the maps all night.

"We've come this far," Keenan said. His finger found their position on the map. "Your friends can't be far away. I've got a tent that connects to the back of the car. We can't build a fire, but I have a sleeping bag I can put over us. We'll find your friends when the sun comes up."

Mary agreed and gave what help she could erecting the tent. While they worked, Keenan asked, "How do you go into another person's body?"

Mary kept her eyes fixed on her labor. "You cannot know. It is *ru.*"

"A mystery," Keenan translated, unconsciously. "I know many mysteries myself, and I would share them with you if you ask."

Mary shook her head. "I will say just this: it must begin with the hand."

"Deina?" Keenan asked, holding up the palm side of his hand to Mary's eyes.

"No. From here." She held up her left hand and pointed with the right. "The t'umb."

Keenan peered at the old woman's hand. At least in the dim light there was no sign at all of the skin being broken and resealed. The sharing of such great magic was definitely a breakthrough. Keenan respected it and maintained his silence until the tent was up and the sleeping bag zipped open and spread. Before leaving Carrick he had bought several candy bars. He brought them out, opened one and offered it to Mary. She gave it a perfunctory sniff and attacked it hungrily.

In the car, Mary had revealed that the other three ancients were also women. There was something about one plus three Celtic women that teased Keenan's memory. Try as he might, he could not dredge it up.

As Mary played with the buttons of her sweater, her eyes

chanced on Keenan's tape recorder. "Do you have music in that?"

"I can put music in it," he answered. He rummaged through his collection of tapes and fetched out the one with the oldest Irish folk music. They both sat and listened in silence through several selections. "It is not like your people's music, is it?" Keenan asked.

"No," Mary replied. "Our music is no so *cas,* no so *cain.*" Not as lively or beautiful.

"Will you sing a song?" Keenan encouraged.

Mary sang a few notes, grimaced at the harsh, hoary sound of her old throat, then began again. Her song was sung in a narrow range, pentatonic and strophic. Keenan guessed that there were about twelve verses, but he had been so intent on understanding the long-dead language that he lost count. When she finished, he begged her to sing it again, and she obliged. This time he understood it more completely. It was a terrible, awesome song of warfare, filled with berserk battle lust, wholesale slaughter and head hunting.

Mary seemed self-pleased when she finished. Keenan mustered his shock and acted as unaffected as he could. "A song of *cath.*" he remarked, to cover his disquiet.

"A song of *cat'buadach,*" Mary corrected. Not just battle but battle victory.

"I would very much like to record it," Keenan said, reaching for his recorder.

Mary stopped him, with a talonlike hand tightening around his wrist. "No. I am *Drui.* No word, no song, no *geis* of *Drui* can be set down. No on paper. No in your machine." The edge in her voice left no room for discussion. The magical bindings of her religion were not to be captured. Keenan withdrew his hand.

"I am tired," Mary declared. The truth of her words showed on her face. The immortal creature was clearly subject to the weaknesses of old Mary Liddy's flesh. "I wish to sleep for a time."

Keenan agreed that she should sleep. He devised a makeshift pillow and arranged the sleeping bag over her. Then he slipped under the opposite edge of the bag and lay as still as possible. The past several days of unsolved problems had exhausted him with fitful nights of rest, but he was sure that he would not sleep this night either. His mind raged like an electric storm, with new knowledge and newer questions flashing out of nowhere and leaving his brain sizzling. A foot from his side lay a woman more than a millennium old. And then there were her three murderous clanswomen who might be nearby. Very carefully, Keenan rolled himself in Mary's direction, so that he could stare at her tranquil face. He had never expected to become great as an archeologist or anthropologist. Academia, after all, had only been his refuge from the Church. He had come to love his work, but he had long ago resigned himself to a life of obscurity. Then this. This miracle could make him the most famous "bone-digger" of all time. Or perhaps the greatest laughingstock. In a modern, media-dominated world, the bizarre sideshow aspects of his discovery could easily overshadow the serious ones. There was more disaster to be feared than that caused by Mary's clanswomen. The hyperbole of scandal newspapers would just be a mild uproar. Entire religions would be questioned. A Roman Catholic basilica and a Byzantine church had been erected, because Bernadette Soubirous had believed she was visited by the Virgin Mary at Lourdes. Keenan could not begin to imagine what a miracle like this, complete with physical evidence, would spawn. Opening the Lamoge cemetery had been like opening Pandora's box. If word of it leaked out, hysteria would sweep the world.

Moses had only been allowed to see the Almighty's back. Staring at Mary Liddy, Keenan felt that he was looking at a reflection of God's face. Keenan's brain ached. Not just around his eyes or at the top of his head, but straight through the middle. Everywhere. Maybe if he forced himself to think of less awesome things. Just close his eyes for a minute and relax.

Keenan saw the cave. He knew immediately that it was enchanted and that it lay in the side of Keshcorran.

It was a splendid Irish morning and the ancient Celtic hero Fionn Mac Uail and his lieutenant Conan the Bald, together with their dogs Bran and Sceolan, were hunting at the peak of the mountain called Keshcorran. They were unaware that they had wandered into the invisible rim of Faerie, the realm of Conaran, king of the Shee of Keshcorran. Conaran harbored a long-standing hatred for Fionn and set his mind to do him harm. The Faerie king had four daughters, known throughout Eire-land as the most cruel and ugly creatures that breathed. The Medusa, the Harpies and the Furies combined could not equal the vileness of these four. Their names were Caevog, Cuillen, Iarnan and Iarnach. Iarnach, the eldest, was by far the most fearsome of the sisters.

Of all Conaran's powers, the means of clouding man's sight was most keen. To Fionn and Conan, the world they had entered looked the same, but suddenly their clansmen and all their dogs had disappeared. Like a giant eye socket opening, the entrance of a cave appeared suddenly in the side of Keshcorran. Inside the cave sat three of Conaran's daughters, spinning yarn. Even from a distance, Conan could see that they were hideous, but Fionn insisted on drawing close, to view the loose flaps of flesh hanging from their arms, the needlelike teeth, the tufts of hair that sprang from innumerable discolored warts.

The instant Fionn and Conan stepped under the shadow of the cave, they became entangled in the yarn, spun about like a spider's web. A terrible weakness possessed them. Their legs had no power; even breath was difficult to draw. Fionn could not even pucker his lips to whistle a warning to his people. So it was that the other hunters followed the barking of Bran and Sceolan into the enchanted cave and one by one lost their strength. They were captured and bound and the grotesque sisters drooled over the meals of human flesh that were to be theirs.

While Fionn and his clansmen languished inside the cave, their dogs bayed and belled fiercely outside. Unlike their owners, the dogs had smelled the danger and refused to venture within.

The sisters honed their broadswords to carve up their victims, but one more warrior figure strode toward their cave. He was Goll mac Morna the "raging lion, the torch of battle." The clann-Morna were the mortal enemies of Fionn's clan, but that did not prevent Goll from greatly admiring Fionn's valor. Goll could see no more than the others had, but he knew Faerie magic well enough not to step forward. Out flew the three sisters, wielding their swords. The wind died, but the clash of the weapons filled the land. Goll's footwork was the champion warrior's dance, a leaping, weaving pattern of mesmerizing intricacy that confused the sisters and left them open to the slashing movements of his arm. Two of the sisters were cleaved in twain; the third begged for her life, promising on her name to lift the enchantment. As soon as this promise was spoken, the warriors stood again in the sunlight of their own land, released through the power of Goll mac Morna's sword.

But then, from the fastnesses of the mountain, the most frightening of Conaran's four daughters—the harridan Iarnach attacked. She laid Fionn under magical bindings, to make him settle all the warriors' fates by selecting just one defender from their number. Again it was Goll to the rescue. Toe to toe he fought the armored Faerie princess, until at last she gave a step. Screaming her rage, she threw herself at Goll, to be impaled on his great sword. A moment later, he severed her head from her shoulders and held it high for all the rescued to witness.

Keenan sat up with a start. His dream was the answer to the question that had scratched his mind so relentlessly. The one plus three combination represented the four sisters from The Enchanted Cave of Keshcorran. It was one of the Fionn legends, retold in O'Grady's *Silva Gadelica*, a volume he had not read since his undergraduate days.

The first light of dawn poured through the tent screening, filtered by the rising damp. Keenan had slept at least five hours. His head twisted to the other side of the tent. Mary Liddy was gone. He felt the pillow—it was cold.

Keenan threw back the tent flap. The boreen and the woods that surrounded it lay still. Keenan swore under his breath and stepped back into the tent. As quickly as he could, he threw his belongings into the rear of the Rover. He noticed that all his candy bars had disappeared. Then he realized that his flashlight was nowhere around. With the tent stowed and everything packed, he discovered that his two ordinance maps had gone with Mary Liddy.

Keenan was not an experienced tracker, but he could see broken twigs and fronds clearly enough, could find footprints pressed into soft forest loam and could tell where sprinklings of night dew had been disturbed. Mary had followed the dirt track eastward. She believed, as he did, that her three confederates had abandoned the highway and were moving cross-country. About a thousand feet in, her trail ended. Keenan saw clear evidence of movement through the brush to the north. He was about to follow it when a thought struck him. He crossed the boreen and searched the south side. Sure enough, the trampling continued there. The three ancients had already passed the spot. Mary had found their trail and gone in pursuit. Keenan followed.

The trail led down into a burbling rill, then up through a glen into a copse of trees. Keenan spotted his quarry from three hundred feet away. All four ancients were in his sight, standing along the edge of a small precipice. Closest to him was an old man who had to be John O'Connor. The man looked near death. He sat on a rock outcropping, with his back against another rock. His shoulders were slumped; his legs hung listlessly, his face was downcast and hung to one side. A trouser leg and one side of his shirt were stained darkly, possibly with blood. The light was still too dim and the distance too great for Keenan to be certain.

The forms of Mick Dunphy and Fergus MacMahon stood farther down the ledge. "Mick" seemed to be dividing his time between listening and standing guard, holding the long-handled pitchfork in a parade-rest posture. "Fergus" kept his attention fixed on Mary, speaking with great animation, waving his arms forcefully and turning in tight circles as he ranted. Mary stood calmly regarding Fergus, with one foot up on a rotten tree stump and her other foot dangerously close to the edge of the precipice. Every few seconds she would try to say something, without success.

Keenan spotted a large tree thirty feet ahead that would offer him a better hiding place. He waited until Mick looked away and Fergus was completing a turn before he dashed to the tree's cover. For a minute, he was satisfied to hide. Then Fergus stopped pacing and shut his mouth, and Mary took the opportunity to speak. Fergus stood with arms akimbo, leaning forward with neck craning and jaw jutting fiercely, like a stone gargoyle erupting out of a Gothic cathedral. Keenan longed to hear them speak. Mary's words were at least staving off another verse of Fergus's tirade. Keenan longed to hear the rhythms and flow of their ancient Irish and wondered if it would be safe to make his presence known, since Mary seemed to be taking control. He decided against revealing himself but moved a little closer.

He had not gotten two steps from his hiding place when "John's" head lolled up and spotted him. Keenan gasped at John's blood stains. His shirt and trousers had been blasted open and his right ear and part of his jaw flesh were missing.

John called out weakly to his companions. Like startled deer, all three heads twisted in Keenan's direction. John lifted a small shotgun from behind the rock.

Mary cupped her hands to her mouth. "Run, *Ollam!*" she cried out. "Run fast!"

Keenan prepared to flee but froze in place as Fergus lurched forward to grab Mary. Mary started back, realized she had nowhere to go, and leapt off the precipice. For an instant, Keenan debated charging to Mary's aid. Then he saw John rise, shotgun in hand. Mick dropped the pitchfork and hurtled rapidly down the incline toward him. Fergus abandoned Mary and followed Mick.

Keenan turned and fled the way he had come. The escape route took him through the trees and into a dry streambed that led toward where Mary had fallen. Halfway down, Mick caught up with him. The only practical experience Keenan had in defending himself were the times he had been forced to act as practice dummy when his brother, Patrick, studied karate. Hearing the ragged breaths of Mick right behind him, Keenan stopped suddenly, pivoted and dropped to one knee. Mick's eyes widened at the surprise maneuver. Between his headlong pursuit and the force of gravity, there was no way he could brake completely. Keenan dove forward, seized the attacker's ankles and thrust upward.

Yelling his surprise and outrage, Mick went head over heels down the streambed, doing a pair of somersaults and landing with a force that knocked the wind out of him.

Keenan stood, in time to meet Fergus's more cautious rush. From above, he heard Mary's old but urgent voice. "Hide your t'umbs! Hide your t'umbs!"

Keenan curled his fingers protectively around his thumbs. He understood the command, but he wondered how in hell he was going to defend himself. One punch with a hand clenched like that and his thumb would be shattered. He turned to run, got three steps and was overtaken. Fergus's bulky shape bear hugged him, then whirled him around. Powerful, mad hands gripped his fingers and pulled, desperately struggling to expose his thumbs. One of Fergus's hands let go and delivered a stinging slap to Keenan's left cheek, then a backhand to his right. Keenan's eyes rolled with the pain.

Keenan pivoted to his left, drew his right knee up and in, then unleashed a swift kick to Fergus's crotch. He watched in triumph as the demon's eyes bulged with agony and the large figure crumpled to the ground. Keenan swung around to flee again. Mick had recovered and took giant steps toward him, arms outstretched.

The victory over Fergus had given Keenan courage. If he had any hope of escape it would be in hurting Mick as badly as he had hurt Fergus. He knew he had to risk his life for one moment. He waited like a lamb for slaughter, his thumbs wrapped within his curled fingers, until Mick was nearly upon him. At the last instant he thrust his hands forward and slapped them hard against Mick's ears. Mick's mouth contorted with silent agony.

Keenan grabbed Mick's shirt at the chest, planted one foot in his midsection, collapsed backward and flung the attacker to the ground.

Keenan dashed down the hill. Out of the corner of his eye he saw Mary's figure disappearing around an outcropping of rocks, several hundred feet away. Keenan could not concern himself with her at the moment; pure survival instincts overwhelmed him, compelling him back toward the wagon at sprinter's speed. Every few seconds he looked back, fearful that an unknown bit of Celtic magic would give them the power to follow and attack again, more lethally than ever. But he saw nothing. He dug his keys out of his pocket as he burst onto the boreen. His mind conjured up images from bad horror movies, where car engines never started. He reached the Range Rover, yanked open the door, threw himself into the seat and rammed the key into the ignition. The engine, mercifully oblivious to clichés of cinematic tension, instantly roared to life.

The path was too narrow for turning. Keenan guided the machine on a careening, backward flight to the roadway. Once on the flat, artificial surface he felt as if he had reached a talisman of civilization that forbade primitive, supernatural attack. For several seconds he lingered at the mouth of the boreen, waiting for sight of his pursuers, keeping one trembling foot on the brake pedal and the other poised over the accelerator while he thrilled to the continued adrenalin rush, exulted over a heads-up escape from some very big time dealers of death. No one had followed. The countryside surrounded the road with lush, green innocence, inviting to the slaughter all the unsuspecting.

A yellow Volkswagen hummed noisily up the highway. Keenan steered the Range Rover from the middle of the road, set his foot a little lower on the gas pedal and drove toward Carrick.

6

August 18, 1988

"Move on, Moira!"

The lead milk cow had never been fleet of foot, but now, pregnant, she had taken on the aspect of statuary. The other four-footed girls—Brigid, Maud, Molly, Kitty, Kathleen, Maggie, Deirdre and Lucy—were not in the mood to hurry Moira. Allan Carradine stepped up to the immobile lead cow and fixed her great brown eyes with his. "Moira, Moira," he complained, theatrically, "the grass won't come to you."

The cow had heard the phrase a hundred times, but from Allan's father. Matt Carradine had a gift for turning a phrase that he had passed on to Allan. Because of the gift, the dairy farmer had lost his elder son to writing and teaching.

Allan, twenty-five, taught literature and creative writing at Cork college. The job brought in the day-to-day money and helped nurture his true vocation, poetry. When he was not yet twenty-three, a Dublin firm had published his *Duncannon Beach and Other Songs.* Devoid of notes, his poems were music nonetheless, contrapuntal themes hurled at each other in fugato, lilting, syncopated measures of sound, built on a wide ambitus of emotions, exalting the beauty of Ireland and its people. Only one minor critic really understood the musical parallels; a well-respected opinion-monger, however, had overpraised the collection, comparing Allan's talent to "that of the young W. B. Yeats, rich in Pre-Raphaelite rhythms and the colours of Celtic folklore." In the same critical paragraph, he wished in print that "Carradine might grow as Yeats did and consider with his own gifts the plight of the Irish as a people political."

Largely on the weight of the critic's words, the young poet had sold almost three thousand hardcover books. Which was why, in one hand Allan held an alder switch to encourage the cows and in the other he carried Yeats's *A Full Moon in March*. His next book was almost completed, and he needed to be sure the growing republican sentiments he was expressing were not unintentionally reconstituted Yeats. Once the cows were driven into the large field, he could perch himself on a flat part of the wall, watch the sun come up and read. This was a labor of love and a duty of guilt. He would never inherit the farm; that would go to his younger brother, Daniel, by default. But he could at least give his parents and brother a week's vacation in Spain, away from the rigors and drudgery of their farm. So he gladly rose before dawn, milked the "girls" and marched them out into the pastures. Poet cum pastor he thought, smiling.

The switch came down lightly on Moira's rump, giving just the right goad to get her moving. The cow raised her head and trotted forward. Chucking and cooing, Allan encouraged the others to follow. He shut the gate and latched it, then paused to look down the slopes to the south, where the rooftops of Carrick barely poked above the trees a mile-and-a-half away. It was all pastel in the morning atmosphere. A good place to compose. Allan pivoted slowly, to take in the entire panorama.

The three figures emerged out of the mist like soldiers fleeing from battle. The two on the outside dragged between them the third. In their free hands they carried what looked like weapons.

The strangers were heading straight for him. Allan had no idea how fast they were. They would be upon him within the next few seconds. The walls were too low and too straight to provide hiding places. Where else?

Hide behind the "hide." Allan duck walked the short distance to the loosely scattered herd, which grazed so obliviously. When he reached Molly he came up into a crouch and shoved the brindled cow toward a little clutch formed by Deirdre, Kitty and Kathleen. Molly protested faintly with a slight kick of a hind leg, but Allan bullied her on, whispering anxious encouragements. Over her rump he saw the trio of men reaching the gate. Maud, ever the shiest of the herd, trotted away from the unknown men toward the safety of her sisters. Allan said a little prayer of thanks for the added protection, shifting his position to watch the men from under Molly's head.

The one on the right carried a shotgun carelessly, letting the barrel graze along the ground. The one on the left clutched a pitchfork. The man in the middle was badly injured, covered with blood, seeming more dead than alive.

Just keep moving, Allan whispered to himself, keep moving. The men stopped. All three had their eyes fixed on the little herd. The one on the left spoke. They were less than twenty paces from Molly. Allan could hear his words distinctly, but he could not understand what the man said. The language he used sounded remotely Irish, but more guttural and hard-edged. The man on the right understood, though. He nodded. Together, they eased their arms out from under the middle man, leaving him to support himself on his own. Together, they advanced on the nearest of the herd—the calf-heavy Moira.

Allan stared in disbelief as they raised both the shotgun and the pitchfork. There was nothing for him to do but watch as the animal took a point-blank blast of pellets in the side. She wailed in pain, lurching several steps away from her attackers, then collapsing onto her side. The one with the pitchfork rushed up with the tines raised, ready to plunge them deeply into the wounded beast. He stopped in midstroke.

At the report of the shotgun, the cows had cried out in terror and fled. Allan reacted a moment after they did, doing his best to stay on the far side of Molly. She betrayed him, cutting and jinking erratically, leaving him exposed long enough for the one with the pitchfork to spot him.

"You bloody bastards!" Allan screamed. He straightened up to orient himself with the spires of Carrick.

The one with the shotgun was quick. He jogged down the slope a score of steps, flanking the herd and the poet. The one with the pitchfork circled upslope. Allan backed toward the east, but found himself hemmed in by the flanks of Brigid and Kitty, who seemed to be cowering close to him for protection.

Dropping his book, Allan grabbed a fist-size stone from the ground as his attackers rushed forward. He dashed around Kitty and threw the rock. It struck the one with the pitchfork, smacking into his shoulder with enough force to spin him partway around. He gave no cry of pain but straightened and came after Allan unfazed.

A little way off, Moira mooed plaintively. Allan could also hear her legs flailing, but he could not risk a glance; he was being stalked. The road was the quickest way to safety. All he could see in his way was the half-dead, unarmed man, weaving unsteadily on his legs. Clenching his teeth, Allan launched himself from behind the cow, head lowered, arms pistoning.

The gun blast caught Allan squarely in the back. His mind functioned long enough for him to reach one arm behind, to feel for the holes that had been bored into him, each pellet searching at supersonic speed for his heart. Before he could tell that he had not been mortally wounded, he passed out, pitching hard into the green sod.

Fergus pumped the shotgun and waited for his target to move. Mick trotted up to his side, and spat a terse command at Fergus, who walked off without demur toward the retreating cattle.

From his trousers pocket, Mick produced a six inch kitchen knife he had found in Johnny O'Connor's kitchen. He tossed it lightly into the air and captured its blade deftly between thumb and forefinger. With equal skill, he let it fly into the sod, six inches from Allan Carradine's head. He surveyed the poet, satisfied himself that this body could not substitute for Johnny O'Connor's dying form any better than the young man at the Walsh's farm.

Mick raised the pitchfork high, then drove down hard into the poet's neck. Allan's eyes and mouth flew open without a sound. His fingers scratched feebly at the sod. Mick twisted the pitchfork and pushed it deeper, watching calmly as the eyes and mouth closed and the fingers stopped clawing the bloody grass.

Mick dropped to his knees, yanked the knife from the earth, wrapped its handle with both fists and began the work of hacking the poet's neck from his torso. The knife was not meant for such heavy duty. Mick worked furiously, hacking at the muscles and severing the cartilage. He pierced the cervical vertebrae by tugging on the scalp hair while chopping with the blade.

As Mick butchered, Fergus pursued the cows. He squeezed the shotgun trigger and let fly a load of pellets into Lucy's hindquarter. The normally docile beast finally had enough. Bellowing with rage, she turned at a trot, lowered her head and ran at her attacker. At the last moment Fergus threw himself to the side, barely avoiding the tormented animal. As Lucy galloped by, Fergus came to one knee, pumped the slide handle again, aimed and squeezed the trigger. This time, the only noise he heard was the metallic click of the hammer. Lucy lumbered on, fixing her attention on the open gate, not caring that another man stood in front of her, one who did not have the ability to get out of her way. She lowered her head once more, bowled Johnny O'Connor over and steamed out of the field.

Fergus pumped the shotgun and pressed the trigger, aiming into the air. Again, no blast. He grabbed the weapon by the barrel and peered angrily into the black hole. He shook the shotgun hard, set it again to his shoulder and squeezed the trigger. This time the hammer did not even click.

In the center of the field, Mick stood up with a whoop. In one hand he carried the bloody knife. In the other, Allan Carradine's head dangled from its hair.

Fergus looked in Mick's direction, gave a complimentary nod, then scowled again and flung the shotgun toward the open field gate. He turned to look at Johnny O'Connor, who lay motionless on the ground. Fergus bent to the battered form and spoke to it. Johnny's lips barely moved as he replied. Fergus called to Mick, who stared at the head with a joyous rapture. Fergus shouted. Mick lowered his treasure and stalked toward his confederates. As he did, the heel of his boot stepped on the book of Yeats, grinding it into the sod, where it would lie undiscovered, swelling with the rains, molding with the months, again becoming part of the earth from which it had sprung.

Keenan had to talk with Sergeant Meagher. But first he undressed and showered. Then he took two aspirin. Then shaved. Then brushed his teeth. Then lay down for twenty minutes because he continued to shake. After he ordered his thoughts, he wrote himself a page of notes. Then dressed in clean clothes. Then swallowed another aspirin. He dreaded his inevitable meeting with the policeman. If he had had a fifth of whiskey he probably would have taken the time to polish it off as well.

Keenan looked at his watch. Nearly ninety minutes had

flown since he had escaped in the Range Rover. He had clocked the distance from the dirt road into Carrick. It was four and a quarter miles as the highway wound. The straight, overland route the ancients were beating, however, would save them no time because of the hills, the streams and the trees. And because of John O'Connor's condition. Nevertheless, Keenan knew that they could reach Carrick well before noon. He had to inform Meagher immediately.

Vickie Ryan swept open the car door and sprang out.

"Victoria, don't you do a thing till you're out of your church clothes!" her mother ordered, through the driver's window.

"I won't, Mam!" Vickie shouted back. Usually, on nice summer days like this, she and her mother would walk the kilometer south into Carrick and then the few blocks over to St. Columba's. Today, however, her mother had many chores, and the time it took strolling back home after Mass could not be wasted. Vickie was pleased. The Ryans had just gotten a spaniel puppy, and Vickie could hardly bear a minute away from it.

As she yanked her way out of her good clothes and tore her play clothes from their hangers, she listened to Tippy barking in the back yard.

"I'm coming, you naughty devil," Vickie answered, glad that the puppy had missed her. She collapsed backward onto the bed to tug on her blue jeans. She was growing so fast that her hips hardly fit into them. She was thirteen and already five-foot-six. As if being one of the tallest kids in her class weren't enough, she also had to bear the cross of braces, put on her teeth in July. Tippy had been the consolation prize.

Vickie finished dressing and raced through the house and out the back door. Tippy was still barking.

"I'm here, already," Vickie called out, expecting to see her puppy tugging on his run line, smiling at her with his dopey grin, tail wagging furiously. Instead, he was faced in the opposite direction. His tail was lowered and snapping back and forth. His little throat gave out a long, menacing growl.

"What's up with you?" Vickie demanded.

Tippy turned to his mistress, gave a bark of recognition, and turned back to whatever was upsetting him. Vickie walked forward, through the damp grasses. At the end of the lawn, almost in the trees that encroached upon the Ryan property, lay a man. Vickie gasped. She took three more steps, near enough to see that he had been badly hurt, in one leg and in his right shoulder and the right side of his face. Vickie saw no sign of life.

"Mam!" Vickie screamed. "Come quick!" She held her position at the edge of her imaginary boundary between safety and danger, staring at the man, praying to the Blessed Mother that he was still alive.

"Good Lord!" Eileen Ryan gasped, coming up beside her daughter, half a head shorter. She paused for only a moment, then she knelt beside the man. She lifted his right hand and felt for a pulse.

"Is he dead, Mam?" Vickie whispered.

"Yes. He's been shot." Eileen stood and hurried back toward the house. "I'll call the *Garda,*" she said as she passed her daughter. "You just watch him."

"Okay."

The back door slammed shut. Vickie was not an especially popular girl in school, but this event, she felt, might help elevate her in her schoolmates' eyes. Even before school began, word would no doubt spread that she had not only found a dead body but that she had touched it. Now all she had to do was accomplish the deed, for sure enough someone would make her swear on her immortal soul that she wasn't lying.

Vickie glided through the grass, hardly lifting her feet, her breath becoming more and more shallow, her eyes never straying from the corpse. She came within touching distance. Her left leg swung out slowly, until the tip of her shoe touched the man's hip. His clothing puckered in. She looked at the ripped flesh of his face, at the missing ear; her lips corkscrewed up in revulsion, showing the gleaming silver dental wires. She carefully squatted down, just close enough to get one finger on the man's body. Behind her, Tippy yapped and growled. The noise was fraying her nerves. She whipped around.

"Shut up, you stupid thing!" she commanded. The puppy obeyed.

Vickie pivoted back and stared at the body. Her eyes went wide. She drew in a sharp breath. She was sure, a moment ago, the man's eyes were half shut. Now they were fully open and looking right at her. Vickie's hand shot toward her mouth.

In the same instant, John O'Connor's right hand swung out toward the girl's leg.

In the same instant, the back door of the house banged open.

The man's hand dropped to the grass.

Vickie sat down hard and skittered backward like a crab. "Mam, mam! He's not dead!"

"Of course he is, Vickie," Eileen declared.

Vickie shot up and attached herself to her mother like a young marsupial. "No, his eyes went wide open an' then he tried to grab me!"

"Hush, now, and let me go!" Eileen said. "Stop acting like a baby. Sometimes when bodies been dead a while they move on their own. It's called rigor mortis."

"Well, it sure did seem like he wanted to grab me!" Vickie complained. "I don't like it, Mam."

"Neither do I," Eileen agreed. "I wish your father was home." She drew her child a bit away from the body. "I tell you what; we'll both stand here together until the *Gardaí* come. I'm sure they'll be here directly."

The man at the *Garda* station desk had informed Keenan that Dick Meagher was having his breakfast at Sexton's

Coffee Lounge. Keenan found the sergeant there hunched over a cup of coffee, studying the menu and looking like he had just celebrated three concurrent New Year's Eves. He spotted Keenan and pointed to the vacant chair across the table.

"Good morning, Dick," Keenan greeted.

"Dia's Muire dhuit," Meagher replied, in a husky voice nearly an octave lower than usual. Keenan had heard the Gaelic phrase "God and Mary be with you" before, but never from Meaghan. There had to be some special significance in the use of an old, religious phrase.

"Dia's Muire agus Pádraig dhuit," Keenan responded, using the traditional addition of St. Patrick.

The waitress approached with another menu and a coffee-pot. "Coffee?" she asked Keenan.

"He'll have a cup and leave the pot, Margaret," Meagher directed. "And I'll have toast, two eggs scrambled and a rasher of bacon. The day demands it."

"I'll have the same," Keenan smiled, dragging out the chair and lowering himself onto it. Meagher regarded him in silence. "So, how did the rest of the night pass?" he stalled.

"Let's go back farther than that," the policeman said. "Why don't you tell me exactly what you think's been happening, since the moment those gravediggers discovered the high cross?"

Keenan reached into his jacket pocket. "Let's begin with this." He fished two folded sheets of paper out of the pocket and shoved them across the table. "The first one is the photocopy of the dental chart you gave me. The other I took from the dentist's office down the street."

Meagher glanced at the professor with surprise.

"Breaking and entering's what we call it in the States. I think there was sufficient reason," Keenan went on. "The second chart, as you can see, is Mary Liddy's. She and Mrs. Smiley are one and the same. Which puts someone else's bones inside the lady we visited in the hospital. The lady the doctor said had had her memory erased. The lady who had

to learn English—how did he say it—just like a foreigner."
Keenan took out his wallet and opened it, while Meagher
remained transfixed by the two charts. Staring in the billfold
section, Keenan saw that half his money was missing. The
new Mary Liddy, it seemed, was a very quick learner.
Keenan extracted a five-pound note and set it on top of the
charts. "To pay for the dentist's broken glass."

Meagher pushed the money back in Keenan's direction
without looking up. "He can afford it. Saints preserve us! I'd
better call the hospital in Clonmel."

"I already did," Keenan said. "She's gone."

Meagher scowled. "You broke into the dentist's office last
night and learned this?"

"Yes. After you left me at the pub."

"And why didn't you give me the news up at the Walsh
farm?"

"Would it have helped then?" Keenan returned. "This is
the supernatural we're talking about, Dick! If you'll remember, you rejected my theories, just a few hours before that. I
wasn't about to lay this miracle out in front of you until I'd
visited the cemetery one more time. Which was where I was
going when I saw you at the farm." Keenan expected that
this half truth would be enough to mollify the angry
policeman; there was no need to drag Mary Liddy into the
discussion.

"Well," Meagher began, and already Keenan could hear
that his tone was softened, "as I said to you last night, I've
been doing some deep thinking on my own. Even before we
got the call from Mrs. Walsh, I said to myself, 'Maybe you
shouldn't have come down on the professor so hard, Dick.
Every Sunday in church, don't you recite the Apostle's
Creed? And don't you say you look forward to the resurrection of the body? Yet when you hear that some bones have
come back to life, you dismiss the idea outright.'" Meagher
reached into his coat for his pack of cigarettes, decided
against it and set his hands on the table. "So now I'm all
ears. Tell me about this miracle."

Keenan spooned sugar into his coffee, spilling half of it on the table. "What the gravediggers discovered was a ritual burial site. Up until about 440 A.D. the people in this area believed in Celtic gods. Then the Catholic faith took hold. We're pretty certain it came from England."

"St. Patrick," Meagher interjected.

"And others. Well, trouble between the Druids and the Christians was unavoidable."

"Naturally. The Druids were pagans," Meagher declared firmly, evincing his Catholic upbringing.

"It was more than just acceptance of Jesus as Lord, Dick," Keenan went on. "It was a clash of cultures." The archeologist recalled the passages of *The Greatness and Decline of the Celts* which he had read only a few days before. "When Christianity was accepted as the official Roman religion, it took on the Latins' predilection for order and hierarchy. Just as the Romans had an emperor and senators to rule their secular empire, the Church had its pope and bishops to lead the sacred one. The Celts, on the other hand, disdained subservient cooperation to a strong central government. Their fundamental nature stressed individualism, and loyalty toward nothing greater than their own clan unit. Even their religion reflected this. As far as we know, Druid priests convened sporadically and made no canonic law."

"Then it wasn't a real religion," Meagher declared.

"Oh, it was," Keenan replied. "Celtic worship used Druid priests but was not limited to their direction. The Druids derived their power by keeping their rites secret and unwritten. People came to them only for divination, intercession with the gods and a few seasonal festivals."

"Which the Church could not tolerate."

"Exactly. Believe me, Dick, the early Church knew how weak it was. It became flexible whenever necessary. For example, when it encountered Mithraism—a very strong religion at the time—it assimilated any elements it could in order to convert the adherents. That's how Jesus came to be born on December twenty-fifth in Church worship; it was the birthday of the God Mithras. The priests declared that these Gods of Light were one and the same. But the priests could not assimilate the Druids the same way. So they made them mortal enemies and wiped them out, just as the Roman armies conquered the independent Celtic groups—one by one. Not by strength—because the Celts were much fiercer and more valiant warriors—but by organization. It's also why the English were able to conquer us, several times in fact."

Meagher looked perplexed. "And how does this relate to what we've found?"

"I think some clan or clans in this area, under the control of Druids, resisted conversion to Christianity. St. Patrick or one of the other missionaries assembled an army and defeated them. When the Druid priestesses were captured, they buried them."

"Alive?"

Keenan nodded. "Brutal times. According to legend, Patrick did not broach opposition. I'm sure he had no idea that burial wouldn't kill these priestesses, however. The one who now lives in Mary Liddy's body must have been particularly powerful, because they felt they had to chain her between two monks with sacred bracelets and bury her face down."

"Why face down?" Meagher inquired.

"Our forefathers believed that if a witch was buried the wrong way, she'd become confused and try to escape into the earth rather than out of it."

Meagher whistled softly.

"When you go up to the cemetery again, you'll see that there's another high cross up there, unearthed late yesterday by the gravediggers."

"I saw it this morning, at dawn," Meagher revealed.

"I suspect both crosses served as sacred paperweights, if you will, to guarantee that the Druidesses stayed beneath the sod. There were three priestesses under the second cross."

Meagher nodded. "I'm following."

Keenan wet his dry lips with a sip of coffee. "I'll bet these three were buried feet up for reasons similar to Mary's face down treatment. There's some tangible proof of what happened up there. Did you find the lead plaque?"

"No."

"It should still be on the ground. I came across it last night. It has Latin writing on it, warning anyone finding it to beware of the sorceresses below. Quite a common thing. *Defixiones,* the Romans called them. Mick and Fergus evidently couldn't read it and paid the price, along with John O'Connor."

"And these creatures killed them and took over their bodies," Meagher filled in.

"All but the bones."

The food arrived, and Meagher made a half-hearted attempt to eat a few mouthfuls. He set down his fork, scowling. "It's bad enough picturing one set of bones pushing out another and the flesh still living. But how can I believe that mere bones kept the spirits of these monsters intact all this time?"

"You want an anthropologist's explanation?" Keenan asked. "Because that's the only way I *can* explain it."

"Go ahead," Meagher welcomed, chewing slowly.

"Since the dawn of man, we've been saving the bones of the dead. In many civilizations *only* the bones. Some of our earliest ancestors saved the crematory ash too, but the ones we're concerned with just saved the bones. This practice isn't unique to Ireland. We find it in Scotland, in parts of India and with some Native American tribes. As soon as a person died the corpse was set out for the animals and the elements to strip of flesh. Excarnation we call it. The bones were believed to contain the essence, the spirit of the dead. That's what all those passage graves throughout Ireland, filled neatly with generations of bones, are about. Ezekial may have been talking in metaphor about bones rising, Dick, but some of our ancestors actually accomplished it."

"But why in Ireland?" Meagher complained. "And why, for God's sake, in Carrick?"

"Where better?" Keenan countered. "There is no land on earth richer in folklore and magic. Ireland's got faeries, leprechauns, banshees, ghosts."

"Some of us are superstitious folk, clinging to our old fears," Dick argued.

"Most of these stories came from a primitive people trying to understand the rules of the world and the tools by which they could control them," Keenan granted. "Some tales were no doubt just campfire entertainment. But some must be based in truth."

Meagher looked befuddled.

"Dragons, for example," Keenan pushed on. Just like we do occasionally today, primitive man must have accidentally unearthed dinosaur bones. The dinosaurs *were* dragons. The only mistake made was that thunder lizards and man never inhabited the earth together. Or take werewolves."

"Now, surely you're not—"

"They're not monsters," Keenan assured. "But there are certain unfortunate people born with a genetic malfunction called lycanthropy. Their bodies are covered with hair, their teeth and nails grow longer, and, because they're regarded as animals and shunned, they behave like animals. Or centaurs —the beasts that were half man, half horse. That legend came from Thessaly, when the inhabitants encountered our Celtic ancestors, mounted on horses. All stories based in fact."

"And you're telling me there are stories of old bones inhabiting new bodies."

Keenan's professorial persona collapsed. "None that I know of," he admitted. "But there are stories of three Irish warrior women who were able to change their shapes, sometimes into animals but especially into male warriors. They were collectively called The Morrigan. Another legend based in fact? I wonder if they're now inside two gravediggers and a farmer."

"Shit!" Meagher exclaimed. He combed his fingers nervously through his hair.

Keenan said, "Why Carrick, I can only guess. Your town sits on a very strategic spot—that's why the castle went up here. I'm sure there was at least one Celtic clan in this valley, and they must have been fiercely ruled by Druids. I'd guess that it was some kind of battle royal between them and the Christians, and when the Christians won, they erected high crosses all around, to symbolize their victory or to hold witches in the ground. They even put a monastery up just north of here . . . perhaps as a spiritual fortress against the Druid evil they suspected still lingered around Carrick."

"Four Druid priestesses: the three who killed the Walshes and their hand and also Mary Liddy," Meagher said.

"I don't think Mary's dangerous like the other three."

"You don't, eh?" Meagher rejoined. He picked up a piece of bacon, then decided he could not eat it. "Impossible to say right now. If somebody buried *me* alive for a thousand years, peaceable as I am, I wouldn't care whose body I grabbed to get out. But why did the other three kill the Walshes?"

Keenan hurriedly swallowed a mouthful of egg. "Our ancestors were a mixture of several races, Dick. Neolithics, Anglo-Saxons, some Viking, Beaker Folk and especially a group called the La Tène. The last two were Celtic and as fierce a people as ever walked the earth. Their greatest legendary hero, Cuchulain, was said to work himself into a 'warp-spasm' in preparation for battle. One eye sucked into his head; the other lay out on his cheek. His mouth opened so wide that you could see his lungs and liver. Black blood gushed from his head, smoking."

"Holy Jesus!" Meagher exclaimed.

"They believed that working themselves into a frenzy— berserking—would make them invincible. Killing was more than a necessity to them; it was a vocation."

"Like a job?" asked Meagher, incredulous.

"Like a way to glory. And for other reasons. For example,

when they'd finished a fort, they'd sacrifice one of their own and bury the person in the foundation, so the spirit would protect the fort. Then there was killing for revenge."

"Which is what this smells like," Meagher reasoned.

"Maybe not," Keenan came back. "In those cases, they buried the person alive."

Roses were Father Flynn's passion. Roses and children. Both were so beautiful, fresh and vibrant with healthy color. "Lovely rosy cheeks" he would say of any child he met with even a hint of pink in its face.

Father Flynn had a collection of roses, some wild, some early cultivations dating back from the Tudor period, but mostly hybrid teas. His garden was the cemetery that backed the grounds of St. Columba's. The elegaic place, with its damp stone wall, its ancient, listing headstones, its moss-sweatered trees and rich green sward, cried out for color. Father Flynn's roses answered handsomely, in bold strokes of red, pink, white and yellow. Despite its sombre purpose, the burial ground had been transformed into a restful place of great beauty.

Which was why Father Flynn was so unhappy about all the freshly dug graves that spotted the yard. The minute he had heard about the decision to move the Lamoge grave-yard, he had known that his cemetery's beauty was in jeopardy. Once he lost the battle, however, he had gritted his teeth and borne the upheaval. But the delays caused by the finding of the high cross were vexing. The American arche-ologist who, the year before, had helped sway the decision to move the burial ground had become a thorn in his side again. His whisk-broom excavating slowed the transfer process to a standstill. The cleric was further convinced that Professor MacBreed monopolized the gravediggers' time on the town's pay.

Father Flynn finished his post-Mass cup of tea and his copy of *The Sunday Independent*. He glanced at his wrist-watch. Just after nine. Half an hour before his round of visits to the elderly and sick began. He slipped his reading glasses into his jacket pocket and scudded into his garden shoes. The graveyard lay just outside the rectory's back door. The priest scowled even before he could see the place. Then he saw it, and his annoyance trebled.

"Too much, too much," Father Flynn fumed, glancing at all the new mounds of dirt and the two open holes, which were protected only by stakes and heavy twine. Leaning against the wall of a mausoleum, under the shelter of its eaves, were the gravediggers' shovels, still clotted with dirt. Apparently, they lacked proper respect for even the tools of their trade. A few steps farther, Flynn found a main stem of his prize Peace split.

"Now someone will pay!" Flynn muttered, his ruddy face turning two shades redder. His eyes cast around for someone whose ears he could borrow to vent his frustration. A hawkish expression replaced the one of annoyance as he looked down the back lane that bordered the cemetery.

"Well, if it isn't the Devils themselves!" Flynn exclaimed.

Mick Dunphy and Fergus MacMahon walked down the lane, heads swinging warily from side to side. They looked tired and disheveled. Father Flynn pressed himself into hiding behind a tree whose branches overhung the cemetery's side gate. "Probably been out drinking all night," he muttered, smiling at the trap he was about to spring on them. He listened sharply for their approach. They spoke, in words too low for him to hear. He held himself hard against the tree until he heard the fall of their feet. Then he launched himself out of the gate and directly into their path.

"Well, well, well . . ." the priest greeted.

Fergus and Mick stopped dead.

"Just the lads I wanted to see. Are you finally here to inter those two coffins in my basement?"

The two gravediggers seemed uncowed by his words. Both appeared to be transfixed by the large brass crucifix dangling from the chain around his neck.

Father Flynn played his ace. "And which one of you louts broke my rosebush?"

In answer, the two figures lunged forward and grabbed the priest.

"What are you doing?" Father Flynn cried out in a small voice, shocked by the attack.

The gravediggers pinioned the priest's arms and dragged him out of the lane and through the cemetery gate.

"Get yer filthy hands off me!" Flynn shouted, flailing wildly. He was neither a young nor a strong man, and he felt totally helpless in the rough grasp of the two laborers. In desperation, he twisted toward Mick and delivered a hard kick to the man's shins. Mick gave no cry of pain; nor was his talon hold on the priest relaxed. The pair hurled Flynn against the nearby tree. The wind whistled out of him, and he collapsed to the ground.

The next thing Flynn knew, he was lying on the ground beside one of the open graves. A piece of white cloth had been stuffed into his mouth; he could just see its edges beneath his nose. He moved to pull it out and found his arms bound. He looked down and saw the twine that had cordoned the grave now wound tightly around his hands and his ankles. He tried to scream and felt the air dam up in his throat. To his left he heard noise. He rolled on his side. The gravediggers were lifting their shovels. As they did, they spoke in a language that sounded remotely Gaelic but was harsher, more primitive.

Flynn rolled away from the hole with frenzied energy, turning over and over through the grass until his legs whipped hard into a rosebush. He felt the vicious pricks of the thorns through his trousers, drew his legs upward and felt the thorns' tenacious hold. Then a boot came hard into his side, driving the air from him once more. This time, only the adrenalin of fear kept him conscious.

The gravediggers booted Father Flynn back toward the open hole. When they reached its edge they pushed harder, so that the priest tumbled down and landed on his back. For a moment he saw only brilliant red. Then his eyes cleared, and he looked with abject horror on the dark, loamy frame that enclosed him. He tried to scream again. The first clod of dirt fell. There was no question now; they were going to bury him alive! His only hope now was that someone would come along and stop them.

The second clod fell, directly on his face. For a moment, it blocked his nose. He whipped his head left and right. The dirt flew. He snorted like a racehorse at full gallop.

Two more clods fell in quick succession. Father Flynn began the Hail Mary, barking it as loudly as he could into the linen that filled his mouth.

The dirt rained down.

Meagher reached into his jacket pocket and pulled out a sheet of paper. "I've been busy making pictures, too, Professor."

The paper was a photocopy of the images of Mick Dunphy and Fergus MacMahon.

"Early this morning I visited Mrs. Dunphy and Mrs. MacMahon," Meagher revealed tossing down his napkin. "I told them I thought their husbands were involved in bad business. Not the kind of news I favor giving. They supplied these pictures. I put them out over our fax machine; they're all over Ireland by now. I also called *Garda* headquarters, up in Phoenix Park."

Keenan winced. "Couldn't you handle this without calling Dublin?"

"No," Meagher said, firmly. "Do you understand how our police system works?"

"I thought it was by borough or county."

"No. The Guards is a national force. I have no authority to take a matter of this magnitude into my own hands."

"But—"

Meagher lifted his hand. "Let me finish. I knew I'd need more men to help me. We have only seven officers in Carrick, and one is on vacation. They're sending several squad cars of men from Special Branch out of Harcourt Square. Except for a great emergency, Special Branch are the only guards who can handle weapons. There will also be a detective arriving from Kilkenny within the hour. Now, all I've told them is we've had some murders, nothing more. That's why I wanted to see you this morning. I'm paying," he declared, and tossed down a bill. "Let's take a walk."

Keenan snatched up two strips of bacon and followed the policeman out of the café. At Keenan's request, they headed for Bridge Street. The Thursday traffic was normal. The people on Main Street went about their business, confident that this would be a typical day, filled with nothing more than the everyday inconveniences, disappointments and annoyances. Nothing was out of the ordinary except for several cars with foreign license plates parked along the curbs. August was holiday month for much of the Continent, and a smattering of French, Belgians and Germans could always be counted on to wander to the farthest European rim, taking advantage of Irish hospitality.

"For many reasons I don't want to reveal everything you and I have spoken of," Meagher declared. "The first is the preservation of dear Carrick. I've lived here all my life, Keenan, and I don't want to see it ruined. We get a small share of tourist trade, and the money is appreciated. But if the world hears what you've told me, people will descend on Carrick like locusts—thrill-seekers of the worst kind.

"Then there's the internal upset. I've spent the past hours imagining the paranoia that would grip my neighbors. What happens if they're told that now murderous Druids inhabit the bodies of people who recently went near the Lamoge cemetery? That must be ten per cent of everyone in the area. Suddenly, guns we never suspected existed are everywhere. People stopping others for the time of day get shot. Or the place becomes a ghost town and looters descend."

"But how can you treat it as just simple murder," asked Keenan, "with *three* murderers?"

"Four," Meagher corrected. "I think you and I must play

dumb to a point. Forget much of what you've observed about Mary Liddy. Just report facts and offer this theory: something unearthed in the Lamoge cemetery has driven a few of the people up there mad. It might be supernatural, but the most likely explanation is a virus out of one of the coffins that has infected the gravediggers' brains." Meagher raised his bushy eyebrows at Keenan for rebuttal.

"And what about John O'Connor?" Keenan reminded.

"Somehow, Fergus and Mick infected him or forced him to go with them."

Keenan paused to weigh the strategy. "Agreed," he stated flatly.

Cautiously, Meagher cracked a smile. "Good! Now, about stopping these creatures. We've found no signs of them on the roads around Lamoge. I assume they've gone cross-country."

"I believe they continued in the same direction they were headed when they encountered the O'Connor and Walsh farms," Keenan answered.

"Why?"

"Because the ancients traveled by the stars and the sun. They surely knew where they'd been buried. They also knew where they came from. Most likely, the first thing they did was take a reading of the stars and set a beeline course."

Meagher's thin smile vanished. "Which puts Carrick directly in their path. But surely, they can't think their village or whatever is still there."

"You're thinking with the benefit of historical hindsight," Keenan reminded. "They lack a perspective of time and probably assume that life stayed the same, even after all these years."

"I understand. So, they're headed this way."

"They could be in Carrick within the next hour," Keenan answered, as they reached the foot of Bridge Street. Before them lay The Old Bridge, the ancient stone structure whose six vaulted sections and massive central piling stretched across the wide Suir, connecting the town with Carrick-beg

and County Waterford. "I suggested we come down here for
a reason. I believe they're headed across the Suir."

"Now, how could you know that?" Meagher asked.

Keenan gave him his best wide-eyed look, knowing how
adept the policeman was at reading lies. "It's not their
village they're headed for. Archeological studies have revealed a sacred Druid ground about five miles southwest of
here." Which was about where Mary's finger tracing on the
map had stopped. "I think they would head there to
commune with the supernatural being that gave them their
powers. There's no other bridge west of here until
Kilsheelan, right?"

"That's true."

"And east to Fiddown." Keenan looked upriver at the
long fishing punts anchored in a clutch just offshore. "Take
all the cots out of the water and lock them up. That will
encourage them to use this bridge."

"Then I post a patrol car at the Kilsheelan and Fiddown
bridges and put a roving patrol along the river line."

"On both sides if you can."

"Agreed. Once we've spotted them, how do you suggest
we stop them?"

"It won't be easy. Don't let your officers just approach
them and expect to get normal resistance. Your men could
easily be flayed alive. Let me tell you my theory of how they
get into their host body." Keenan explained to Meagher
what Mary had revealed about the thumbs.

"Incredible!" Meagher exhaled. "And I've got evidence
you're right."

"Really?" Keenan rejoined, eagerly.

The sergeant held up his hand, for demonstration. "When
Mary Liddy was being captured by Fergus MacMahon, his
thumb was split open, right down to the bone. Strange cut.
Hardly bled. I thought it had been done by a rock. Later,
Fergus said it healed up very quick."

"Classical literature backs it up," Keenan added. "According to the Ossianic Cycle, when Fionn Mac Uail was

invited by a certain beautiful woman to sit beside her, he
tested her real nature by putting her thumb between his
teeth and biting. The woman instantly transformed into the
hag that she was. Bad spirits in those days were thought to
be cast away if one chewed on a thumb. I'm sure you've
heard the old saying, 'By the pricking of my thumbs;
something evil this way comes.' Or the tradition of kissing
the thumb before using it to make the sign of the cross. It
seems all these superstitions have a rational basis. Druids
throughout Europe may one time have entered other bodies,
thumbs first. I don't know if it will work, but I'd have all
your people's thumbs wrapped in the heaviest tape you can
find."

"Which will make them stand out like sore thumbs,"
Meagher riposted, sourly. "What I haven't told you is that
these creatures have a shotgun. And they know how to use it.
They blew out the brains of Walsh's hired hand. It was
registered for hunting—a small gauge bird gun."

Keenan nodded. He knew that firearms were strictly
regulated in Ireland. Gun collecting was all but impossible,
and anyone who owned firearms for hunting had to bring
them into their local *Garda* stations once a year for registra-
tion. The legacy of "The Troubles." Keenan also knew that
Irish police operated on the "civilized nation" principle of
England; patrolmen carried no firearms.

"Then you'd better waive the rules and carry firepower
yourselves," Keenan counseled. "It won't destroy an ancient's soul, but a well-placed bullet should render the
borrowed body useless."

"What *will* destroy them completely?" Meagher pleaded.

Keenan shook his head impotently. "Decapitation?" he
ventured. "The Irish Celtics were big headhunters. In fact,
one of their words for battle was *árcenn*—head-harvest.
Maybe they lifted other warriors' heads to prevent the bones
from rising up."

"And if that doesn't work?" Meagher persisted.

"Then do what the early Christians did, only better,"

Keenan said. "Bury them, feet up, under a high cross. But this time encase them in concrete."

Meagher flicked a piece of crumbling concrete from the top of the wall down into the swirling water. *"If* we can find them." He stared down at the weir which angled across the river just upstream of the bridge. The tide was such that the weir was partially exposed. The water hissed and foamed, tumbling back on itself. "And who knows if they can't hop from one body to another any time they please."

"I don't think so," Keenan answered. His response was sincere, but he knew that he would now have to bend the truth a bit. "The last time I saw Mary Liddy, she told me she hated her body. Obviously, she had plenty of opportunity to grab a younger, quicker one, but she didn't. I think the body these old bones take has to die first. It's called metempsychosis."

"What?" Meagher asked.

"The passing of the soul at death into another body, either human or animal."

"There's a word for that?"

"There are two words in English, maybe more," Keenan imparted. "Some people call it transmigration. It's not an uncommon belief."

"Among Hindus maybe; not among the Irish," Meagher opined.

"Not *Catholic* nor *Protestant* Irish," the archeologist emphasized. "We're pretty sure the Celts originally came from northern India. That's where we get the term Indo-European. The Celts definitely believed in transmigration."

"But transmigrations can only occur post-mortem, right?" Meagher asked, anxiously.

"As far as I know."

"Let's hope so," Meagher said. "And speaking of Mary Liddy—whatever she is will have to be dealt with as well."

"I'm certain we can handle her peacefully," Keenan assured. "If we find her, I can reason with her."

"If you want to risk your life," Meagher replied, stepping

away from the wall and thrusting his hands deep into his trouser pockets. "Remember, she was the one with the golden manacles. The one who needed two monks to hold her under the sod. She's probably a hundred times more dangerous than the others. And more subtle, like Satan himself. If one of the Special Branch lads shoots first and asks questions later, I'll be quite forgiving."

Tim McGrath, sexton of St. Columba's, turned the corner into the graveyard. There, in the shade of an old oak, Mick Dunphy and Fergus MacMahon were throwing the last clods of dirt on a new grave. Tim waved to the gravediggers and trotted into the church, smiling broadly. He could hardly wait to deliver the good news to Father Flynn.

The ambulance pulled up to Carrick's little hospital. It was what the Irish called a cottage hospital, intended only for emergencies, outpatient treatments and terminal care for the aged when they were too sick to be kept at home. The hospital also functioned as a morgue, where bodies were stored until they could be moved to one of Carrick's churches for burial rites and thence to a cemetery.

A *Garda* car followed directly behind the ambulance. Jimmy Driscoll killed the ambulance engine, set the parking brake and eased his considerable bulk through the driver's door. It had been a slow, quiet summer for Driscoll. But with this and the Walsh disaster, things were picking up.

Jimmy opened the rear door of the ambulance. Rory MacCullen, Dick Meagher's second-in-command, stepped from the police car to lend a hand. Rory had no fear of work; he was thirty-eight and healthy, cocksure of his vitality and intellect. As he walked, he carefully stroked back the forelock of his thick, sandy-colored hair.

"Just give me a hand liftin' this down, Rory," Jimmy directed, "and I'll take it from there."

Dr. Noel Dunne appeared at the hospital's double doors

and locked them into open positions. Dunne had no trouble reaching the tops of the doors; in his stocking feet he stood six-foot-four. "This is positively the last one we'll take, Rory," Dunne declared, only half joking. "The lockers are all full. We'll have to put him in the emergency room and hope no squeamish patients show up."

"It had better be the last," Rory rejoined from his side of the gurney. "I'm sure I don't have to tell you, doctor, but he's not to be touched until the state pathologist arrives from Dublin. There's been a crime committed, and it's got to be handled by the book."

"Understood, understood," Dunne affirmed. Gaunt as famine, Dunne looked like a character out of a Dickens novel. For all his height, he weighed in at only one hundred sixty-eight pounds, fully clothed and invariably dressed in black. His liquid brown eyes were dominated by polished black pupils. A lugubrious smile constituted his bedside manner and he had a perpetual allergic catarrh that made him sniffle once or twice a minute, causing more than a few dubious patients to wonder why this physician could not heal himself. The doctor would have made a perfect mortician. Funeral parlors were just coming into fashion in Ireland. Until recently, people who died at home were laid out in their beds, or else died in hospital and were sent directly to the church. For those who lacked a funeral director's attention, Dunne did his unintentional best by creating a specter of the inevitable approach of Eternal Rest.

Dunne unzipped the body bag and gave the corpse a professional glance. "Gunshots. What happened?"

"We think he had something to do with the Walsh murders," Rory answered.

"How so?" Dunne probed.

Rory smiled lightly. He had dodged Dunne's inquiries a few hours earlier and knew the doctor was curious as hell, but Meagher would be furious if his order of silence was ignored. Much as Rory liked inflating his importance by doling out crime-related information, he was not about to get himself fired and lose his chance at sergeant. His boss was getting too old to last much longer.

"Sorry, doctor. Privileged information, for now. I'll fetch Sergeant Meagher and be right back," Rory replied, moving toward the patrol car.

"Do that, do that," said Dunne. He signalled for Driscoll to push the gurney into the emergency room, through the double swinging doors that isolated the area. "Am I allowed to know the fellow's name at least?" Dunne persevered.

"Johnny O'Connor," Driscoll reported. "From the farm just above the Walshes."

Dunne sniffed. "Feud was it?" Dunne asked Driscoll, since MacCullen had already climbed into his patrol car and shut the door.

Driscoll shrugged.

"Help me remove the bag!" Dunne ordered, annoyed not only at being kept in the dark regarding the four corpses but also at having so much ruckus while he was on call. Three doctors rotated the "graveyard shift" duties for the little hospital. Three-quarters of the time he could sleep the night away but not last night or this morning.

"But Rory said you weren't to touch—"

Dunne cut the hospital orderly cum ambulance driver off with a stern look. "Surely, the state pathologist will want the body stripped," he pronounced. He glanced at his watch. His own patients weren't scheduled until two. He could catch a few hours' sleep. Since he was now wide-awake, he might as well satisfy his curiosity and examine Johnny O'Connor's wounds.

"You need help, doctor?" Jimmy asked, once the body bag was removed.

"No, thanks. Why don't you go down to the lab and clean the glassware?" Dunne affixed his "Ignore the way I just acted; I'm really a nice guy" smile.

Driscoll was not fooled. He shuffled through the swinging doors and down the hall, moving at his usual slug's pace.

Jimmy was Hardy to Dunne's Laurel, Mutt to Dunne's Jeff. He stood seven inches shorter than the doctor but outweighed him by ninety pounds. Only youth had made it possible for him to manage his own bulk and the dead weight of Johnny O'Connor at the same time. Never, even in winter, was he without a handkerchief to wipe away the perspiration caused by the slightest effort. When he moved fast, which was seldom, he puffed like a freight yard switcher.

Dunne listened to the orderly shamble away. It had been an unusually healthy summer; not one bed was occupied on the second floor. The two nurses were not due in for another half hour. Dunne enjoyed the quiet. He picked up a pair of well-honed scissors and made the blades snick several times.

"Well, Johnny O'Connor, Esquire, let's take a look. Let's take a look." Dunne sniffed. He started at the trouser cuffs and cut up both legs, right past the belt loops. Then he did the same with the shirt cuffs. He raised a professional eyebrow as he snipped the shirt buttons and peeled cloth from the shoulder wound. He was inured to the visual ravages of old age, disease and the occasional accident. Dunne was not startled by the shotgun wound, but he recoiled at the sight of the entire body. It looked like a used-up husk, as if the old man had been death-marched a thousand miles before he was blasted.

A drop of mucus hung off the tip of Dunne's nose. The doctor set the scissors down beside the body and crossed to the countertop that held the tissue box. Damned allergies! They really bloomed this time every August. He blew forcefully, first one nostril then the other, stepped on the garbage can foot pedal and let the used tissue fall.

Dunne turned back to the body. His eyes blinked in surprise. The corpse's right hand was balanced on its belly. Dunne did not remember leaving it there. But he had to have moved it. This body was the proverbial doornail. With the clothes cut off he could see the post-mortem lividity. Gravity had worked on the uncirculating blood and settled it bluely in the lower back, buttocks and thighs; the upper torso looked like chalk.

Dunne set the right hand down on the gurney, directly on top of the scissors. Just to be 100 per cent sure, he stepped to the top of the gurney, reached around the head of the corpse and felt both sides of the neck for a pulse.

John O'Connor's eyes popped open. The sight registered in Dunne's mind, freezing him in place. O'Connor's right hand, wrapped around the scissors, swept up and back. The twin blades drove through Dunne's neck and chin, through the root of his tongue and into the roof of his mouth, pinning his jaw shut. Even lock-jawed, Dunne bellowed out his agony.

The corpse's left hand stretched up, grabbed a hank of Dunne's hair, and yanked down. Blood erupted from the throat wound and out the corners of the physician's lips. O'Connor's fingers relaxed around the scissor grips just as Dunne's fingers fluttered upward to extract it. The gray-white hand coiled back then shoved up through Dunne's fingers, driving the point of the scissors into the base of the struggling doctor's brain. He stopped his frantic motions instantly. His legs failed him and he collapsed to the floor.

O'Connor's hands relaxed back down to his side.

"Dr. Dunne?" Jimmy rushed through the swinging doors, worry deepening the folds in his obese face. He stopped short as his gaze settled on the corpse. The pale countenance was spattered with fresh blood. He glanced left and right. "Doctor?" Then he saw the figure on the floor beyond the gurney. Gasping in tiny, clavicular breaths, he edged around the gurney. Blood had sprayed everywhere. Jimmy caught sight of the scissor handles protruding from under Dunne's chin, then saw the look of horror frozen on the doctor's face. Jimmy glanced away. It was not because of the gruesome image; the orderly's pronounced morbid streak had led him to choose his job. He turned because an intuitive sense, a bone-chilling premonition of doom redirected his attention to the corpse on the gurney. Johnny O'Connor's eyes were wide open and staring at him. The dead fingers sprang out to fasten around Jimmy's hands, the white bones already erupting through livid flesh.

"Let me see Smiley's and Mary's charts again," the sergeant bid Keenan. He set the two pieces of paper side by side on the quay wall. "No doubt about it; they're identical," Meagher declared. A slight breeze fluttered the papers. Suddenly, one slipped out of Meagher's grasp and sailed over the water. The sergeant stretched forward to catch it and, in doing, his belly pushed the other paper over the edge of the wall. The first swooped and dove down and away. The other plummeted then made a last-second curve so that it landed face down on the surface of the undulating water.

"Shit!" Meagher swore, softly. "Stupid thing to do." He offered Keenan a sheepish look. "Ah well, it's not as if we need them to prove anything, right?"

"Right," Keenan agreed, privately relieved that the evidence of his break-in was drifting toward the Atlantic Ocean.

"Just forget about them, Professor," Meagher advised. "They served their purpose. I believe you. There are other things to do; come with me!"

Keenan followed Meagher's quick about-face and pulled alongside, matching the older man's rapid strides. Meagher's brows were tightly knit.

"This is the worst thing's happened in my fifteen years as sergeant, and it's not even over. In 1979 a woman skidded on the ice and drove through the quay wall. She and her five children went down into the Suir. Even with the cold water they might have escaped but for the weir. When the tide's in, a fierce back pressure forms under the drop. They call it a hydraulic," he imparted. "The pressure held them all under until they drowned." Meagher drew air through his teeth. "Never thought I'd see worse than that."

Meagher and the professor trudged up Bridge Street toward the *Garda* station. Keenan noted that the short incline and a few long sentences were all that were necessary to make Meagher draw his breath through his mouth.

A *Garda* car roared down Main Street in their direction and came to a grinding halt at their feet. Rory MacCullen leaned across the front seat and called out the window. "I got O'Connor!"

Meagher raised his forefinger quickly to his lips. Rory pursed his lips and threw open the passenger door. "Found him sprawled out on Mickey Ryan's back lawn."

"Dead?" the sergeant asked, opening the car's back door for Keenan.

Rory waited until his boss had climbed in before answering. "Couldn't be deader. He felt like a block of ice. Blasted in two places. Looks like the Walshes used the gun on him before he turned it on their hired hand. Vickie—the Ryan's girl—found him. How he got so far from the Walsh place blasted like that is beyond me."

"Is he still there?" Meagher asked urgently.

"No. At the medical center. And I know we wouldn't ordinarily move him before examination but—I wanted to find you before we called the state pathologist in Dublin."

"You did well. Let's get over there," Meagher directed. "How long do you think he was lying at Ryan's?"

"Long enough for rigor mortis to set in," the young officer remarked. He laughed lightly. "Young Vickie was ranting about its hand moving by itself, trying to grab her."

Meagher gave MacBreed a baleful glance. "Put your foot down, Rory!"

The fire engines arrived at the same time as the guards and the archeologist. The little hospital was already engulfed in flame, orange-yellow tongues of fire darting out of the exploded windows.

"Holy God!" Rory exclaimed.

"So much for John O'Connor," Meagher said, darkly. He swung his gaze up and down the street, studying the growing throng of onlookers. He seemed disappointed. "But who knows who he's infected," he finished.

"What?" Rory said.

"I've got a great deal to share with you and the other lads," Meagher told his subordinate. "Have the officers arrived from Dublin?"

"Yes," answered MacCullen. "One car's working The Sweep; the other's patroling Carrigadoon."

"Call everyone back in," ordered the sergeant. "Then bring them all over here. What I have to say can't go over the radio. Get moving!"

"Yes, sir!" Rory returned crisply. Without a backward glance, he trotted to the patrol car.

Meagher eyed the conflagration. His throat worked up and down. "Well, it's come to Carrick. What odds will you give me that the thing inside Johnny O'Connor has traded bodies?"

"No bet," Keenan answered. "The others could be nearby now as well."

"Lovely. Bloody lovely," Meagher fumed.

The fire engine crew had hooked up to the town's water line. Powerful sprays arched from the hose to the hospital's second floor. A pair of firemen in flameproof wear and oxygen masks dashed through the front doors and disappeared in the smoke.

"The important thing now is that they don't get across the river," said the archeologist.

"Is it?" Meagher countered. "Letting them go across might prevent the entire town from going up in flames."

"I don't think that's a concern," Keenan said. "They must know they can't afford to stay in an area with so many people. In fact, when they were buried there wasn't a town in all of Ireland this large or imposing. They might be too afraid to enter it at all."

"My luck isn't that good," Meagher lamented. "They seem a brazen bunch to me. This fire might be a diversion precisely so they can sneak across."

"True," agreed Keenan. "And once they pass the bottle-neck, they can move off in any direction. I'll watch the bridge until you can position your men."

"I can't let you do that," said Meagher. "You're a civilian."

"I am, and I wouldn't do it if I thought it was too dangerous, Dick. Believe me."

Meagher glanced past MacBreed's shoulder. "All right. Be on your way; the hordes are descending on me."

"You're going to stick with the story you gave me in the café?" Keenan asked, turning to see a firefighter and the reporter from the previous night bearing down on them.

"Yes. And so are you. Now get the hell out of here before you're questioned."

Keenan lowered his face and walked off briskly, moving against a stream of chattering townsfolk. He was fairly certain he knew what had happened at the hospital, fairly sure that the sergeant understood as well: the body Keenan had seen just after dawn, sitting so lifelessly on the rocks had finally died of its wounds. The creature inside had either compelled it to walk several more miles before it dropped or perhaps had been carried until the Druidesses again encountered civilization. Fergus and Mick may have hidden near the lawn, in hopes that someone from the house would come out soon and be taken. Or perhaps they had moved off, certain that the third Druidess would eventually grab another body and link up with them at a preappointed place. With O'Connor's body dead, she was free to move to another. She had been trying to grab the Ryan girl when someone else had come on the scene.

Keenan's step took a hitch. He wondered just how big the Ryan girl was. Were the bones as supernatural as the spirits they held? Could they somehow conform to any size, or must the stolen body be close to the Druidess's own former stature?

Keenan kept his eyes moving warily. He was unsure about the ancients' fear of the town and very concerned about not becoming their next victim. The latest one had undoubtedly been inside the hospital. Keenan looked for a figure dressed in hospital whites, about John O'Connor's height.

And where had Mary Liddy gone since the confrontation in the woods? She could undoubtedly save lives—either by telling Keenan how to kill her three fellow creatures or at least how to contain them.

The wail of a police siren echoed through the town. Keenan glanced back and saw black smoke billowing in the blue sky. Reaching Main Street, he found the center of town unusually deserted. The absence of people heightened Keenan's sense of danger. He whistled an old Irish tune and hurried into the middle of the street. Volunteering to play Horatio at the Bridge suddenly seemed a foolhardy offer.

Keenan made his way cautiously down Bridge Street to the place on the quay where he and Dick Meagher had stood minutes before. From his vantage point, he could look down the quay, up Bridge Street and across the bridge into Carrick-beg. He narrowed his eyes and peered south. Three people hurried toward him over the slight curve of the bridge, their faces studying the sky. He saw no one else. In the last minute or two, nobody had crossed the bridge from the Carrick side. Keenan glanced back over his shoulder. He could just barely make out wisps of smoke in the sky between the walls of the tall buildings that lined Bridge Street.

The three curiosity seekers passed by, and Keenan found himself alone again. He peered over the edge of the quay wall and down to the swirling waters. The dental charts had floated out of sight. Gone forever.

Keenan watched the sunlight glinting off the water in a hundred sparkles, vanishing as a hundred other starbursts replaced them. It was an exhilarating image, equaled only by the dance of firelight. Transience embodied. The very evanesence the Impressionist painters had struggled to capture. Until the past few hours, Keenan had been sure that religions also struggled for the same control. Man refused to accept life as a sparkling, temporal gift. All the invented gods, the prayers, the hymns masked a stubborn refusal to accept the fact that one day we stop existing and the gift of life is gone.

Keenan had awakened every few months quaking at the stark reality of death, but he refused to let blind faith numb his feat. Whenever he could not block the subject from his conscious mind he regarded it with heavyhearted resignation. Until Mary Liddy. If she herself was not immortal, she at least had communed with a supernal force that allowed her to transcend normal death. Beyond this terror also lay hope.

But where was Mary, and why was he standing here guarding a bridge when he should be finding her?

Keenan blinked his way back from these abstractions and glanced to his left. The figure of a man, backlit by the sun, moved rapidly along the east side of the quay. Keenan squinted to make out the man's face. He was clearly aware of Keenan and seemed headed straight for him. A moment later, Keenan was sure that the shape was that of Fergus MacMahon.

Escape up Bridge Street was impossible. Fergus had the angle on that avenue of flight and on the bridge as well. His right hand trailed behind his hip, concealing something. Keenan spun around. The figure of a second man closed stealthily from the west, hugging the building walls. The second was at a greater distance but had the light shining directly on him. Keenan saw clearly that it was Mick. The creature held a length of metal pipe.

For a moment Keenan considered jumping over the quay wall. He swam well, and the water could not be that cold.

The problem was that the current was swift and treacherous. He remembered well Dick Meagher's comment about the weir which, like a cobra, hissed a warning of death.

Keenan looked toward the buildings that lined the quay. Most were warehouses with locked doors and without windows. A little way down stood a house, but its wall was high and jagged with glass. The only avenue of salvation seemed an alleyway, halfway between Mick and himself. Keenan broke into a full-out dash, gaining a slight lead before the two hunters reacted. He entered the alley still accelerating. To his dismay, he saw no doors at all and more jagged glass on the wall to his right. The alley emptied into a T intersection. As he rounded it, he glanced behind him. Neither man had yet entered the alley.

Then Keenan saw why. Mick had ducked down another lane and cut off Keenan's escape west. The professor turned around. The alley ahead of him was blind, dead-ending at the unloading dock of a hulking, two-and-a-half story, yellow building. The alley was wide enough to accommodate two trucks, side by side. At the T where he stepped out his nervous, indecisive dance, three garbage cans stood empty, with their lids thrown on the ground.

On his final turn-round, Keenan saw Fergus enter the alleyway to the south. Mick closed at full tilt from the west, the pipe now raised with lethal intent. He was almost a hundred feet closer than his partner and posed the immediate threat. Keenan picked up the flatest garbage can lid and twisted his body to the left. As Mick entered the T, Keenan flung the lid in a discus motion. Mick pulled up short, eyes going wide, mouth changing from savage to shock, hands moving to ward off the flying lid. It caught Mick hard in the chest. His legs skittered out as if on ice, and Mick was suddenly on the ground.

Keenan did not see the effect of his throw; he was already halfway down the alley, knees high and arms pumping. He mounted the loading dock in one leap, hit the door lightly, found its handle and yanked. It was locked. Keenan turned. Fergus was helping Mick off the ground. Both looked in his direction. They did not seem in any hurry. Keenan's entrapment was as obvious to them as it was to him.

You had to daydream, Keenan scolded himself as he ran. He had let the professor part of him drift off into reverie when he knew his life might be in jeopardy. No wonder he had chosen academia to hide in. The real world, even when it proved far less threatening than this, would have eaten such a man alive. He made a swift but solemn promise to himself that, if he got out of this alive, he would change.

Keenan looked to his right. A sturdy-looking downspout ran along the length of the building, secured by massive iron U-clamps. He reached up to one and tested its anchoring. It remained fast in the wall. He climbed. On the second level, another rainspout fed in, providing a firmer foothold. One brick had been mortared slightly forward of the rest, leaving room for finger tips. At summer camp, Keenan had scaled small precipices with lesser holds. Back then he was twenty years younger and half his present weight, but the two creatures bounding up the alley below him tilted the balance. He avoided looking down and concentrated on the roof, which lay almost within his grasp.

The impact made Keenan swing out like a monkey on a stick, one hand and one foot all that saved him from death. He had been hit squarely between the shoulder blades by something hard and sharp. In spite of himself, he looked down. A large rock lay on the loading dock—the missile Fergus had been carrying. Mick still clutched the pipe. Both were clambering onto the dock. Keenan gasped in a breath, stretched up hard and caught the corner of the gutter. His arms were killing him. He got his other hand up and held tight while his free foot found the last clamp.

The building formed an inside corner where the spout was anchored. Keenan used the roof angle to throw one leg up and haul himself onto the roof. The cant was not too steep, but he stayed low, working his way to the ridge. He shuddered at how much higher the place seemed when looking down rather than up. In a moment of leisure, he might have lingered to drink in the view of Carrick and the surrounding valley. Now all he craved was salvation. A *Garda* van rolled slowly along the bridge, heading for the Carrick-beg side. Far west, in the town's river-edge park, he could see two guards hauling the cots from the water. He cupped his hands to his mouth and hollered for help. A solitary man on the north side of the quay turned as if he heard. Keenan yelled again. The man scanned the river and all around on ground level but refused to look up.

Keenan paused to catch his breath. He heard the telltale groans of a mistreated downspout. Keenan watched the gutter quiver. The Druidesses were not about to let him escape, evidently equating their safety with his extermination. He was sure the indignities he had dealt them in the woods only added to their fury. For the first time in his life Keenan wanted to kill. Within sight were any number of slate and tile roofs, which could provide plenty of missiles for him to break the heads of his pursuers. The roof he stood on was asphalt. All he could do was keep fleeing. Keenan started down the roof's opposite side.

The building's roof almost touched the neighboring wall of a three-story building. Its third-story windows had been bricked up. Its roof, four feet above, was flat, surrounded by a ledge. Keenan hopped up, hauled himself over, scrambled to his feet and ran to the opposite edge. He looked down onto Bridge Street. The only people in sight were two old women. They strolled toward the river, directly below him.

"Hey, help!" Keenan called down.

The women looked up, startled. "What's the matter?" one asked.

"I'm being chased by two men who want to kill me!" Keenan shouted. He pointed across the river. "Get the *Gardaí!*" The women looked at each other and began debating in voices too low for Keenan to hear. "Goddamnit, do what I say!" Keenan screamed. The women both started, then hurried to follow his command.

Keenan watched their agonizingly slow progress. He looked over his shoulder. By the time they reached the police, his two pursuers would be throwing him from the roof. He leaned out over the edge. To his right and left, about three feet below, large windows stood open. A young woman's head popped out of the one on the right, looking everywhere but up for the source of his shouting. A thick barb of iron stuck straight up from the top of the low wall ledge in front of him. It was covered with rust but remained rigid when Keenan grabbed it and rocked back with his full weight. As quickly as he could, Keenan stripped off his belt and threw the buckle over the metal barb.

Half a minute. Unless the Druidesses were completely inept at climbing, they would be on him in that time or less. Keenan threw his left leg over the roof's ledge as he held onto the belt with an iron grip. Any lesser hold would almost certainly spell his end; the fall was three stories down onto concrete. He clutched the ledge with one hand while he aimed his legs at the windowsill below. An involuntary groan escaped him as he let go of the roof ledge and dropped to the window. His free hand clawed out for the frame. When he had it fast, he flicked the belt up several times, until the buckle leapt free of the metal barb.

Two young women worked in the third-story room within. First one, then the other shrieked as Keenan swung in. He blocked out the noise in his mania to get the window down. He lunged for the second window and repeated his action.

The women had stopped screaming, fascinated by Keenan's unexpected movements. He turned to them and tried to speak. Panic had a stranglehold on his throat. All that came out was a squeak. He swallowed hard. "Don't open these windows! Please," he urged, huskily.

The brunette stared past Keenan at the windows; the

blonde fixed her gaze on the belt in his hand and on his drooping trousers.

"Sorry," Keenan muttered. He hitched up his pants and threaded the belt back through the loops as he rushed from the room and clattered down the two flights of stairs.

When he exited into the sunlight, Keenan looked up. Mick's face glowered down from thirty feet above. Then it glanced riverward and disappeared. Keenan saw the *Garda* van speeding over the bridge. The officer in the passenger's seat pointed excitedly at the rooftop. The professor pivoted abruptly and walked at a quick-march up Bridge Street. He was done with the hunt; he wanted out of the action completely; this, as Dick Meagher had so astutely pointed out, was police work. The *Gardaí* had photographs of Mick and Fergus; they didn't need him to identify them. They also didn't need him to lead them on any rooftop chases. In fact, he didn't need to be within fifty miles of these banshees from the fifth century.

Halfway up Bridge Street Keenan slowed his pace. His arms ached, his shoulder sockets burned, his calves had shortened into hard knots. He still puffed like a steam engine, but he had a strange feeling of exhilaration. He had again outwitted not one but two adversaries and had again cheated death. And he had pulled it off not with luck but with élan. True, Indiana Jones would not have groaned with fear when swinging onto the window ledge. James Bond would have tossed off some clever apology to the women about "dropping in unexpectedly." But they were fictional characters; he was real flesh and blood. He'd had all the horror and derring-do he wanted for a lifetime, more than enough stimulation to borrow on forever. He marveled at his light-headed feeling, then realized that he was hyperventilating. He held his breath for several steps and forced himself to breath shallowly. As he walked, he cast anxious looks behind him. No more goddamned reveries for this boy!

At the top of Bridge Street, where it ran into Main, Keenan spotted a hulking figure leaning on the far end of the corner's guard rail. The blond-haired man, in his mid-twenties, had to be no less than six-foot-three and two-hundred-ten pounds. He rested with his arms folded across his chest, as if on lookout. A colossal improvement on Johnny O'Connor's body.

Keenan shrank back a step as the man's blue eyes fixed hard on his, widening at the same time. "Excusemecanyoutellmewhattimeitis?" Keenan blurted, unconsciously recalling Dick Meagher's words about people in Carrick shooting each other over the time of day.

The man's eyebrows knit; he gave a shake of his head as his arms came down to his sides. He took a step toward Keenan. The professor glanced around the street for the best avenue of escape.

"I can tell you what time it is, sir," an accented voice said, from the entrance of the store on the corner. Keenan looked and saw a female version of the blond-haired man emerging from the store toting a shopping bag. Before she could consult her watch, the blond man spoke to her in what sounded to Keenan like Swedish or Norwegian.

The woman replied in the same tongue, then raised her wristwatch to the level of her eyes. "It's fifteen minutes after ten," she said. "My brother doesn't speak any English. He's afraid he has upset you."

The large, powerful-looking man did indeed look concerned and not at all threatening now. Keenan told himself that the man had probably never looked dangerous; his mind had supplied what it expected to see. The professor could well imagine the expressions his own face had just held. "No, no, it's my fault entirely. Please tell him I'm sorry."

Keenan caught the woman's gentle smile as he rushed past. Swedish or Norwegian tourists. Nothing more. No harm done. But if he had had a gun and the sister hadn't emerged when she did, the blond-haired man might be lying on the sidewalk, staining it Belfast red.

Doing his best to control his shaking, the professor ducked into the Bessborough Arms, collected his key and took the stairs up two at a time. He locked himself inside his room and shoved the wardrobe against the door. These were not rational creatures on the loose. Otherwise they would have searched for a less populous river crossing point or might at least have hidden in shadows until Keenan abandoned his lookout. These ancients were indeed like the legendary Irish berserkers who went into "warp-spasms," working themselves into such frenzies before battle that they threw off their armor and shields and conducted the business of slaughter with little more than sharpened iron and shrill war cries. Definitely a deadly trio. Finally, satisfied that he was safe, Keenan collapsed on the bed. If anyone wanted him, they could damned well call on the telephone.

The phone rang, shattering the stillness of the room with its raucous jangle. Keenan sat bolt upright on the bed, lids snapping back like those on an uprighted porcelain doll. He gave his head a couple of hard shakes to slip the torpor. His eyes searched out his travel alarm clock as he groped for the phone. Twenty minutes to three. He had slept, or more precisely had passed out, for a good while.

"Hello," Keenan managed.

"Dr. MacBreed, there's a gentleman here from Trinity college," announced the receptionist. "I thought it best to ring you before sending him up."

Keenan managed a smile. The receptionist had evidently learned his lesson after the chewing-out he got over the mysterious redhead. "Thank you. Yes, send him up." The redhead. What in hell *had* that been about? In all the furor over the resurrections from the Lamoge cemetery, he had forgotten about her fleeting visit and fleeter flight.

Moving the wardrobe back was not an easy task. Not only

had MacBreed's muscles stiffened during his nap, but he was sure that excess adrenalin had helped him move the heavy piece of furniture against the door. By the time he had pulled it back into place, a knock sounded on the door.

The face in the hallway was a familiar one. "Come in, Dennis," Keenan said to the Trinity college graduate student. "Do you have that report on the femur bone?"

"Yes, here it is," Dennis answered, handing the professor a manila envelope. Inside, the formal document told Keenan that the bone had radiocarbon dated at 445 A.D. plus or minus twenty-five years. Exactly the date range MacBreed expected.

"The report pleases you," Dennis observed.

"It does. This is a significant find."

"Wonderful!" Dennis enthused. "You've merited a good dig, sir."

Keenan dropped the report on the desk and set a hand on the graduate student's shoulder. "Come down to the Rover with me; I've got something else to date." He guided Dennis out the door and locked it behind him. "There was a wooden cross under the stone high cross. I want some slivers analyzed as well."

On the way down the stairs and out into the street, Dennis said, "By the by, there's been some fantastic news from the Dublin Institute of Advanced Study. Supposed to be hush-hush." Keenan knew what that meant: the public was not yet allowed to share the discovery. "The passage tomb at Newgrange is definitely the oldest structure with an astronomical function. A computer program set the heavens back 5,150 years to compensate for the change in the earth's tilt. First light would have hit the back wall precisely on the winter solstice!"

"Amazing," Keenan responded. And it was indeed. This was six hundred years before the first of the great Egyptian pyramids went up. That long ago, his Irish ancestors had the science to build a tomb so precisely aligned that a ray of sunlight shone sixty feet deep into its main burial chamber on December 21.

"And the opening, viewed from the chamber, is exactly the width of the sun," Dennis finished. "Well, the archeology Challenge Cup moves to Ireland this year!" he crowed.

Newgrange Tomb was indeed a rival to the Great Pyramids and Stonehenge. But Keenan wondered in silence what Dennis would have said about the four Druidess' accomplishment—surviving burial for fourteen hundred years. In a matter of days, Ireland had emerged from archeological insignificance to preeminence. But, like the joke about the priest who takes Sunday off to golf and gets a hole in one, who could Keenan tell?

The professor unlocked the Range Rover and opened the door. He saw the map immediately. There was no question of its origin; it was one of the two that Mary Liddy had stolen. Keenan slid it aside as casually as he could and clambered into the wagon to fetch the metal box holding the ancient wood.

"You don't have to come back with this," Keenan told the student. "I don't expect to be here much longer. I'll read the report when I return."

Dennis seemed anxious to head back to Dublin. Probably a date, Keenan mused to himself. The young man was bright and good-looking, with money from his assistantship and, Keenan suspected, from a well-heeled family. A good catch in a depressed country. Keenan waited until the college's car disappeared past the town hall before reaching into the Range Rover for the map. A small hole had been poked through it, about a half mile east of the center of Carrick. At that point, the little Lingaun River fed into the Suir.

Keenan took the map with him to his room and studied it while he telephoned the Carrick *Garda* station. "I'd like to speak with Sergeant Meagher," he told the male voice that answered.

"He's not here. Who's calling?"

"Officer Rory MacCullen, then."

"Not here either. May I say who's calling?"

"Professor MacBreed," Keenan said. "Can you tell me if the gravediggers, MacMahon and the other, have been caught yet?"

There was a pause on the other end of the line, then, "I'm afraid we can't be giving that sort of information out over the telephone. Perhaps if you were to stop by the station and wait for Sergeant Meagher."

Keenan hung up. He had gotten his answer; somehow, the two had eluded the police. Keenan laughed ruefully. All his neck-risking acrobatics for what? He hoped the police would at least have had the presence of mind to keep the bridge guarded while some of their number ran across Carrick's roofs. Keenan snatched up the map and hurried out of the hotel.

Keenan took the Rover down to the quay. Neither Dick Meagher nor Rory MacCullen were in sight. The guard, however, had been doubled, so that a police car stood conspicuously at either end of the bridge and officers paced warily back and forth in plain view.

Carrick was so small that all its streets could be driven within the space of a few minutes. Keenan had no idea how long ago Mary had put the map into the Rover, and he didn't want her to give up hope that he would find her. Despite this, he needed to make his own quick patrol, to see if he could spot MacMahon and Dunphy. He could not turn his mind to the scholarly aspects of the Lamoge cemetery discoveries until the terrifying aspects had been resolved. After a full but futile turn of the town, he headed the Rover toward the confluence of the Lingaun and Suir Rivers.

Mary Liddy sat under a tree near the river bank, about a hundred yards from the dead-end lane that served the area. When she saw the Rover she stood, but she made no effort to close the gap between them. One frail arm extended to the tree for support. Keenan took a metal survey stake from the wagon, the most harmless-looking weapon he could feel safe with. He took his time approaching the woman, assessing the shape of every bush and stand of weeds as he neared them, ready to make a wild dash for the Rover if anything looked suspicious. A third hairbreadth escape from death in one day was too much to ask of Fate.

When Keenan was almost beside the old woman, he noticed the reason she had not moved. The weight was completely off her right foot, and her ankle was plainly swollen. The flesh above her shoe protruded in a mottle of angry pink and purple. A makeshift wooden crutch leaned against the far side of the tree. In spite of her injury, Mary smiled broadly. When Keenan stopped short in front of her she made a rapid, formal bow.

"You stole my maps, my flashlight and my money," Keenan accused.

"Yes," Mary replied, straightforwardly. "And I have lost your flashlight. I will pay you. Will you eat?" She gestured to a simple fare lying in the crotch of the tree—a half-eaten bag of unpeeled carrots, most of a small box of fresh berries and the remains of a loaf of Irish soda bread. A bottle of Tipperary spring water lay unopened.

"No, thank you. You can repay me with answers," Keenan returned, scanning the area. "You knew your three friends were dangerous, so you left me sleeping."

"Yes."

Keenan reached for the bottle of water. "You couldn't convince them that the people they meet are not their enemies."

"Yes. They are . . . like the people in the hospital." Mary put her hand up in front of her face and waved it erratically.

The professor knew she referred to the Clonmel mental hospital. "Insane," he said, and when she did not react, "You couldn't make them understand what has happened."

"Yes, insane." Mary paused to watch Keenan unscrew the bottle's metal cap. He offered it to her. She drank thirstily, then said, "But to kill was always their answer for problems. Even before they went in *cael teg.*"

147

"In the narrow house," Keenan translated unconsciously, knowing precisely what the woman meant and marveling that the familiar Irish expression for *grave* had survived for so many centuries. "You have to stop speaking your old language," he insisted. "It's dangerous."

"No with you," Mary answered, looking offended.

"Not with me," Keenan corrected softly. "I'm only trying to help you."

"I know. T'ank you, *Ollam."*

"If I made your life difficult by following you, I'm sorry," Keenan apologized.

"No," Mary answered. "What you say—they are insane." She held out the bottle.

Keenan shook his head. "They're here in this town . . . Carrick," he revealed. "They tried to kill me again, but they couldn't. I also know that they want to go across the river."

Mary arched one gray eyebrow in appreciation of his knowledge. She did not, however, seem particularly surprised by the intelligence he had gathered. She wobbled unsteadily on her good leg.

"Sit!" Keenan said, offering his hand to help her down against the tree. He scanned the area one last time and sat himself opposite Mary, with his back to the water. "Where are they going?"

"They go to awake the Tuait'e de Donn," Mary replied, fixing Keenan's eyes with a hawklike stare.

Keenan felt his body go cold. "How many of your people are still alive?"

Mary's eyes blurred momentarily as she counted. "Seven hundred warriors, t'ree hundred children, eight hundred and more women, maybe two hundred old people. And slaves."

More than two thousand souls! Keenan felt lightheaded, as the blood pooled in his center. Goose flesh gathered on his arms and neck. "Where do all these people sleep?" he ventured.

Mary shook her head. "Most *ru."* She winced and flashed

a look at her ankle. "Most secret. I and the t'ree sisters went under the sod for this secret."

"Sisters. The three who are killing are sisters?"

"Yes. All one. All of one age," Mary told him.

Identical triplets, Keenan told himself. He knew of the power the Irish Celts ascribed to the number three. Not only were The Morrigan, the triple goddesses of war, a manifestation of this; the goddesses of Ireland—Eriu, Fodla and Banbha—personified the land itself as the triune Earth Mothers. Little wonder that triplets had become Druidesses.

"You need my help," Keenan declared.

"I do not want the Tuait'e de Donn to wake," Mary replied, evasively. "The sisters have no t'ought but killing and to bring our people to home. They must be stopped."

Keenan raised his right hand, hoping the gesture would signify a pledge to the ancient woman. "I promise on the souls of my ancestors and on all the magic powers I command to help you stop them. First you must tell me how the Tuatha de Donn came to sleep."

Mary studied Keenan's face for a moment. Her lips pursed with the weighing of her thoughts. She nodded her agreement and crossed her arms over her chest. Then she spoke.

The Lady of the Flaming Hair rode a dappled mare, and at her flanks rode Eogan and Oillil, two champions of the Tuatha de Donn. Once beyond the western march of their clan, where the waters of Slievenamon Peak gouged the earth into deep ravines on their course south to the Suir, the soldiers of Aenghus of Munster became a common sight. Their camps at every ford and pass were too well entrenched and too crowded for normal times. But they gave her and her companions no trouble; Aenghus's warriors had been well instructed.

They had mounted up at dawn, having camped inside the westernmost ring-fort of the clan-Donn the night before. The frequent challenges by Aenghus's men slowed them through the day, but they imposed a self-enforced leisureliness on themselves. The spies who no doubt galloped ahead to inform Aenghus of their progress would have attributed their slowness to calculated arrogance, but The Lady had more purpose in mind for their late-afternoon arrival than manifesting disdain for Aenghus's invitation.

Ireland in A.D. 445 was a land of more than one hundred petty kingdoms, and movement of each clan-chieftain's population was zealously restricted to prevent losing population. Many inhabitants, however, had the right of free travel throughout the island, the poets and lawyers, historians, physicians, and the "base" craftsmen—those who created tools, weapons, musical instruments and jewelry by hand. These travelers, both with selfish purpose and unwittingly, spread the news and the schemes of the powerful throughout the land.

Thus it was that Caicher, the king of the Tuatha de Donn, learned of the exile of another Aenghus. This one was Aenghus of the Deisi People, from the High-kingdom of Meath and known as The Raven. The meaning behind his name was shrouded. Most thought it came from his black beard and the bushy black eyebrows which swept upward like wings. Others said it was due to his intelligence, since the raven is among the smartest of birds. To his enemies he was the harbinger of death, the carrion-eater that circles the battlefield. The Deisi People had fled into the region of Cashel, the seat of Aenghus, High-king of Munster. The Raven had avenged an insult to one of his Deisi kinswomen, killing the offending prince Cellach in the presence of Cellach's father, Cormac Mac Art. During the battle, The Raven also put out the eye of the monarch, causing Cormac to lose his throne because of the immutable Brehon law that no man disfigured could hold a kingly position. Before Cormac stepped down, he made sure that the rash Deisi prince and those who chose to follow him would never again set foot in the central kingdom of Meath.

The Lady's king, Caicher, was certain that Aenghus of

Munster held no especial love for The Raven. The lands of
his people would not be freely parceled out to an exile.
Conquered land, however, was another matter. For more
than three hundred years, the land of the central Suir valley
had belonged to the Tuatha de Donn. Although among the
shortest people on the island, their valor was legendary,
even among the fierce Celts. No less legendary were the
powers of their Druid priestesses. The clan, in fact, owed its
independence more to other tribes' fears of their supernatural powers than to the skill behind their swords. The
Tuatha de Donn pledged a tenuous allegiance to the High-
kingdom of Leinster, the southeastern of the Five Kingdoms
of Ireland, but in reality no other clans dictated to the
clan-Donn. Because of this unsteady relationship, Aenghus
of Munster, the High-king of the southwestern kingdom,
saw the possibility of extending his sway eastward and
southward. He knew it would have to be done indirectly.
Although the High-king of Leinster held little love for the
clan-Donn, he would surely not allow Aenghus to conquer
them and occupy their land. Only a king without declared
allegiance to Meath or Munster could vanquish the Tuatha
de Donn. The Raven was made to order.

Now Aenghus of Munster had invited Caicher to his
fortress on the Rock of Cashel. No mention had been made
of the Deisi People. No provocations such as the obligatory
cattle raiding had come prior to the invitation, which would
precede claims over pieces of the region. Safe conduct had
been pledged, but breaking of pledges and wholesale slaughter was not unknown among the tribes. Caicher doubted
such blatant treachery from Aenghus—only because it
would unite the superior forces of Leinster against him.
When Caicher had demanded a retinue of two hundred
warriors, however, Aenghus had demurred. If Caicher
would not honor his invitation, Aenghus counteroffered,
then perhaps he would send his celebrated Druid high
priestess, The Lady of the Flaming Hair. Unlike the Conti-
nental Celts, the Irish held their women in high regard and

granted them, except for the holding of land, virtually all the same rights afforded men. In religious, astronomical and magical arts, moreover, it was accepted that women could excel. And so it was agreed that a woman would answer the invitation of the High-king of Munster.

The sun had fallen halfway to the horizon when The Lady of the Flaming Hair first saw the awesome Rock of Cashel dominating the fertile plain of the Golden Vale. Before the fortress was erected on its heights, her people had called it *Sheedrum*. But now it was the place where Munster's wealth was collected, so it was renamed *Cios ail*—the Rock of Tribute. The isolated hill rose three hundred feet above the unleveled stands of forest, lush green mottled with the gray stone that thrust up through the earth here and there. Every few minutes, as the Rock grew with their progress, The Lady and her fearless companions passed a huddle of wooden huts, each the nucleus of one *fine*, the fundamental family unit. The Munster farmers labored at their soil and tended their flocks and herds just like the clan-Donn. Their day-to-day and season-to-season survival far outweighed their desires to wage war and change boundaries. The songs of the poets exalted the war-lust in every Gaelic Celt. To be sure, martial exploits were beloved among her people, and they would fight to the last man and woman to defend what was theirs, but the heart-kept desire in each farmer was for peace and security for most of his days.

At about one mile distant from the Rock, a troop of King Aenghus's men stretched across the road. The avenue from there forward was as broad as the *Slighe Cualann*, which ran from Tara into Leinster. Fully forty warriors on horseback blocked the road, each carrying a thrusting spear. On first sight of them, The Lady slipped a ring onto the third finger of her right hand, then set the hand lightly on her hip.

The captain of the guard trotted his steed forward to meet Aenghus's guests. He smiled with manly appreciation at The Lady of the Flaming Hair, his eyes roaming boldly along the length of her figure. Her shoes were of deerskin and beaded

with colored glass. Beneath her dress, which consisted of a
fine weave dyed in scarlet, were trousers that protected
against the chafe of riding. Around her narrow waist was a
girdle of leather studded with bronze medallions. From it
hung a comb bag, and out of that protruded a rowan stick.
The mantle draped over her right shoulder was secured by a
large and ornately decorated gold brooch. The Munster
warrior could see that the hand which gripped the reins had
long, well-trimmed and red-painted nails. Her face, which
had benefitted from cleansing in a stream an hour earlier,
shone whitely, contrasting with the black berry-juice darkening her brows and the natural shades of her arrestingly
beautiful red hair. She wore her tresses in traditional plaits
down to the middle of her back, decorated on the ends with
hollow, gold spheres. Just before she and her companions
had stopped, she had pinched each cheek, to heighten their
rosy glow. She smiled broadly at the captain. The Lady had
seen such bold looks of appreciation many times before, and
this time she welcomed them. He would be too occupied by
her beauty to worry about her brains.

The captain introduced himself and offered escort to
Aenghus's Great Hall. The Lady returned her appreciation.
The enemy horsemen closed in around them. As they
trotted forward, she studied the plains on either side,
counting, assessing. In a short time, they came to the edge of
a copse. The dust of the highway rose high from the two
dozen horses ahead of her. It masked the sharp downward
movement of her right hand, a movement that jabbed the
needlepoint on the underside of her ring into the flank of her
mare. When they had stopped at the stream, The Lady had
dipped the length of the needle into a clay vial containing
bee venom, an added spur to the sliver's prick.

The mare reared up hard, snorting and rolling its large
eyes. Then it cried out and bolted off the road, heading for
the forest. The Lady dropped the reins and lay flat along the
line of the mare's neck, gathering hanks of its mane among
her fingers. For effect, she glanced backward with a plaintive

expression and cried out for help. Eogan and Oillil gave chase, but only quickly enough to look convincing. The captain called to two of his men, and these three set out in swift pursuit.

By the time the mare had cleared the woods, it had regained its composure. It was, by its nature, a docile animal. In fact, not long after its initial pain, it was responding to the accustomed guidance of its mistress's hands on her mane. As soon as the horse slowed, the Lady jabbed it again with the ring, making it lower its head and gallop forward. Each second put the rider farther from the main road and deeper into the masking woods and hillocks. By the time the mare was overtaken and forced to a shuddering halt, The Lady had seen much of what she had desired to assay. The ring had also disappeared into the sod.

The walk back to the road was protracted. The Lady insisted on examining the horse minutely, then allowing it to regain its strength. The captain seemed relieved that his charge had neither hurt herself nor eluded him for long. He was the one who suggested a bee had stung the mare; they were, after all, just north of Cluan-mealla—the plain of honey.

They did not return by way of the copse but rather angled toward The Rock of Cashel, so that soon enough they cantered along the edge of its outer defenses. The High-king's *dun* was a formidable fortress. The first wall, halfway up the steep hill, stood the height of three men. When they passed through one of its gates, The Lady saw that it was more than a horse-length thick. Beyond this lay a deep trench lined with sharp, outward-pointing stakes, and then a second, lower wall. Inside, stood half a dozen wooden structures, dominated by the Great Hall. The three guests were given basins for cleansing and mead for refreshment.

The sun lay four lengths above the western horizon when The Lady and her escort were led into the Great Hall. Although the poets' tales had somewhat prepared them, none of the three had ever stood inside a High-king's chamber of power. It was almost a hundred feet long, some thirty feet wide and thirty feet high. A primitive stone buttressing held the main walls in place, but otherwise the entire structure was of wood. A large fire burned at either end. The smoke did not hang thickly in the hall; a wind had picked up with the falling of the sun, drawing the smoke out the roof holes. Tables lined the long walls. Behind them, on the walls, were hooks for the shields that announced the warriors when they dined. No warriors dined now; the hour was yet too early. On a raised dais just beyond the center of the room were several camp chairs, sturdily built, with animal-figure legs. The chairs were filled with men. Other men stood behind and to the sides. Some of them were dressed in plain brown robes. All of these wore identical decorations on their necks. The Lady had seen the shapes only once before. They were crosses, made of bronze or stone. The other standing men, some twenty in number, were soldiers, dressed in light battle regalia, each wearing a buckler with sword and holding a javelin at rest. The men in the chairs were variously dressed. The Lady recognized their rank and expertise by the cut of their costumes and by the number of colors they wore. The man seated in the center wore seven colors, the maximum allowed. The Lady knew without having seen him before that this was Aenghus of Munster, the High-king. Many of the colors he wore came from bright bird feathers. The most striking color on his person, however, was a swath of white cloth that bandaged his left foot. The foot was elevated on a stool.

To the High-king's left sat a man with a fierce black beard and six colors to his costume. On Aenghus's right hand sat an intense-looking man who wore pure white. Other than The Lady, the hall held no women.

Aenghus excused himself from not rising due to the wound to his foot. He introduced the man on his left as Aenghus of the Deisi, his honored guest. The man on the right he called simply Pádraig. He had chairs set for The Lady and her escorts, directly opposite and below the dais.

The High-king deplored that the respected Caicher of the Tuatha de Donn could not himself attend, but was sure that The Lady could transmit the news of their meeting with no trouble. With little more delay, he announced that he had just been converted from the worship of pagan gods to discipleship of the Lord Jesus Christ. He introduced the man, Pádraig, as a Britain and the holy man responsible for his conversion. He was anxious, Aenghus declared, that his friends, the clan-Donn, be brought into the light of this new religion from the East as soon as possible.

The Lady declared her willingness to listen. Pádraig rose and spoke for nearly an hour about the One True God, His only Son and the Trinity with the Holy Spirit. He spoke of the fulfillment of the ancient prophecies, of the virgin birth, of Jesus' miracles and His final sacrifice for all mankind's sins, of original sin and God's forgiving, infinite love. Finally, he spoke of the Kingdom of Heaven, which was a reward only to those who believed in Christ and who followed his teachings of love, forgiveness and self-abasement. Not once did Pádraig speak of the Heavens of the Celt, the many other worlds earned by those who proved brave of heart in battle, those who killed with valor and took no affront from any man.

"Now you have heard the Word of the Lord of All," Pádraig said, using his metal, cross-topped staff to draw himself up to his full height. "What do you have to say?"

"Have you seen this Christ with your own eyes?" The Lady asked.

"No," replied the missionary, undaunted. "But I have received His word and am filled with His love."

"You received his word directly, through visions or through dreams?"

"No. From other men."

"Then you have taken the word of others that this has happened," The Lady said.

"I have taken the words the Holy Spirit has placed in men,

the testimony of the thousands who believe. I myself am a rustic, unlearned man; I serve only to echo these saints."

"These men you spoke to; did they know the Christ?"

"Through His message."

"But not himself. When did he die for our sins?"

"Four hundred years ago," Pádraig answered.

"You said he would return in glory. Why has he not done so?"

The holy man did not seem daunted. "He alone will choose the day of His coming, the day of wrath and judgment."

"We already have a God of all. He is the Dagda Mor, the Great Good, and we know him as the God of Light also," The Lady announced calmly.

"He is a false god," Pádraig declared.

"He also has one son, who walked among men and passed down his word."

"Ogme is just one of many gods," Aenghus broke in with anger. "What of Ned, the god of war, of Boann, the Dagda's wife, Lug of the games, Sama of the moon?"

"These are not the gods of the Tuatha de Donn," The Lady assured calmly. "We have had our own revelations, which are not of any other people of the Five Kingdoms."

"You see?" Aenghus shouted down to the missionary. "She is a Druid witch who will jealously hold her people in her power in spite of the light you shine on her! She and her people will always be bloodthirsty pagans."

"I have already heard of your God from a man named Ailbe," The Lady declared, lifting her head slightly to listen to the wind above them. It had increased its velocity, so that the two fire holes moaned deeply from its flight.

"So, you have rejected the Christ twice," Pádraig said.

"I reject a God who invites you to drink his blood and eat his flesh."

Pádraig moved back to the dais, shaking his head. As he did, The Raven leapt up and said, "This sorceress and her people are the very reason why the south of our island has not embraced the Christ, why those before Pádraig were rejected!"

Pádraig came near to Aenghus of Munster's side. There was no show of anger in him. "Saint Peter himself denied Jesus three times. The Tuatha de Donn must be given another chance. I will go myself to Caicher and—"

"First kill the woman!" the exiled Raven cried out. "Then Caicher will be free of her spell, to choose the True God."

"I have heard enough," The Lady said, rising. "I will be no more part of this display for gain."

"What gain?" Pádriag asked. "We preach not ourselves but God."

The Lady laughed loudly.

"Kill her!" The Raven shouted.

"I cannot," the High-king said, firmly. "She and her escort have my oath of protection."

"But not mine!" returned the exiled prince. He looked to the file of his soldiers. "By my order, kill them!"

Before his words were halfway out, The Lady had reached into her comb bag and drawn out her wand of rowan. "Get behind me!" she ordered her escort.

Eogan and Oillil sprang from their chairs, knocking them backward. "No, Lady!" Eogan shouted. "It is we who must protect you."

The Deisi soldiers rushed to the front of the dais, twenty javelins arching back as they came.

The Lady pointed her wand at the rear fire hole and uttered a stream of words. Immediately, a blast of air whistled down into the hall, throwing all near the dais to the ground. Half a dozen spears shot forward without aim. Eogan and Oillil had tossed tables in front of them to block the way.

"Now you see," Aenghus of Munster shouted at Pádraig, over the shocked outcries and the powerful susurration of the wind. "They must be killed."

The Lady's expression was of fierce concentration; her

thick red hair stood back straight from her body in the stream of air. "To the doors!" she cried out, gliding backward, the wand still raised. Her companions gave ground with her. Before them, the warriors, monks, poets, kings and lords struggled to regain their feet.

By the time the woman and the two warriors had reached the rear doors the hosts in the hall had regained their balance. Many held onto hooks in the wall, others to tables and chairs. A few of the soldiers had braced themselves on their knees. Three threw their javelins in quick succession. The last missile caught Oillil between the shoulder blades as he wrested open the door. He crumpled without cry.

The Lady gestured to the fire hole directly above them. The wind plunged down, snatching up bits of the flaming wood and sending sparks and glowing coals raining onto the enemy. Braced as they were for the wind behind, the new force completely confused them and sent them tumbling and skittering backward.

"Alarm! Alarm!" the High-king of Munster shouted.

Eogan thrust open both of the main doors at once. Running toward him were four guards. He gripped his sword hilt in both hands and charged forward, screaming. The Lady followed close behind. The moment Eogan had dropped the first guard, the woman snatched up the fallen sword and threw herself into the struggle. Eogan despatched a second warrior but was himself stabbed deeply in the side by the third. The Lady pulled him roughly from the opening of the doorway and circled her wand down and forward. The wind followed it, throwing the two enemy guards backward down the stone steps with stunning force.

For all the warrior strength in the hall, few soldiers had been posted on the grounds of the *dun*. Those who rushed forward at the commotion were all women and unarmed "people of poetry." The Lady and her champion reclaimed their horses quickly and followed the howling stream of wind through the main gate of the fortress and out into the dusk that was rapidly cloaking the plains of the Golden

Vale. Rather than head back the way they had entered, they rode immediately due east, skirting a large military encampment.

"It is as we thought," The Lady called out to her companion, still at the gallop. "Aenghus has gathered Munster's forces, the Deisi clan and soldiers of Tara as well to war against us. This is Tara to the east, and I myself saw Munster's battalions hidden to the west. The High-king of Meath has embraced this Christ, and he has lent a force of his soldiers to the man Pádraig. Aenghus has used his guile to turn Pádraig and his force against us."

Eogan nodded grimly from his horse but made no reply. Behind them echoed the warning notes of war horns. Just ahead, appearing suddenly out of the gloom, sat three warriors on horseback, guarding a stream ford.

"Can you use your powers against them?" Eogan asked, in a husky voice.

"No," The Lady replied. "There is no force here I can compel."

"Then I will take them alone," Eogan declared. He threw back his mantle, showing her the quantity of blood that had spread across his under-robes. "I am a dead man already. Go!"

"To your glory!" The Lady exclaimed, saluting the warrior. She cut her steed's reins hard to the south and dug her heels into its flanks. One of the guards gave chase while the other two held the ford. The dying sunlight was just strong enough for the woman to look back and see Eogan overtake him, cut him from his horse and wheel around to face the others.

"We must decide in this hour," The Lady told Caicher and his council. "By my estimate, Aenghus has assembled at least four thousand warriors against us. They can camp before this place within two days."

"We can fall back along the valley little by little, until our allies in Leinster are marshalled," Caicher suggested.

"And be slaughtered day by day while Leinster purposely delays," said Colm, a clan elder. "They would let us kill half of Aenghus's force for them, then drive him back to Cashel and take our lands for themselves. We have no true allies."

"Then what is left but to face these odds and fight nobly to our deaths?" asked the king. The seven assembled heads swung back and forth, searching for the impossible solution.

Responding to the silence, The Three ventured forward from the gloom into the bonfire light. They formed a blunt wedge, three identical figures. Each stood five-foot-seven, three inches taller than the average man of their clan. Cuarveg, at the point, was their spokeswoman. Heads pivoted to face the young Druidesses.

"We must not wait for the enemy," Cuarveg said. Although her stance was one of bravado, her voice came out timid and choked. "They have used trickery to make war; we should annihilate them with even greater guile. In the morning, all our warriors must hasten to the slopes of the Sacred Peak and make themselves as one with the forest. When Aenghus's army reaches the march of our land, they will stop to assemble all their men. In that night, while they sleep, we will descend from hiding and attack them."

"They will have many scouts and guards," Caicher reminded. "It is not possible that we could enter their camps without alarm."

"But we shall have speed and alertness," Cuarveg answered, her voice emboldening. "Moreover, every one of our warriors has courage and skill to equal three of theirs."

"But they have *six* men against each one," Caicher said. The tone of his voice was gentle, the same tone he used to deal with the fantastic suggestions of the clan's children, so not to offend their delicate sensibilities. "Have you not heard the numbers your mentor has observed?" Caicher nodded in the direction of The Lady of the Flaming Hair, who sat under a broad-branched ash tree within the yellow-orange throw of light and directly across from where The Three stood.

"But our attack will only begin the slaughter," Cuarveg argued, her words spilling out in her haste to present the sisters' total plan. "When they have exhausted their sword arms with chopping, our warriors will retreat, and we will visit the enemy with the fell forces of nature."

Seven sets of eyes turned toward The Lady for her assessment. She shook her head slightly. "Perhaps there would be opportunity, but such control of the forces of nature cannot be guaranteed. Especially at this season of year."

Cuarveg glowered at the elder Druidess. "The Dagda Mor will provide for us. He surely wishes our enemies torn limb from limb, wishes to see a thousand heads on pikes."

"If you are certain our God speaks through you," The Lady replied, in a low and controlled voice, "I bow to your sacred knowledge. I, however, am more willing to believe that The Dagda gave us brains as well as sword arms."

"Yes," agreed Erc, the eldest of the leaders, contemptuously. "We cannot even be sure their army will stop at the limit of our march. They might go right past our men and get between them and the rest of our people." He turned his back on The Three and regarded The Lady. "How do we use our brains?" he cued.

The Lady stood and advanced a pair of steps. "By fighting on the day of our choosing," she said.

"Go on," Caicher commanded.

The Lady tossed her red and auburn hair out of her eyes. Among the more than two thousand members of her clan, less than a dozen had such hair; brown prevailed. She had inherited it from her mother, who was not of the Tuatha de Donn but negotiated for many years earlier at the Leinster Fair of Carman. Her mother, too, had been a powerful Druidess.

"With our combined powers," The Lady said, "we can place our entire clan in a long sleep. In one night, we will all seem to have disappeared. For a time, Aenghus's army will search the hills and valleys for us. Then they will stop, and his minions, the Deisi, will be allowed to settle here. They will take our homes, rebuild the fires and put away their weapons. And then, one dark night, we will awaken together and slaughter every one. The word will travel the length of the land. We will need to slaughter but once, for no one will ever bother us again."

The old king's eyes sparkled at the words. "Where will we sleep?"

"In a cave known to few of us and to none of our enemy," said The Lady."

Colm the elder smiled. "The cave beneath *Loch Céo?"*

"Yes," The Lady replied. "Even if they knew about it, they could not pass through the water to get to us."

"And how would we know when to awaken?" Colm asked.

"The Three and I must stay awake and watch for the time of killing," answered the woman.

"It is a good plan," Caicher proclaimed. "Who opposes it?"

"How safe is your magic for this spell?" asked Erc. "Have you cast this before?"

"No," The Lady admitted.

"And what if the Druidesses are captured and killed?" the old warrior asked the council.

"We may be captured, but we cannot be killed," The Lady assured.

"Perhaps not," the warrior rejoined. "You say that you have the power of The Morrigan, but you cannot know the power of this Christ. His followers spring up throughout our land and Alba as the summer thistle."

"True," Caicher granted. "I am in favor of this plan, but those who fear it may take flight. Let the word be spread to each *fine:* either sleep with the Tuatha de Donn or flee. Those who flee will be forever banished and forfeit their land. I have spoken."

The Tuatha de Donn disappeared, through Druidic magic. Cunning as they were at their own art, however, none of

the four Druidesses was a good tactician. In leading the
enemy away from their people, they allowed themselves to
be isolated from the cave of *Loch Céo* by the wide Suir
River. The patrols of Aenghus of Munster and his cohort
kept the riverbanks within view day and night. The enemy's
fear of the vanished clan was so great that the search for
their number persisted far beyond the time The Lady of the
Flaming Hair or The Three had anticipated.

Although The Three had had nine years of training in the
Druidic arts, they had only reached their nineteenth year.
Youthful impatience made them foolhardy. On the last
night of a dark moon, they dared to cross the river at a
relatively shallow place, where a stream fed in from the
north. Ten Deisi bowmen lay in wait. In less than a minute,
all three sisters and two of their horses lay dying.

Then the Deisi took their turn at underestimation. Two of
their number rode off to fetch The Raven, who had led the
troops into the nonwar with the Tuatha de Donn. Six men
lay down to sleep. One patrolled the shore. One guarded the
bodies of the three women. The last of these uttered one
feeble cry as the skeleton erupted from the middle corpse
and fastened its boney fingers on his. Five minutes later, the
soldier on patrol greeted his friend and was promptly
knocked unconscious, never to wake again. Ten minutes
after that, five of the six sleeping Deisi men had been hacked
to death as they slept or were waking. The one allowed to
live was the one nearest in height to five-foot-seven. The
minutes of life he was spared were traded for a personal
view of his own flaying.

The shock of their deaths and the vengeful bloodbath that
followed began the unraveling of the three sisters' minds.
Always attuned to each others' emotions and pain, the
collective experience overwhelmed them. With the ambuscaders slaughtered, the ford lay open and inviting for
crossing. Instead, the sisters decided to turn back north and
collect their mentor, The Lady of the Flaming Hair. The feel
of male muscle and sinew, even on their less sturdy skele-

tons, gave the sisters a sense of invincibility. Moreover, their faces and costumes allowed them to stride within arm's length of the enemy. Their gory trail was not difficult to follow; time was wasted hacking off heads in traditional manner and tying them to the horses.

The Raven and his honor guard of fifty, along with two men of Munster royalty and five of Pádraig's monks caught up with The Three on the far side of the mountain range north of the Suir. Had they been ten minutes slower, their wolf dogs would have tracked The Three right into the rock defile where The Lady had dug in her hiding place. As it was, the belling of the giant dogs warned the older Druidess and sent her to high ground, a vantage from which she could see for a mile in every direction, to be able to head away from danger in plenty of time.

The Deisi and their companions were extremely respectful of The Three. By means of long ropes and their attack dogs, they were able to ensnare them with only one more soldier's death. The two ambuscaders who had ridden to fetch The Raven had surely told him that The Three were dead when they left. The female corpses without skeletons had also given them potent information about what forces they dealt with. The Three were not tortured to the point of death for fear of what they would become when their spirits were again released. When it was determined that they were either too valiant or too insane to tell where the rest of the Tuatha de Donn were hidden, a deep trench was dug and The Three forced in alive and feet up. Their screams were terrible as the dirt slowly enclosed them. Terrible also was the laughter of the horde who entombed them. A huge cross of wood was roughed out of two fallen tree trunks and set on the surface of the fresh mound. As dusk approached The Raven climbed behind the driver of his four-wheeled war chariot, and his retinue followed him over the mountain in the direction of the Suir.

The Lady knew she should have waited. She had, after all, all the time in the world. But her passion for the suffering of

The Three, in bodies now suffocated but with souls alive and entrapped, clouded her better judgment. She waited until the sliver crescent of the reborn moon had swung low in the night sky before she left her lookout point. For hours her keen eyes and keener ears had detected nothing of human movements. She had found a large, flat rock which she would use as a shovel. She could wait in hiding no longer if she expected to have The Three dug out by dawn.

The Lady had succeeded in moving the cross and scraping away the first inches of earth when the enemy thundered in from three directions. First six, then ten, then thirty men appeared, keeping a wide, respectful circle around her. Finally, The Raven returned, this time on foot, followed by the monks, who carried newly-lit torches.

"And will you blow us all away, Lady?" the black-bearded prince asked, with a trace of anxiety unsuppressible through his sarcasm.

"Leave this place at once or I will indeed destroy you all," The Lady said, calmly.

The Raven smirked. "If you had that much power, you would have destroyed the Great Hall of Munster days ago. You would have faced our army alone." He glanced at her ragged clothing. "You would have drawn those three from the earth without sullying your fine raiments. Tell me where the rest of your clan cower!"

"They are all around you. I have made them invisible." The Lady watched with dark pleasure as many of the enemy glanced with fear into the gloom.

"I do not believe that even you can do that," The Raven said.

"No?" his captive replied. "You can search all you want, but you will never find them. But they will find *your* people, when they are ready. In the first night you believe they will never return, they will reappear and kill you all."

"They will have to do it without you!" The Raven shouted, to distract his sheep-eyed men.

"You will fail even in that," The Lady told him. "Like your Christ, I can conquer death. No matter what you do to stop me, I will return to kill you."

The Raven leaned on his spear. "Let us see what we can do, then, to slow your vengeance. Since you have no fear of death, we will never learn more from you." He reached into a pouch slung over his shoulder. "I did not believe you could be captured so easily; I am glad I had my smith reforge these bracelets this very evening." He held up the two pairs of golden bracelets, each pair linked by chain, the torchlight revealing the crosses engraved in their smoothness. "The holy men are in awe of the powers that the Devil has lent you, but they have an answer of their own for ridding this land of your evil. Bind her!"

Coils of rope hissed through the air, capturing The Lady and fastening her arms to her sides.

"What?" mocked The Raven. "Can you not turn the ropes into snakes? I have heard that is a favorite Druid trick."

The woman refused to dignify the remark and maintained her silence while a contingent of soldiers dug a second grave, some thirty feet northwest of the first. The prince was well aware that her perfect composure frightened his men. He distracted them by a recounting of how The Three had been initially trapped, then followed and disposed of, obliquely telling his followers that they would succeed in doing the same to this awesome creature.

"A pity such beauty is wasted on a witch," The Raven commented, while they waited.

"Her beauty is no doubt magic," declared the leader of the monks. "She is probably an old hag."

The Lady responded, with derisive laughter. The spear of the soldier nearest to her clattered to the ground.

To The Lady's surprise, the grave had been made far wider than was necessary to bury her. When it was finished, the monks took the bracelets from the exiled king and cautiously attached them to the woman. The leader and a young man, not yet old enough to shave, moved to the open ends, with their backs to the woman's front. Each man wore a simple stone cross around his neck.

"You are certain you wish to make this sacrifice, Brother Ruman?" the head monk asked.

"For the good of thousands, this sorceress must be kept under the sod," the young man responded, as if in an ecstatic trance. "Death for such a purpose will ensure my place with Jesus."

"Yes," the older man affirmed.

"You die in vain, boy," The Lady admonished. "Save yourself!"

"Thrust now!" the young monk shouted. Two soldiers raised their spears and stabbed them deeply into the unresisting monks. The weight of their collapse dragged the woman down. The moment all were on the ground, a score of hands dragged them toward the hole and let them fall. The woman's face struck a stone protruding through the damp loam. She felt the blood well from her cheek. Then the dirt began to rain down.

"Do your worst, sorceress! If you escape from this, it will be an honor to die by your hands!" The Raven cried.

Keenan wiped the perspiration from his forehead. A heat of passion suffused him. Because the woman had told her tale with little display of emotion and spoken modestly of her powers, her beauty and her people, the story became all the more potent. Keenan felt himself outraged on behalf of the Tuatha de Donn. The story bore out Hubert's theory in *The Greatness and Decline of the Celts:* the Brown Haired clan's fierce independence had proven their undoing. Ironically, it would prove the undoing of the tribes of Aenghus of Munster and of the other Aenghus, called The Raven. Not for any substantial passage of time was Ireland gathered into less than four kingdoms, and these were kingdoms only in name. Keenan pictured the hundred or so clans like the islands of the Caribbean, separated not by water but by their remarkable self-sufficiency and disdain of centralized government. As isolated entities, the islands of the Caribbean were regarded as banana republics and easily conquerable by a nation of any stature. If, however, one morning they were magically united into one great landmass and one people, they would overnight have become a formidable nation in the Western Hemisphere. Nature would never perform such a miracle for the islands; nor would human nature perform such a miracle among the Irish Celts. As the Tuatha de Donn were doomed as a clan, so were all the clans the moment the English Normans turned their aspirations on Eire.

Other aspects of the woman's saga made the professor much happier. When he had read the ancient Irish legends, first in translation, then later in the original, Keenan had delighted in them. But hearing their equivalent from a women who had lived during that era was intoxicating. He had always believed that his beloved legends and fairy tales had a core of truth; The Lady's recounting proved it. So much of St. Patrick's life, for example, was unverifiable and often discounted as exaggeration. Now Keenan knew that at least one story about the saint was true. In baptising Aenghus of Munster, Patrick had thrust his pastoral staff not into the earth as he had intended but into the High-king's foot. Aenghus made no outcry. Only later did Patrick learn of the injury. When he asked why Aenghus had not complained, the king had said, "I thought it part of the ceremony." The Lady had seen the king's bandaged foot, without knowing the source of the injury.

So many other ancient puzzle pieces fell into place. The Christian monk transcriptions, lovingly and carefully set down, albeit hundreds of years after the first tellings, held so much of what Mary Liddy had told Keenan. The monks recorded that the main supernatural powers concerned with ancient Irish warfare were wielded by females. Women, in fact, seemed to have actively participated in battle. The fairies, those magical inhabitants of tiny stature, were said to have belonged to a tribe called the Tuatha de Danann. Scholars attributed the name to an obscure goddess named Dana. But could the name have been a corruption of Donn? Could the "little people" have been the Tuatha de Donn, who stood several inches shorter than the tall La Tène Celtic stock?

Was The Morrigan, the triadic war goddess who changed shapes, purely a legend? Mary had referred to The Morrigan as an entity outside her tribe. Were they a trio of warrior women who had passed down their powers of entering other bodies to The Lady and The Three?

Most exciting was Mary's reference to the hidden cave, with the entrance under water. According to *The Book of Leinster,* the Tuatha de Danann had lost a great war to the invading Milesian race, but they were so valiant in defeat that the Milesian judge, Amergin, awarded all land under Ireland to the de Danann. Enchanted caves holding great heroes abounded throughout the British Isles. Fionn Mac Uail had not only been lured into the Keshcorran cave but ended his days with his warrior followers sleeping in a cavern, to be awakened by three blasts of a horn if ever Ireland was again in danger of invasion. A cave in Glamorganshire, Wales was said to hide the sleeping King Arthur and his men, also ready to save Britain. In Cardiganshire, a cave protected the sleeping Owen Lawgoch, whose "Red Hand" held the sword of English kings and whose dormant body was ringed by armored and weaponed warriors.

The legends most strikingly similar to Mary's story were the dozens of flooded cave or flooded plain tales. Keenan knew at least three wherein one woman had been charged with keeping a fortress or village safe only to let a flood submerge her people. By enchantment no one died, however; they all slept, to be awakened. Some water stories even pitted Christianity against Druidism, where a man of one faith was lured beneath the waves by a woman of the opposite belief.

As Keenan stared at the harmless-looking old woman, he

knew in his heart that parts of the legends had come from her people, her person and her ordeal. Some of them must have originated with those of her tribe who chose to flee rather than sleep in a cave beneath water. The invisible fairies came from the tongues of Aenghus's terrified soldiers. The long Dark Ages had clouded the truth of the tale. Like the children's game Whisper Down the Lane, fragments of the truth had been passed on by so many tongues eager to embellish for entertainment's sake that only the strongest elements could survive. Keenan recognized that the living entity before him was the most important historical find of all time.

Yet Keenan could not think long in an abstracted, academic way about the soul inside Mary Liddy. He pondered with icy horror the destruction of The Lady in her prime, a woman of great beauty and intelligence. How could he begin to imagine the sensations of live burial, of a soul locked in earth to feel its body die, forced to feel it decay and become one with the soil?

"I am most honored for your story," Keenan said, respectfully affecting a speech form of the ancient Goidelic. "And I am one with you in its sorrow. May I ask if you were awake during all these hundreds of years?"

"No," The Lady said. "Not all the years. We have the . . . *up-tha* . . ."

"Sorcery," Keenan translated. "Power?"

"Yes, power," Mary agreed. "The power in our minds to be like in sleep, to live in dreams for much time."

"But sometimes you would awaken?"

"Yes."

Keenan struggled with the unnatural concept. "What did you think about, to keep your mind from becoming like The Three?"

"The beautiful," she answered. "Have you no walked under the sky on a day of brightest sun? When every leaf on the tree can be seen? When the shadows are dark enough to lift in your hands? And when the sun falls it makes the sky of fire? Have you no . . . not on one such day said 'This . . . nah, wait! . . . this *moment* is enough to have lived for?' In my life, I had many such days to remember, many friends, much love, much laughing."

In that instant Keenan wanted to reach out and gather the soul inside the old shell into his arms. Despite abundant evidence that her race bred exquisite poets and writers of just and compassionate laws, the surviving literature seemed to dwell on her people as a fierce and curiously cruel race. He had expected her to speak of revenge, of the bloodlust which had made her laugh when back-lot Indians had scalped day-player cowboys. On her behalf, Keenan thirsted for some sort of long-delayed vindication.

"The monks who buried you feared you greatly," he offered. "They put two great crosses over you and many more across your people's land. They also built a monastery—a place where monks live and pray—near where you were buried. But the monks did not live long. Nor did the people of the Deisi. Another race, the Vikings, came from across the water in boats such as the one I drew for you."

Mary nodded in remembrance.

"They killed the Deisi, destroyed the monastery and built a town where this river turns south to the ocean."

Mary nodded again, with no smile on her cheeks but with an intimation of deep satisfaction in her eyes. Keenan refrained from telling her how long the Deisi had lived in her valley in peace, but, unless some ninth-century local popped out of the earth to tell her, she would be none the wiser.

Keenan followed Mary's change of focus. A *Garda* car rolled slowly along the river road on the opposite bank of the Suir.

"The Three . . ." Keenan said. "It was here, you t'ink, that they failed to cross the river."

"Yes."

172

"And now they try again."

"They are insane," Mary declared. "Otherwise, they would have listened to me this morning. They would understand the lessons of their own eyes. All they can t'ink of is to open the cave."

Keenan nodded firmly. An *idée fixe* fourteen hundred years in the setting. "Can they open the cave without you?"

"Yes. In the body of men, they can. But this must not be allowed."

Keenan agreed, but needed to know Mary's reason. "Why?"

Mary's gray eyebrows knit. "When I first came above the sod, I t'ought that I had traveled to the Land of Many Colors." Keenan understood. The Land of Many Colors was the first level of the ancient Irish afterlife, which ended in *Tir na n-Og*, the Land of Perpetual Youth. "Not even Aenghus wore colors so . . . *alainn.*"

"Vibrant . . . beautiful," Keenan aided.

"And more beautiful in books and in the television. So wonderful. Houses which are cold in the summer. Airplanes. So many old people live. Places to help the sick." Despite her glowing praises, she kept her frown. "But I have also seen your atom bomb. Of world wars. I have watched this chemical warfare all over your world, where clouds of death fall from the sky and kill even the little children. The television shows me that there are too many people in the world. The diseases which cannot be stopped. The many who die of hunger."

Keenan recalled her fascination watching *The Day After*. God only knew how many news programs, eco-disaster features and good old murder and mayhem movies she had been exposed to at the hospital. She had had a swift baptism into the modern world. He doubted if he could have survived it sane if he were in her place. He doubted if many of those who slept in the hidden cave would either, if allowed to wake.

"What has happened to the people of this time, to make such good with such bad?" Mary beseeched.

"We call it Progress," Keenan answered, sardonically. "Man has learned much about the world, and he has made it work for his good. Unfortunately, he hasn't studied himself nearly as well."

"Then much worse t'ings will happen. Your people will kill themselves," Mary declared with certainty. "After this happens, then will it be the time for my people to wake."

Keenan was not about to debate the simplistic conclusions of the ancient woman. Ultimately, their goal for the continued sleep of her clan was the same.

Keenan was no expert on caves, but his profession had compelled him to spend time in them. He knew that the good-size ones were almost always in limestone or dolomite rock. As far as he knew, the land to the southwest had a red sandstone base. "The cave, *Loch Céo,* is that way?"

"Do not ask of this," Mary said, firmly. "I cannot let you know more."

"I understand. But you want me to help you stop The Three before they can reach it. That's why you put the map in my car."

"Yes."

"I believe that the third one—the one who was wounded —has taken another body. I saw only two in Carrick, however." He dug into his jacket pocket, for the photocopies of the gravediggers' faces. "These two," he said, holding up the sheet.

"I remember," said Mary.

Keenan had little doubt that she could have forgotten, considering her altercation with her sister Druidesses only hours before. Evidently, she had attempted to reason with them about keeping the cave closed, and they were incapable of truly seeing the changed world around them. That was probably why they roamed the streets of Carrick with such audacity.

"What can you tell me about The Three," asked Keenan, "to help us stop them?"

"They are of one mind," Mary offered. "They are sad if they are not together."

The first two had been obliged to leave the third when Johnny O'Connor's body had given out. But, if what Mary said was accurate, they would have preset a rendezvous point.

"You hoped they would meet here, didn't you?" Keenan asked.

"Yes."

"If they had come, would you have killed them?"

"No. They are . . . *óc.*"

"Young."

Mary held up ten fingers, then nine. "I wish there is a way for the mind doctors to help them."

Keenan grimaced. "I think they're too dangerous for that. *Gábud.* If you want to keep your people safe in the cave, you may have to kill them."

Mary shook her old head vigorously. "I cannot. Strongest *geis.*" Again, Keenan understood. The *geis* was the strictest Celtic taboo. *Geasa* were at once mystical prohibitions and bonds of honor that often demanded death if broken. "If I kill them," Mary revealed, "I lose all my powers and die also."

"What if someone else killed them?" Keenan suggested. "You know how to do it; all you need to do is tell me."

"I cannot. *Geasa,*" Mary affirmed.

"But you think you can stop them without killing them?"

"I must. I wish to ask you—"

"Before anything else, we have to find them," Keenan cut in.

The *Garda* car again passed the point directly across the river from them. The patrolling was vigilant; The Three would not have an easy time of reaching the hidden cave.

Keenan thought. He remembered the excuse he had given

Dick Meagher why he believed the ancients needed to cross the river. "If I were they, I wouldn't come to the place where I'd been killed," he told Mary. "I'd go to a place where I felt safe. A place where I'd gotten direction. Did the Tuatha de Donn have a *fidnemed* on this side of the river?"

Mary's eyes brightened. "Yes, *Ollam!* Not far."

Keenan stood and offered the woman his hand. "My name is Keenan." Mary nodded, and wobbled unsteadily on one foot. Keenan clucked at the swollen ankle. "The first thing we have to do is bind your ankle." He helped her collect her food and other belongings and lent her his shoulder to the Range Rover. In the wagon he had an enormous field kit for first aid. He found an Ace bandage and wrapped it carefully around the frail, discolored ankle. Mary praised the cleverness of the toothed hooks that held the elastic bandage together.

"Now," Keenan said, clutching Mary around the waist and lifting her from the rear of the wagon, "you find us this sacred grove."

The "grove" lay about three-quarters of a mile to the northwest, beside the Lingaun River, which in the late summer was not more than a frisky stream. Keenan was sure that, fourteen hundred years ago, the spot had been hemmed in by dense stands of oak, rowan, hazel or hawthorn. Now, the trees were sparse and the area open to distant view. The rocks, immense and leaning together like cromlechs, did more than the trees to mask the area. The flowing water spilled over successive flat outcroppings of rock just above the level sacred area, providing a picturesque series of cascades as it sought the Suir River below.

A careful circumambulation determined that The Three were not in the local area. Keenan let Mary lead the way toward the ritual ground. For a time, she seemed confused as to the *fidnemed's* exact location, so much had its appearance changed. Once they neared the spot, however, there was no question that the three sisters had recognized it. A young pig lay dead on the naked earth, its guts spilled out and its blood soaked into the soil.

"Well, they've been here," Keenan concluded, moving toward the pig to feel its body for lingering warmth. "I hope not too long ago."

"Do not touch it!" Mary cautioned, halting Keenan with her left hand and circling the pig twice before kneeling in front of it. After long moments of silent study, she insinuated her fingers under the entrails and lifted them. She murmured a litany too low for Keenan to understand. Then she dropped the intestines and other organs, stood and moved toward the stream. Keenan followed.

"What does it tell you?" Keenan asked, knowing such divination was a common act of the Druid.

Mary smiled. "You are a Christian. You must not believe I can read anyt'ing in an animal's belly."

Keenan lengthened his stride, to pass the hobbling woman. "I don't know what I believe anymore, since you and your friends came out of the sod. Tell me what you read."

"The pig has been dead an hour or so. It warns the sisters not to cross the river until it shines wit' light at midnight."

"Until the moon is full?" Keenan asked.

"Until the river shines wit' light at midnight," Mary repeated.

The opposite of the moonless night, when they first tried to cross the river, Keenan mused to himself. It seemed a thoroughly logical supernatural instruction to him: to achieve success, cross the river under the opposite moon from the time when you failed. "So, if they follow this sign, we have some time before they'll try to cross the river."

"I believe."

"Is there some chance that you have not interpreted the pig the same way as they have?" Keenan asked. The flashing eyes that fixed on his told him without words that his question was an insult. Mary knelt down beside the stream, to wash the blood from her hands. Keenan searched his mind for a tactful change of subject.

"You have told me that this cave is under water. I'm *not* asking where it is; I only wish to know one thing: did all your people have to swim under the water to enter it?"

"No," Mary answered, intent on her ablution. "I moved the water."

Keenan looked up at the sun. As if by its own direction, his stomach started shaking. After what he had already witnessed in the past few days, he had been sure that nothing more could surprise him. But here his belly was forcing nervous laughter out of him, making him sound like he was on the verge of a mental breakdown.

Mary's eyes again met the professor's. Instead of shifting to an innocuous subject, he could see that he had only succeeded in annoying her more.

"You t'ink I lie to you?" Mary challenged.

The image of Moses parting the Red Sea came into Keenan's conscious mind. Like the dry bones rising, again from the Bible. The word of God. Not to be doubted. But instead of reassuring Keenan, the thought only redoubled his involuntary laughter. He held up his hands in apology. "I'm sorry. Nuh . . . no, I believe you."

Despite the age of her body, Mary shot up into an erect posture. "Stand away!" she cried out. The command instantly halted Keenan's paroxysm. "There!" she indicated, pointing to a place some twenty feet behind her. Keenan retreated. Mary turned her back on him. From under the folds of her clothing she produced a length of wood, a branch plucked clean of leaves and twigs. She murmured a burst of ancient words.

The water of the stream ceased to tumble down the cascades. Instead, it flowed straight out, at ninety degrees to the pull of gravity. It continued that way for some hundred feet, then made a twenty-foot drop through thin air to the riverbed.

Keenan's shock drove him back a step, where his heel thudded into a large fallen tree trunk. He lost his balance and sat down hard on the trunk. "Jesus Christ!" he muttered as he sat, regretting the unfortunate expression only after it had escaped and glad he had stood far enough away so that the partially deaf Druidess had not heard it. His eyes followed the gravity-defying liquid back and forth, from end to end. Real goddamned magic! Just like the lady suspended in air, with the rings passed around her. Not a trick, no mirrors, no wires, no masking curtains. Right out in the middle of the countryside, under the blessed sun.

Mary waved her wand again. The entire length of water collapsed at once, with a booming roar that echoed against the hills to the north. Mary turned and looked at Keenan, one eyebrow arched in disdainful triumph.

Keenan opened his mouth, but no words came out.

"Yes?" Mary invited.

"You weren't exaggerating when you spoke of making the wind blow through Aenghus's hall."

"I do not lie," Mary asserted.

"If you could do that and you can do this, why couldn't you defeat the army that marched against your people?"

"If the Dagda had wished, we could," Mary said. "But he did not. I can only . . ." She paused to find the right word. ". . . command t'ings in nature which . . . are moving. Water, wind, fire."

"Not these rocks?" Keenan asked, pointing to a jumble of huge stones, doing his best to suspend his disbelief and understand the forces at work.

"No. They do not move. The land moves almost never."

"Earthquakes," Keenan hazarded.

"Only then," Mary agreed.

"But water doesn't move any more than these rocks do," Keenan argued. "If one of these rocks was like this . . ." He angled his arm at forty-five degrees. ". . . it would fall. They both move from gravity. Wind blows only because of the unequal heating of the earth."

"You do not understand," Mary said, walking past the professor, with no intention of further discussion.

"I guess I don't," Keenan muttered, looking again at the

stream, which flowed as naturally as it had for a thousand years. "But I sure in hell would like to." He reached back blindly to push himself upward. His hand came down not on wood but on something softer and far more common to his touch. He jerked his hand away even before his eyes focused on the gruesome sight. When they did, the professor leapt from the trunk with no help from his hands.

Propped up just behind and slightly below the tree trunk was the head of Allan Carradine, hair disheveled, eyes open and glassy, mouth yawning in a rictus of horror. His cheeks and chin were stained with dried flecks of his own blood. The neck sat on a bed of velvety moss, with muscle, bone, cartilage and assorted gore splayed wide to keep the head more or less upright.

Keenan gave a yelp of fright and revulsion and stepped slowly away from the severed head.

"They are insane," Mary declared calmly from the professor's flank. He was grateful for her pronouncement until she added, "Never would they forget such a treasure if they were in healt'." While Keenan struggled for a reply, she turned away toward the pig.

"This is *really* going to get people upset!" Keenan anguished aloud. "Murdering's one thing, Mary, but taking heads is another."

"What do you mean?" Mary asked.

"I mean murder still happens many times these days. But *nobody* cuts heads off anymore."

"The T'ree do not know," Mary pointed out. "To them, the time is still of our people. I am sure they stayed in dream always in the eart'."

Keenan fought back his rising gorge. He forced his eyes from the head. "Goddamn, God damn!" he shouted. Mary did not react. He followed the gimpy old woman. "Do you know where the sisters are hiding?" he asked.

"No."

"Can you . . . do some magic that will tell you?"

"No. We will take this pig for cooking," Mary proclaimed. "And you will have the hind joints."

Keenan registered the compliment. In her society, the hind joints of a pig were reserved for the champion of the clan. In the ancient Irish legends, blood had been spilled more than once over the giving of this symbolic portion. "I am honored," he told her, "but we must leave it here."

"Why?"

"If the police came here right now, we'd be put in jail for your friends' theft. Not to mention the hell to pay over that poor man's head." The professor stole a glance back at the tree trunk. His mind held the horrific sight indelibly. He willed it from his consciousness and thought of Mary. "You've been living on porridge and berries," he said. "You need something more substantial. Since your friends won't cross the river for a while, we can relax and let your ankle heal a little. I know where we can both eat the hind joint of a pig."

Mary nodded and began shambling downhill toward the Range Rover. "We shall leave the pig. You are the *ollam* in this land."

Keenan let out a ragged sigh. Yeah, he was the *ollam*. Just like she was little old Mary Liddy from Lamoge.

Waterford lay less than twenty miles east-southeast of Carrick. Keenan drove there with purpose. The pall of horror and the supernatural had fallen so heavily upon him that a temporary escape from its touch was needed. With any luck, the three sisters had obeyed the signs of their sacrifice and were withdrawn for a time into some remote fastness. Keenan and Carrick would both be allowed a second wind. Tomorrow he could figure out how to present his knowledge to Dick Meagher. He knew he wouldn't sleep comfortably until somebody else knew where that poor man's head lay.

Keeping his mind on the highway was almost too demanding a task, especially with a resurrected Druidess in the passenger's seat beside him. He no longer feared her, but The Lady's powers made his head spin every time he thought about them. He decided, for sanity's sake, to forget for a while just who and what she was.

An excellent restaurant near Waterford's old round tower specialized in pork. Keenan purposely dawdled on the sidewalk, so he could vicariously enjoy Mary's wonder at the shops of clothing, toys and the world-famous Waterford cut glass. At each place she refused his offer of gifts. Only when she came upon an open flower market did she clearly show her desire to possess something. The colorful bird-of-paradise flower, flown in all the way from South America, fascinated her. She would only take one; keeping more, she told Keenan, would not increase her joy. And if she greedily took more, then she would be responsible for the death of another beautiful plant. Her smile at Keenan's gift was radiant, showing the straight young teeth that had betrayed her to him. She had not admired anything so much, she confided, since her first head—a Munster warrior's she had severed and had preserved in cedar oil.

Keenan winced inwardly. Fundamentally, she was of the same cloth as the three sisters. Perhaps casting off his fear of her was not wise. Certainly just being and not thinking around her would be more difficult than he expected.

The meal started shakily. Keenan had forgotten that boxty, a traditional potato bread, was divided into four sections, called farls. The pattern created a cross. Mary looked at the bread, then at Keenan. Before he could stammer out an explanation, Mary took the bread in her hands, tore off a piece and put it in her mouth, obliterating the pattern.

"Do you put *uiscebeat'a* in the car to make it go?" Mary asked.

Keenan smiled at Mary's naive question. He did his best to explain that it was gasoline and not whiskey, the "water of life," that fueled engines. Throughout their dinner, Mary kept Keenan busy describing the complexities of modern life. Directly after they had finished the main course, she grinned at him, spreading the wrinkled webbing of her cheeks.

"I believe truly you are a friend. Now I tell you why I put the map in your car and have you come to me."

"Please do," Keenan answered.

"The T'ree must not die," Mary said, fixing her piercing gaze on Keenan's eyes.

"Yes. *Geasa*. You've already told me."

"I wish them to sleep, so that I may place them in the cave wit' the Tuat'a de Donn."

"And how can I help you put them to sleep?"

Mary looked around, to make sure none of the other diners listened. She leaned across the table and spoke in a softer voice. "You must get guns from the spaceship."

Keenan's easy smile vanished. "Spaceship?"

Mary nodded vigorously. "The men shoot the enemy wit' the guns, and the enemy goes asleep."

The pork felt like a rock in Keenan's stomach. "The guns of Captain Kirk and Mister Spock?"

"Yes!" Mary exclaimed, beaming. "Of the starship *Enterprise.*"

"That's only a story, Mary," the professor told her. "It's not real."

"No, no. I have seen it."

Keenan winced. Kipling, who wrote "East is East, and West is West, and never the twain shall meet," should have lived to see a Druid priestess meeting Hollywood.

"Say you there are no spacemen?" Mary challenged.

"No, there are spacemen," Keenan admitted.

"Have they no walked on the moon?"

"Yes. But there is no starship *Enterprise*. What you've seen is just a toy. About this big. They put the camera up very close to it, and it looks real. But it isn't. Believe me. I do not lie either."

"And no sleep guns?"

Keenan saw the door opening back into reality. He lunged for it. "Yes, there are sleep guns. Guns that fire darts with a drug in them. At least there are in the United States. I don't know if they have them in Ireland."

"Can you shoot such a gun?" Mary asked.

The look on the old woman's face demanded an affirmative answer. "I could, if I was trained," Keenan hedged. "I'll see what I can do about finding such a gun."

"Good," Mary cooed, almost to herself. "Good." An aura of tension seemed to dissolve around her. "This is one good t'ing about your time."

"There are a lot of good things," Keenan defended. "You'll learn as you're here longer."

"No t'ing is good enough to . . ." She raised one hand and lowered the other, then reversed the act. Before Keenan could register the imitation of scales, Mary remembered. ". . . to balance for the atom bombs or the deat' from the clouds."

"I won't give you a fight there," replied Keenan. "As I said before—the price of Progress."

"It is the evil when so many men are ruled by few. This is the belief of my people. When all people can not hear of judgments or stand to speak when judgments are speaked, then the want of only a few come. If that want is evil, the world gets atom bombs."

There it was: the philosophy of the Irish Celt expressed in crude English. Keenan understood fully. Democracy only works when everyone is at the town meeting to hear it all and have a say. As soon as government gets beyond the town meeting, the common man relinquishes his input to a representative and forms his opinions based on the second-hand reports of others. Progress. Today, the news of a coup in Africa could reach him half an hour after it had started. But how the report was biased probably depended on their relationship or value to the U.S.A. All The News That Fits We Print.

"The Tuat'a de Donn could kill a t'ousand people," Mary

continued, "but each enemy warrior would have his sword arm to live. The Tuat'a de Donn would not kill women and children wit' gas from the sky, wit' never seeing their faces."

So, the price of your convictions and your proud independence was extinction, Keenan thought. Extinction at least as a people free to rule your own island as you saw fit. Why had history not given you an ancient Benjamin Franklin, to convince you that you must hang together or you would most assuredly hang separately?

Before the professor could sink himself deeper into melancholy, another challenge was thrust at him.

"This Jesus Christ," Mary assayed. "Pádraig preached love for every man. Never to return evil for evil."

"Yes," Keenan answered, bracing himself for rough philosophical seas. "If a man strikes you on the cheek, you must not strike back but turn the other cheek."

"To be striked?" Mary asked, incredulous.

"Yes, to be struck. The idea is to win over your enemies with love and understanding."

Mary shook her head gravely. "This is not what Pádraig and the monks did to my people."

Keenan pursed his lips, ruefully. "I think Pádraig may have been a bit zealous in converting people, but he was not your enemy. I think he was afraid of you and . . ."

Mary snorted softly. Keenan watched the muscles tighten under her jaw, saw her focus shift from him to another place in the room. She did not want to hear what he had to say, and he understood.

"The person you should hate is Aenghus," Keenan said. "I know that, at first, he was very much opposed to Patrick . . . Pádraig. The people of Leinster and Tara, his enemies, had become Christian. But Aenghus was a smart man, wasn't he?"

Mary nodded.

"He must have realized that his people were listening to monks like Declan and Ailbe, even before Patrick came to Cashel. They wanted to become Christian. Aenghus knew he had to accept Jesus also if he wanted to remain king. Then, when the other Aenghus came to him for protection, he saw how he could gain your land for his kingdom. He used religion for politic reasons."

"Politic?" Mary asked, finally meeting his eyes again.

"It means crafty, unscrupulous. You understand?"

"Evil."

"Yes. Many, many times over the centuries, rulers have misused people's faith in their God to steal land and kill their enemies."

"Tell me," Mary said.

Keenan knew he was out of his depth. He searched his memory and began with the Protestant Reformation and the atrocities committed between Catholics and Protestants such as the Huguenot massacres. He spoke of the Crusades of the Catholics against the Islamic Empire, the driving of the Moors from Spain, the thousands of years of persecution of the Jews by Christians, the separation of Pakistan from India because of intolerance between Hindu and Muslim.

"This very island," Keenan concluded, "suffers the same kind of separation. Where we sit is Catholic. To the north, Ulster is controlled by the Protestants. This also happened for political reasons."

Mary had rested her chin on her right hand, frozen there in fascination by Keenan's words. "How?"

Keenan glanced at his watch. He had drained his second cup of coffee, and Mary had refused to drink the strong beverage. The waiter was hovering to get rid of them and reset for other customers. "It's very complex, but I'll tell you how I understand it. About four hundred years ago, a king wanted a boy child, so that child could be king. His wife could not give him a son, so he wanted to divorce her. To end their marriage."

"This is a right t'ing," Mary commented.

"Well, not in the Catholic faith. The High-king . . . *Ard-rí* of all Roman Catholics is the Pope, and he refused to give this king, Henry, the divorce. So Henry divorced Britain . . . Albion . . ."

"Yes. Across the sea." Mary pointed due east.

"Right. He divorced Albion from Roman Catholicism and made his own Catholic religion. Now, Henry was a very powerful king. He had many enemy kings who feared him. These kings used religion to attack Albion. When Henry died, his daughter, Elizabeth, became queen."

Mary smiled proudly at the news that all of Britain was ruled by a woman. "Tell more," she ordered.

"Elizabeth had two great enemy countries to her south, France and Spain, who wished to attack her. She could not let the island to her west, Ireland, remain in the control of Catholics. So she colonized Ireland, put many Protestants from her country and Scotland into the north of Ireland. Over the years, the politicians, businessmen and the religious leaders controlled their people by stirring hatred and misunderstanding between the two faiths."

"Who do these Protestants worship?" Mary asked.

"Jesus."

Mary's jaw dropped slightly. "The same Jesus Christ as the Cat'olics?"

"Yes."

"Scuitemail!" Mary exclaimed.

"It is ridiculous," Keenan agreed. "Many people say that The Troubles, all the killings and hatred still going on in Ireland, have nothing to do with religion. They say it's simply a dispute between Unionists—people who want to be part of Britain—and Nationalists—people who want all of Ireland to be by itself. But religion is still being misused, as it was against the Tuatha de Donn. And all the common people, of both sides, suffer." As he finished speaking, Keenan had a flash recollection of the joke he and Dick Meagher had been told at Delaney's, the one about the priest, the minister and the policeman. It was just such jokes that were considered harmless but which cemented prejudices deep in hearers' psyches. In light of hundreds of years of sorrowful history, in light of the slaughter of young men he had personally witnessed in Lisburn, the joke seemed neither funny nor harmless.

"And the God of Jesus does nothing to punish these people who misuse his name," Mary remarked.

"I think if there is a God—"

"There is a God," Mary declared.

Keenan nodded. If he was about to believe anyone on the subject, it was the creature inside Mary Liddy's flesh. "Then we trust that God will punish such people after they die."

Mary's eyebrows furrowed. Keenan knew that the ancient Irish had no concept of reward and punishment, heaven and hell, in the afterlife. To them, death did not mean inevitable judgment; it meant only moving on to another plane of existence.

"Sometimes God punishes here on earth," Keenan offered. "Perhaps my people have been paying a long time for the sins against your people."

The dusk of midsummer settled in as Keenan and Mary drove back toward Carrick. The music they listened to on the Rover's radio was briefly interrupted for a news update. The events that interested Mary most were the killing of twenty Russian soldiers during the withdrawal from Afghanistan, the slaying of several school children by a semi-automatic rifle-toting American madwoman and the blowing up of a man in the Republic of Ireland. The last had interested Keenan most. A man had been assembling several large plastic bombs with illegal explosives when something had gone wrong and detonated the entire cache. The person's identity was not yet known, but the destination of the bomb was almost certainly Northern Ireland. Mary repeated her firm belief that this was not the right era in which to awaken her people.

As he neared Carrick, Keenan tried to decide where to shelter Mary. He knew that she could do well on her own.

Even sleeping outdoors on such a balmy night could not harm her. But he wanted to be sure The Three did not stumble upon her. In their enraged, insane states, they could not be counted on to treat her with the reverence she showed them. He did not think it wise to rent a room at the Bessborough Arms and advertise that she was there, instead of in her house in Lamoge, where she ostensibly belonged. The only answer was to smuggle her upstairs to his room.

Main Street had several empty parking spaces catercorner across the street from the Bessborough. Keenan backed the Range Rover into one and shifted into park.

"Pay attention, Mary," Keenan said, drawing the old woman's focus from the shift lever. "We'll go into that building now. I'm going to get the key to the room I'm staying in from the man at the desk. Then I'll walk over to you, and we'll talk. When the man isn't looking, I'll tell you to go up the stairs. I'll wait a minute, and then I'll follow you. *Tu-dam?*"

"We speak only English," Mary said, smiling, her door already open and one foot outside. "I understand."

Keenan stepped into the deserted street and waited for the hobbling woman. "Oh. One more thing . . ."

The red Ford Granada jinked out of its parking space at the end of the block and accelerated toward Keenan, headlamps off. The professor watched it in amazement, unable to believe it was heading straight for him. The car sped under a street light, which illuminated the two persons in the front seat.

A solid force struck Keenan from behind, propelled him across the street and between two parked cars. He fell, just catching the curb with his hands before his face struck it. Mary Liddy came down on top of him, in the same instant as the Granada nicked one of the sheltering cars, making a dull *clang* that was almost drowned out by the roar of its engine. The car's wheels squealed as it cornered sharply. It could be heard a block away, gunning off at full throttle.

"Damn!" Keenan swore, as Mary struggled off his back

and retrieved her bird-of-paradise bloom. "Are you all right?"

"Yes," she said, although she took all the weight off her injured ankle.

Keenan stood and checked for blood. Across the street, a couple discussed the near-fatality, wondering whether or not to offer assistance, finally deciding that the man and old woman were fine and moving off.

"Thank you!" Keenan told the old woman. "I owe you my life."

Mary dusted off her pants. "You are my friend. No t'anks must be made."

Keenan looked in the direction of the vanished Granada. "Did you see the faces of the people in the car?"

"Yes. I will remember the faces."

"Well, if you see them again don't confront them! Don't go up to them. They're dangerous."

"Not mairbfet," Mary said, lapsing into ancient Irish.

"I know they want to kill me, but we have to let the police catch them."

"No," Mary said, quietly. "I will kill them. Your . . . enemies are my enemies."

Keenan's thoughts flashed to the Bible. The Lady as a cold-blooded Ruth. He put his hands on his hips and glanced around the town in impotent frustration. He had also seen the two faces well. The passenger was the same woman who had come to his room several nights before, the woman who had also fled so quickly. The beautiful redhead was the same, the car was the same and probably so was the driver. What-the-hell did they want with him? Why would anyone want to kill a harmless archeologist?

"Relax, Mary," Keenan said, his breathing finally normal. He patted his jacket pocket. His horn-rimmed reading glasses were unbroken. "You'd have to catch them to kill them. Besides, I'm sure they won't bother me again tonight."

"Who are they?" Mary asked.

"I don't know. Did you see the numbers on the back of the car?"

"No."

"Neither did I. I'll talk to the police in the morning. Come on."

Smuggling Mary into the Bessborough Arms was easier than Keenan had anticipated. The receptionist was beleaguered by a group of vociferous German tourists. Mary went up the stairs first. They entered Keenan's room without seeing anyone else.

Mary was amused by the Odds and Evens finger game Keenan used in deciding who would take the first bath. He won. When he emerged from the bathroom, he found the bedroom in modest turmoil. Mary had ferreted through his belongings. She sat on the bed paging through a book she had taken from his attaché case. It was Keenan's doctoral dissertation, published by the Harvard University Press, a meticulous catalog of Irish Celtic artifacts, from 5,000 B.C. to 500 A.D.

"Who has wrote this book?" Mary asked.

"I wrote it," Keenan answered proudly. He pointed to the cover. "This is my name."

"Wonderful! I owned a *fail* like such," Mary said, reopening the book and pointing to a photograph of a bracelet, ornate with curvilinear bird motifs, screaming the hallmarks of the La Tène people in its thick-lobed spirals and trumpet curves. She flipped to a page that her forefinger had been marking. *"Ballan.* I know where are many."

Keenan's heart sped up once again. Mary pointed to a large ceremonial bowl, only one of which had ever been uncovered.

"My people did not bring such to the cave," Mary explained. "Such and much other they buried."

Keenan hoped the scholarly greed he felt did not show in his eyes. "And you remember where these things are buried?"

"Yes."

Keenan nodded, delighted.

It took five minutes to restore the room to order. During that time Mary got into the tub and splashed with obvious pleasure. Keenan picked up the telephone to call Dick Meagher. He checked his watch and decided the conversation could wait until tomorrow. Meagher, who had looked bone tired early in the morning, surely needed no requests for sleeping-dart guns or news about people trying to kill an out-of-town professor. Keenan also worried that Mary would be confused in hearing a one-way conversation. Instead, he searched through his clothing, realized that the only pair of pajamas he had brought with him lay folded on the toilet seat, and changed to a polo shirt and lightweight, baggy cotton trousers.

Mary stepped out of the bathroom wearing Keenan's pajamas. She lifted her left sleeve, sniffed it and smiled at its owner. The expression on her face was that of a giddy young girl. The situation became grotesquely bizarre when the professor remembered that this face was linked to a twenty-two-year-old mind, a seventy-odd-year-old body and fourteen-hundred-year-old bones. Mary yawned without covering her mouth.

"We're both tired," Keenan said, turning down the bedcovers. "Let's go to bed and make some plans in the morning." The hour was just past nine o'clock; the professor was reasonably sure that sleeping with the dark and rising with the sun were normal practices for Mary.

Mary moved wearily to the double bed and sat. "Keenan," Mary said, using his name for the first time, "have you a . . . *linnaun?*"

The question momentarily jolted MacBreed off center. With rare exceptions, Mary had shown little interest in his personal life, concentrating her questions instead on understanding the flow of history since she had been buried and the skills necessary to cope in the modern world.

"No," Keenan said, remembering his promise not to lie to her. "No sweetheart. Not really."

Mary lay down, twisting to face her bed mate, resting the curve of her jaw in the palm of her hand. "You have many women?"

Keenan laughed lightly. "No." As an academician, he would love to have heard firsthand about the sexual and connubial ethics of the Tuatha de Donn. The handed-down stories of the Irish Celts said that they tolerated almost any kind of sexual relationship outside of marriage. Marriage was a contract of exclusivity no more unbreakable than any other legal understanding. Since the Celts recognized that the planning of one's entire future at any early age was folly, marriage was held to be a temporary institution. At the same time, however, it was not regarded lightly while it was in force. Adultery was punishable by death. Checking the facts with a woman of that age was tempting, but the *quid pro quo* question deal still standing with The Lady would have demanded that Keenan open up to her. Maybe at some later time. Not this evening, though, with him so tired and her wearing that silly schoolgirl look on her face. "I'm going to turn off the light now," he warned. Mary made no objection. She voiced no surprise when he stabbed his legs under the bedclothes wearing his trousers. The light went out, and only the throw of street light from the window illuminated the room. Keenan relaxed back into the pillow, waiting.

"And you have no been married," Mary persisted. "I know this because you are Cat'olic."

Keenan clucked his tongue. Did he have a *linnaun!* What he seemed to be caught in was a case of puppy love. She had been buried alive at the height of her sexual desires, desires which originated in the body but had obviously had time to mold her libido. After centuries of sensory deprivation, the need for sex was no doubt irresistible. Unfortunately, the body she chanced upon was that of a frail, old woman. As far as Keenan knew, she was imprisoned in it until it died.

"That's right," Keenan confirmed. "I've never been married."

"I am your friend," Mary declared.

"And I am your friend," Keenan assured. "Now, go to sleep." He turned his back on her and let his upper leg hang partway out from under the covers. Mary said no more, but two minutes into their silence, her upper hand stole around his middle and her thin leg crept over his. Keenan stayed still. Moments later, she was sound asleep. He patted the boney hand lightly, then cleared his mind for rest.

7

August 19, 1988

In Boston or Dublin, the distant sounds of a police siren would not have disturbed Keenan's sleep, but in tiny Carrick he was fully awake before the faint echo died away. Mary lay undisturbed in a fetal position beside him, her good ear pressed into the pillow. Keenan grabbed his keys and shoes and crept out of the hotel room without waking her.

Keenan had to find out if the siren had something to do with The Three. If it didn't, he had to check in with Dick Meagher anyway, and he had to do that without Mary beside him. Guessing, he headed toward the bridge. His watch told him it was twenty-five minutes past midnight. He spotted the police cars as soon as he reached the top of Bridge Street. The entire force seemed concentrated on the quay. The blue lights atop one *Garda* van splashed beams of light across the scene, highlighting the bustling movements of men in uniforms. The blue provided a contrast to the more powerful searchlights that flooded the area. Blinding white rays knifed through the darkness from several places, one beam concentrating on the length of the river.

As Keenan walked closer a white van pulled up. Several long poles with hooks were unloaded and handed to waiting guards.

"So, he shows at last." Dick Meagher had appeared from around the corner, wearing a thermal vest against the evening chill.

"I tried reaching you all afternoon and early evening," Meagher told him, in a slightly annoyed tone. "Thought maybe you'd finally had the spit scared out of you and you'd fled back to Dublin."

"No," Keenan said. "Still here."

"Well, you're either very brave or very stupid," Dick judged. "That was you they were chasing over these rooftops, wasn't it?"

Keenan stuck his hands in his trouser pockets. The night was cooler than he had expected, with ominous, thick clouds scudding through the dark sky. "Yes," he admitted. "Unfortunately, they got away."

"Not for long," said Meagher. He nodded in the direction of the river. "They tried to get across by boat and got caught in the weir. We're fishing out the bodies now."

"You're sure it's them?" Keenan asked. The news caught him completely by surprise. Could the redoubtable Lady of the Flaming Hair have been wrong in her reading of the pig entrails? Or were The Three so crazy that they had chosen to ignore the divination?

Meagher started across the street to the bridge. "Let's see."

Keenan followed. As soon as he could see over the quay wall down to the river he knew why the three sisters had chanced the crossing. The river had indeed shone with light at midnight, as the entrails had warned it must; the police beacons had made the little waves brilliantly luminous.

A dark shape was being guided by two poles into a net. Behind it, a second floating figure was being hooked. A fishing boat tumbled noisily in the weir's backwaters.

"They couldn't have stolen that cot from near here,"

Meagher declared. "I'm sure we hauled in every one in town. Why they floated all this way without getting across is a puzzle."

"You may be able to ask one of them," Keenan said, grimly, "if you're not careful handling them. Remember, the bodies they steal can die but *they* don't. If you're lax, they'll jump into someone else's skin and slip away again."

"You're right," said Meagher, moving toward the guards. "You lads, make sure not to touch these bodies! We think they're infected with some kind of virus."

The policemen were working professionally, dividing their labor so that some kept the lights trained, others retrieved the bodies and the rest herded the curiosity-seekers away from the action. A murmur ran through the onlooking crowd at Meagher's mention of the virus.

A pair of men stood next to an unmarked car, dressed in plain clothes. The taller of the two, a craggy-faced man with a cigarette dangling from his mouth, ambled toward Meagher.

"Keep your voice down about this virus business, Dick," the man advised. The dip of his head indicated the onlookers. "It's only your theory."

"Right," Meagher agreed. "Frank Williams, this is Professor Keenan MacBreed. Keenan, Detective Williams."

Keenan and the detective silently assessed each other through perfunctory smiles. "Do you subscribe to this virus-from-the-grave theory, doctor?"

The professor hadn't given any thought to the fleshing out of Meagher's fabrication. He dissolved into a mild fit of coughing to buy time. "Excuse me. It is a rather . . . uh . . . exotic notion. But I *do* know that when they opened King Tut's tomb there was an anaerobic bacteria inside that had survived for two thousand years. It killed the first man who entered the tomb."

Williams's cigarette drooped as he grunted his amazement. "All right, then. We'll be careful."

The guards had set the first two corpses on the quay and

covered them with tarps. They continued to struggle with the third body, unable to lift the netting until a fifth policeman lent a hand.

"Holy God!" exclaimed one of the guards, as the body came into the light. "It's Jimmy Driscoll! What was he doin' with them?"

Williams turned to Meagher for explanation.

"He's the attendant from our hospital."

"That solves one more missing body," Williams said. "But why was he with them?"

"Hostage?" Keenan hazarded, hoping to save his friend from any more lies to a superior. "Fergus and Mick must have come looking for John O'Connor. They found him dead, took Jimmy prisoner and set the hospital on fire."

Standing alongside Williams and unseen by the detective, Dick rolled his eyes at Keenan.

"Could be," Williams granted. "We'll see if the state pathologist agrees." He consulted his watch. "If we hurry back to Kilkenny, Jack and I can catch a few hours' sleep in our own beds. We'll be back tomorrow as soon as we can. I hope we're not pulled into that bombing business."

"Do they have any clues to that?" Meagher asked.

"Some, including the body. Fingerprints burned off, but all the teeth are intact. The teeth will tell us who he is," Williams assured.

Meagher gave Keenan another look as he steered the detective around with a light hand. "You be off, and we'll get *our* bodies into someplace safe."

The detectives drove off.

The storage barn of a nearby turf and gas supply firm was commandeered for the three bodies, which a troop of policemen carried in one by one via the large net and dumped onto the concrete floor. When they lay in a ragged row, Meagher turned to the company of guards.

"Who came on duty last?"

The men shied glances at each other. They guessed that

Meagher's next words would mean work for someone. Finally, two men raised their hands gloomily.

Meagher's right hand made an involuntary reach into his vest pocket but stopped short. "All right, Meeny, O'Hara. Make doubly sure this barn has no other entryways. Then do a patrol around it until you're relieved. I want no unauthorized person in here. The rest of you are dismissed."

As the guards dispersed, Meagher said, "Keenan, stay a moment." After the last man had passed through the double doors, he closed them and faced the professor.

"I'm going out to my car for a knife and a shotgun. I want you to stay and watch them."

Keenan laughed and backed toward the doors. "Oh, no, Dick! I don't want any more to do with this."

An expression of anger twisted Meagher's face. "Then why did you come down here tonight?"

"Wait just a minute." Keenan jerked his thumb in the direction of the corpses. "These two almost killed me yesterday, when I volunteered to help you at the bridge. It's one thing to show up as a bystander, to watch the police end a nightmare I've been part of; it's another to be in here alone and have them jump out of their skin at me."

"Bystander?" Meagher snorted. "You leapt in for the penny, Dr. MacBreed; you're in for the whole pound. I've got to find out right now whether or not these creatures are dead. There's no way we can turn them over to unsuspecting officials unless they are. You're the only one capable of helping me. I can't have my men see me examining the bodies, *especially* if they're supposed to be highly contagious."

"Don't you think they're still alive inside those bodies?" Keenan asked.

Meagher shot the bodies a quick glance. "No."

"Why not?"

"I think there's a good chance they've drowned. Why did the three of them go through so much trouble finding a cot?

They could have swum across the Suir; it's not that formidable. In fact, this time of year, if they'd gone west, there are places they could have waded much of it. I think they drowned." Meagher lowered his rear end to a stack of skids. "You've given me your theories about how legends arise from truth? I have one for you. People say witches are afraid of water."

Keenan smirked. "This isn't *The Wizard of Oz*, Dick."

"Well, I'm willing to prove my theory, and you're gonna help me, because I've helped you." Meagher crossed his arms. "You think I dropped Mary Liddy's dental chart into the river by mistake? I know you and her have put your heads together somehow. I don't know when—maybe at the hospital, maybe *after* sometime. I don't think it's a wise thing for you to do, but I can understand it. If she is from Druid times, she's like the Rosetta Stone to you. I respect that. I don't *like* it, but I respect it. And you haven't been harmed by her. But all this while I've let you act wide-eyed and innocent and I haven't said a word." He stood. "So you'll help me now. If I could, I'd send *you* out to the car for the weapons. But I can't. So you stand by this door and watch. If one of them twitches, dash outside and set the lock. I'll have my answer."

"All right," Keenan agreed.

Meagher muttered his thanks and lumbered out the doorway.

A shudder ran through Keenan as he watched the water dripping off the three corpses. He did not ascribe to Meagher's theory. As far as he was concerned, The Three were very aware inside the bodies, playing dead, waiting to make their move for new flesh. Alone, he was their first opportunity. Keenan imagined one of them turning its head and fixing its dead eyes on him, immobilizing him with fright as it rose and finally enveloped him. In the silence he could hear the blood pounding in his ears.

Keenan stepped slowly around the bodies. A muffled noise from the opposite wall made him look up. He realized it had to be one of the guards making a circuit outside the barn. His eyes chanced on the dimly lit shape of an axe, held to the barn wall by a pair of hooks, all but hidden by bags of turf. Keenan moved quickly around the edges of the open area, never glancing from the bodies for more than a second. He sprang onto the bags, lunged for the axe, tore it from its fasteners and whirled around to face the bodies. Swift as he was, he felt as if the action had taken a full minute. As he stared again at the corpses, he was sure he detected a flash of light from Mick's eyeballs. A trick of the light or trouble controlling a body all but dead?

Keenan raised the axe blade to the level of his head and dared two steps toward Mick's form. "Come on, you sneaky bitch, try it," he hissed. "We'll see how you like losing *your* head."

"What's that?" Dick asked, from a good distance.

Keenan jumped anyway. "Just doing a little coaxing," he muttered, sheepishly. He lowered his weapon.

"Wish you'd found that two minutes ago," Meagher said. "Would have saved me the trip. Put it down and take this; it's more effective." The policeman handed Keenan the shotgun, transferred the knife to his right hand and drew in a fortifying breath.

"Can't we think about this a second, Dick?" Keenan asked. "Stabbing them won't—"

Meagher turned. In the barn's dim light, Keenan read the resolve in the taut muscles of the policeman's face. His words came out softly, through lips that barely moved. "I'm not in the best of health. If somebody's got to go it might as well be me. I have to test them."

"Couldn't we set fire to this place?" Keenan argued, looking at the propane tanks and the piles of peat. "We'd avoid the state pathologist, and then we'd have only the bones to worry about."

"I can't do that," said Meagher. "I trust you know how to shoot that thing."

"Yes."

"Then blast it in the face if it moves. That may give me time to escape it." Meagher approached the first corpse in the line, Mick Dunphy, and kneeled. Keenan chambered a shell and angled around for a clear shot, letting his eyes rove back and forth among the corpses. Out of the corner of his eye he watched Meagher stab deeply into Mick's chest, twist the knife and withdraw. The corpses remained quiet. Meagher set the knife down on the concrete floor and turned Mick on his side. Water trickled out of the wound, second after second, until a generous puddle lay on the floor. Keenan's arms began to tremble from the weight of the raised shotgun. Again, the light tricked him into thinking Mick had flinched, and he aimed the weapon at the grave-digger's head, but it made no move.

Meagher rose and sighed.

"That doesn't prove they're dead," Keenan argued. "All they can prove is that they *aren't* dead."

Meagher gestured for the shotgun and stepped back toward the door. "You're right," he granted. "But at least we know they really drowned. Your theory is that they can't jump bodies until the ones they're in die. If these three hadn't died by drowning, if they'd just been abandoned and dumped in the boat, we'd know that wasn't true and that the real game was still afoot. Now at least we know they're in here, alive or dead." He wiped the knife against the material on his thigh. "I'll tell the pathologist the wound was made by one of the pikes."

Keenan nodded. "Good thought. He'll know it was made after death. But we're still not sure if the water really finished off the creatures. As you said, you can't just release these three to an unsuspecting examiner."

Meagher's shoulders lowered another notch. He looked thoroughly drained. "At least we've got them in here. I'm so exhausted I can't think straight. Let's both go back to bed and get a few hours' sleep. I'll meet you at nine for breakfast and we'll thrash it out."

As Keenan thought about bed, his face brightened, then

took on the expression of a child caught lying. "I know how we can tell if they're really dead."

"Tell me," Meagher said.

"Mary Liddy. I found her again this afternoon. She's sleeping in my room at the Bessborough right now."

The professor led the way back to the hotel. He was forced to slow his pace for the lumbering policeman. Although he looked quite peeved, Meagher asked no questions about Keenan's relationship with Mary or how she came to be in his room. Whether this was out of deference to the archeologist's judgment or from shortness of breath Keenan did not know.

Keenan unlocked the hotel room door and softly called to Mary. There was no response. He flipped on the light switch. The pajamas lay neatly folded on the chair; Mary's clothing was missing.

"She was here, Dick, I swear," Keenan said, rushing into the bathroom.

"I believe you. But she's gone now."

"We should go out and find her."

Meagher smirked. "I don't believe she wants to be found, and I *do* believe that will make finding her difficult."

As Meagher spoke, Keenan crossed from the bathroom door to the bed. A mark of black stained the white of the bedclothes, just barely appearing from under the rumpled covers. Keenan exposed the bed sheet. From the pillow down there was an unbroken line, made with the professor's felt marking pen. Its length was bisected and touched upon in many places, by short lines either at or slightly angled from the perpendicular, grouped in ones, twos and threes, with spaces in between.

"That's Celt writing, isn't it?" Meagher asked, softly.

"Yes," Keenan said, sitting on the top corner of the bed. "Ogham."

"Can you read it?"

Keenan nodded. His lips moved soundlessly until he uttered the word *blorc*. "It seems I'm under a *geis,* a mystical taboo," he told the officer. "If I value my skull, I won't try to find her or interfere with her."

"Like I said; she *don't* want to be found. You're lucky you didn't end up like Fergus, Mick or Jimmy Driscoll."

Keenan offered no reply.

"Well," Meagher said, moving toward the hall door, "get some sleep, Professor. I certainly intend to. I'll meet you at eight. Sexton's. We'll figure this thing out together."

Once Meagher had gone Keenan examined the rest of the room. All that was missing was the ordinance survey map of East Cork-Waterford. The next day's search could be narrowed. He took a sleeping pill and set his clock for seven-thirty. As he lay in the dark, eyes staring at the invisible ceiling, he could swear that a chill emanated from the Ogham writing beneath him.

For ten minutes Mary had watched the drama at the river quay, observed until the three bodies were carted around the corner. Using curiosity seekers as shields, she had moved as close as she dared. Her old eyes were not blind, but neither were they keen. Whenever car lights swept in her direction, she turned her back on the bridge. Keenan, the *ollam,* was talking with several men and never gave a glance in her direction.

Mary had not spent much time looking at the bodies as they were hoisted over the wall; her eyes fixed instead on the people around her, then ones not directly involved in the midnight work. She paid especial attention to the ones grouped in threes who spoke to each other in muted tones.

As the street drama ended and the guards moved down the quay and into the barn, Mary turned in the opposite direction, heading east toward the town's castle. Her gait was unsteady and halting. The ankle had been hurt again when she had pushed the *ollam* out of the way of the car. She stopped and looked down at the swelling and discoloration. Her face contorted into an aspect of rage. Through her straight, white teeth she spat a string of ancient oaths. Then her head straightened up. Her wet eyes darted back and forth in thought. She cocked her good ear to listen to the town. Somewhere, not too far away, part of it was still awake. She limped up a dark thoroughfare toward the steady pattern of a drumbeat.

The music came from a pub in the middle of a narrow street just off of Main. Another bar, three doors down, was also open. No one moved in the street. Mary leaned against the cool wall of an alley, a place from where she could observe the road and both pubs.

Presently, the music stopped. A few minutes later two couples emerged from the nearer pub, leaning on each other out of affectionate comaraderie and common need for support. The lead pair carped loudly at one another and punctuated their words with laughter; the trailing pair said nothing, but held their heads together like Siamese twins. Just before they rounded the corner, they paused to kiss. Mary watched without expression.

A small, thin woman holding a flute case exited the bar and walked toward Mary's alley with a sprightly step. Mary pulled back, made herself invisible among the shadows and silently watched the woman go by.

From the pub three doors up emerged a man of medium height and burly build, wearing a shopworn tweed coat and a snap-brim cap. His movements were not at all sprightly. He set one foot in front of the other with comic deliberation. In spite of his caution, he weaved along the sidewalk like a sloop tacking into the wind. His eyes studied his shoes as if they had compasses on them. He staggered within six feet of Mary before he knew she was there. When he did become aware he stopped short, teetered for a moment, then dropped one foot backward to keep his balance.

"Hello, grandmam!" he said overloudly, through a dopey grin. "Out a little late, no?"

"Can you help me?" the old woman asked, carefully.

"Sure! What do you need?" the drunk returned, affably.

"There is something in this alley too heavy for me to lift," the old woman said. The words flowed with rehearsed smoothness.

"And what might that be?" the broad-shouldered man asked, already moving into the alley's deep shadows. "Let's take a look."

Mary glanced over her shoulder, assured herself that the street was deserted, then followed after the man, hands rising, fingers spread.

The alarm clock never had a chance to clatter. Keenan awoke at quarter to seven, bathed in perspiration and gasping for breath. The tang of mortal fear lingered in his memory. All he remembered clearly of the dream was looking at his own hands and seeing bloody flesh hanging off his finger bones.

Keenan took a long shower. Long after the heat of the water had left his body he continued to sweat. His stomach ached from tension. With nothing more to do until his rendezvous with the sergeant, Keenan turned on the radio and listened for the news. As usual, little of it was positive. The peoples of the planet continued on their grim, collective way to hell. He switched off the radio and practiced deep breathing.

Eight o'clock found Keenan sitting in Sexton's Coffee Lounge, sipping tea. His stomach could not bear coffee at the moment, it felt much like the day looked—foul and turbulent. Nasty clouds, the kind that gathered in December and made the short days even shorter, hugged the earth. Rain descended in a light drizzle but was whipped by sporadic blasts of wind. Keenan watched the street through the rivulet courses winding down the windowpanes, finally recognized the bulky, hatless silhouette shambling toward the cafe.

Dick Meagher entered the coffee shop, shrugged out of his raincoat and shook the raindrops out of his hair. He gave Keenan a faint approximation of a smile. To Keenan, the sergeant looked like Willy Loman in the second act of *Death of a Salesman*.

"You okay?" Keenan asked, rising to take the policeman's coat.

"I'm fine," Meagher insisted. "I always look like this before my coffee. Margaret!" He dropped onto his chair and rested his chin on one hand. The waitress took his order, identical to the one he had placed the day before. When she left the table, he asked, "You have any relatives in the area this summer?"

"No. Why?"

"Before I came here I stopped at the station. They identified the fellow who blew himself up. A Canadian by the name of MacBreed."

Keenan's eyes went wide. The waitress arrived with her pot of coffee, giving him a few moments to think. When she sauntered again out of earshot, he said, "He'd just entered Ireland, hadn't he?"

Now Meagher's eyes betrayed surprise. "How did you know that?"

"He was the guy that redhead mistook me for. Remember the one I told you about?"

"Right." Meagher whistled softly.

"The girl asked me how my trip had been. I assumed she meant down from Dublin."

Meagher nodded. "This other MacBreed had entered Ireland illegally. They think he was in Libya last month. Dealing with Colonel Qaddafi."

"The girl mentioned a colonel!" Keenan revealed.

"We're pretty sure there's a connection there with the I.R.A. This MacBreed must have been the courier and supposed explosives expert. Mistaken identity, eh?"

Keenan quickly told Meagher about nearly being run over by the red Granada the night before. "Goddamned I.R.A.," he concluded. "Just a bunch of criminals, hiding behind the Plough and the Stars, extorting and destroying."

Meagher's reaction was pronounced. His mouth stiffened, and he pulled his lower lip inward. His forefinger went up toward MacBreed's nose. "That's an ignorant generalization, Professor. I'm disappointed in you."

Keenan blinked hard at the stinging words. He found it impossible to hold Meagher's angry eyes and looked away.

Meagher's finger went down slowly. "I hope you know me to be an honest man, Keenan. Because I value you as a friend, I must speak my mind on this. I'm sure there are thugs and common criminals amongst the Provos," Meagher granted, "but that isn't the essence of the I.R.A. We are a people divided by an outside power. Since the British occupied this country, they've taken our land, our language, our right even to teach our history. They have at times denied us freedom of religion, freedom of speech, even freedom to wear green or sing the songs of our heritage. They've hanged us without fair trial, and when they saw that they couldn't hold all of Ireland in their Union, they repartitioned it to keep all they could."

"An Irishman actually invited the first English forces," Keenan offered, timidly. "In 1169—"

"Oh, shove your learned histories," Meagher quashed. "The real problems started somewhere around Henry the Eighth's time. The Brits realized they could finally control the Irish uprisings by importing their own people, stealing the land, colonizing it piece by piece in plantations, and establishing loyal subjects permanently in place. The notion worked so well that they built a world empire using it.

"Then times changed. Now all that's left of their glorious empire is their first colony. And they're damned if they'll let it go. It's become a fixation with them. They're heartless in their obsession, and *that* is exactly what makes the I.R.A. possible."

"Most people of the Republic I talk with," Keenan observed, meekly, "don't seem all that keen on one Ireland."

"In their hearts they are," Dick affirmed. "It's their minds that keep them from shouting out. They think of the burden all that Northern unemployment would put on them and they fear the economic reprisals from the British, on whom they absolutely depend. Don't get me wrong; I don't condone the I.R.A.'s violent method but I certainly understand it. *Your* country's founding fathers threw the British out with bullet and sword. Over stamp and tea taxes, for God's sake!"

Keenan sighed. "I'm sorry, Dick," he offered. "I had no call to say what I did."

Meagher's face softened. "Understood. But you of all people can't make such harsh generalizations. You're someone people look up to."

Meagher flicked a crumb off the table. "You really do surprise me, Professor. Someone mysterious tries to run you over, right in front of your hotel, and you fail to call me?"

"I didn't know it was the I.R.A.," Keenan answered.

"And you were anxious not to let *me* learn about the creature in your room," Meagher added, archly. "These people who're after you know you can identify the redhead. They want to silence you before the other MacBreed's identity comes out and you get wise."

"Great! More trouble!" Keenan lamented. "Now what do I do?"

"Stick with me," said Meagher. "You were going to do that anyway. Once this business with the Druids is resolved, we'll deal with your other problem. Speaking of Druids . . ."

The cafe door swung open smartly, and Rory MacCullen rushed through it, bearing straight for Meagher. "Brendan's found a Citröen abandoned off the road at Ballinderry," he reported. "French license plates. Looks like it was hidden on purpose. Nobody around."

Meagher's complexion turned more sallow. "I don't like the sound of this."

"Neither do I," MacBreed agreed.

The sergeant rose slowly and placed money on the table. "Hold the food, Margaret!" he called. "Stick close by me,

Professor," he cautioned. "I can't bear any more losses today."

Before driving to Ballinderry, Sergeant Meagher stopped at the *Garda* station and suggested that Keenan accompany him inside. His reason for the stop was explained indirectly, through a call he placed to Kilkenny.

"Detective Williams, please. This is Dick Meagher," he said into the phone. While he waited, he leaned over to the officer on duty and asked, "Any word about Father Flynn?"

"No, sir."

"Now the good Father's missing, as well," Meagher told Keenan. "You'd think this was New York City." When Frank Williams came on the phone, Meagher related Keenan's chance connection with the smugglers. "I'm hoping you haven't given this Ian MacBreed's name out to the media yet. You haven't? Good! How long can you keep it off? Well, it'll have to do. That will keep the other two after the professor. Yes, he's agreed to act as a decoy for us." Meagher winked at Keenan. "That he is, that he is—for a Boston Paddy. All right, I'll stay in touch with you." Meagher headed for the door, not waiting for MacBreed to follow. "He'll try to keep the name quiet until tomorrow," he imparted.

"What am I, for a Boston Paddy?" Keenan wondered.

"Brave, me buck-o," said Meagher, wheezing as he stepped back into the rain.

"What did Ireland ever do to deserve such sorrow?" Keenan asked.

"Eire," Meagher corrected. "That's the country's real name." He ducked into the *Garda* van. When Keenan had entered his side, the guard continued, "But sorrow it is. Two months ago, it was the I.R.A. blowing up British soldiers in Lisburn. A month from now you'll be reading something like Ulster Freedom Fighters bursting into the home of a Catholic lawyer and killing him at Sunday dinner. Right in front of his family." Meagher started the car engine. "Solomon himself couldn't straighten this out. But right now I'd trade duty in Belfast for what we're facing here." He steered out onto the road and headed west.

Ballinderry was a flyspeck on the map, between Carrick and Clonmel, no more than half a dozen houses. The Citröen sat nose down in a small ravine just off the road, concealed from passing motorists by a stand of dense bushes but visible to a morning cyclist. Other than a dented front fender, the car had no appreciable damage. Brendan O'Dea, a red-cheeked Carrick *Garda* in his late twenties, sat in his patrol car waiting for his superior's arrival. On the opposite side of the road, in his wagon, sat Rory MacCullen. Seeing Meagher arrive, they stepped out into the weather, umbrellas rising.

"I haven't opened the car," O'Dea told Meagher, "but the engine's stone-cold. It's been here awhile."

Meagher looked at the Citröen's license plate. "French, all right."

"Shall I call it in?" MacCullen suggested.

"No, wait until we've looked inside." Meagher circled in front of Keenan, who stood a respectful distance from the car, wanting not to get in the way of the police work.

The car was a large, four-door model. Meagher peered inside the driver's window, saw nothing and used his handkerchief to open a rear door. A handbag lay open on the backseat, with its contents strewn about. The sergeant sifted through them.

"Tourists," Meagher announced, looking at several pieces of paper. "Here's a reservation for the Ardree Hotel in Waterford. For last night. Never used it, I'll wager." He collected three passports and studied them, with O'Dea and MacCullen crowding in for a view. "From Rouen," he told them.

"I saw him!" Rory declared, pointing at the passports. "Her, too!"

"When?" Meagher asked.

"Last night. At the bridge. Just after we fished the bodies out of the river."

Meagher glanced at Keenan with a crestfallen face, then back to MacCullen. "Did they walk across to Carrick-beg?"

"Yes," said MacCullen. He pointed to the third passport. "I think this one went over, too. I'm not sure."

Keenan moved forward at last, to look at the passports. They were of a family—mother, father and sixteen-year-old son, all looking rather somber.

"There's a fourth passport," Brendan observed. "Halfway under the driver's seat."

Meagher retrieved the passport and opened it. The face staring out of the picture was that of a ten-year-old girl, smiling with adult teeth still too large for her young mouth, her angelic face framed by blond ringlet curls. Meagher sighed.

"They didn't need her," Keenan murmured.

"I know, I know," Meagher answered, faintly. "Everyone spread out and search the area!"

Brendan O'Dea was the one who found the girl's body, concealed within a stand of bushes. He announced his find with a cry of sorrow. The girl lay with her body prone but her face turned almost straight up, her neck viciously snapped. The look frozen into her delicate features was one more face of Horror, Keenan thought as he averted his eyes.

Keenan knew that the Walshes, John O'Connor and Jimmy Driscoll would have disagreed, but the little girl's death seemed so much more savage and vicious than the previous murders. The fury of the three sisters had not abated.

"The bloody bitches!" Meagher wailed.

His words did not register with Brendan, who had turned away from the corpse and was wiping away tears with a trembling hand. Rory MacCullen, however, had taken the murder in stride and reacted to his chief's strange phrase.

"What do you mean?" he asked.

Meagher handed Rory the passports. "Give me a minute, Rory. You two call this in," he said quietly. His men moved off, MacCullen shooting a quizzical glance over his shoulder. Meagher waited for them to cross the road. His face was ashen. He clasped his left arm with his right, then rubbed it.

"They took the three bodies with the largest bones," Keenan said. "But how did they get the car to stop?"

"That's not important," Meagher said. He let his weight sag against the Citröen. "We were wrong, Keenan; they *can* leave a body before it dies. Clever bitches. They knew we'd be looking for Fergus, Mick and Jimmy, so they gave them to us. With the tourists' bones inside. But how could they get water into their lungs?"

"The river's just over there," Keenan said. "They had to drag them down there anyway. Maybe they submerged them before folding these people's bones inside."

"To fool us?" Meagher asked.

"Just because they lived fourteen hundred years ago doesn't mean they didn't know how drowning worked."

"Why are they so damned determined to get across the river?" Meagher's breath was suddenly ragged.

Keenan absorbed the sergeant's pasty color and labored breathing. "Are you all right?"

"No," Meagher admitted. "My arms feel like they're made of lead."

Keenan moved close to the older man. "Do they hurt on the undersides?"

"Yes."

"Lie on the back seat," Keenan ordered. "Right now."

"It's a heart attack, isn't it?" Meagher said, sliding along the car frame and onto the seat.

Keenan stripped off his jacket. "Maybe."

Meagher closed his eyes. "Damn."

"Relax," Keenan advised. "Breathe slowly and deeply. It could just be stress."

"Wrong." Meagher smiled grimly. "And me miles from a priest."

MacCullen's voice echoed into the ravine. "Sergeant! They found Father Flynn."

"Speak of the Devil," Meagher gasped, as Keenan tucked his jacket under the policeman's head.

MacCullen halted at the top of the ravine. His umbrella and his jaw dropped as one. "What's the matter?" he called.

"Call an ambulance!" Keenan shouted. "Dick's not well."

"I already did," MacCullen said, sidestepping down the slippery decline. "For the girl."

"What about Father Flynn?" Meagher asked.

"Stay calm!" Keenan advised, undoing the sergeant's top buttons.

"Not knowing will upset me more than anything. Where is he?"

"At St. Columba's," MacCullen said, struggling to maintain a professional detachment. "They found him buried in the cemetery. Trussed up and gagged."

"Busy bitches," Meagher muttered.

"What's he talking about?" Rory demanded of the professor.

"One way or the other I'm out of the fight," Meagher said, huskily. "You've got to tell him what we're up against, Keenan, so we can stop them once and for all."

Keenan looked into Meagher's glazing eyes, frowning his opposition.

"We've got no choice," Meagher told him. "Rory's a good man. He'll understand what we've done and why. We *have* to confide in him!"

Keenan patted his friend's hand. "All right, Dick." He turned from the sergeant and moved under MacCullen's umbrella. Choosing his words carefully, he detailed the rising of the bones from the Lamoge cemetery, their origin and the reason they would not stop until they had crossed the Suir River and freed their clan. Dick Meagher absorbed without comment the facts he had never heard. Keenan did not mention Mary Liddy. He knew that MacCullen had watched Mary Liddy's strange behavior in the cemetery, just after The Lady had possessed Mary's flesh. The guard was either too overwhelmed to connect her with the rest of the events or else was keeping his mouth shut for his own private reasons.

"It's unbelievable," MacCullen said, when MacBreed had finished.

"It is," Keenan agreed, "but it's also true. And if you *won't* believe it, pretty soon two thousand Celts are going to wake and begin slaughtering the people on the other side of the river. It's a rural area. I'm sure some folks don't even have telephones out there. A hundred people could be killed before the area was evacuated."

The shrill noise of the ambulance pierced through the rain.

"You work with Professor MacBreed now," Meagher directed the guard.

"I will, Dick," Rory vowed. "I'll finish the job." A smile seemed to steal through the firm set of his face.

O'Dea led the ambulance attendants down from the highway.

"You're hanging in there fine, Dick," Keenan encouraged. "You'll be okay."

Meagher shook his head as he was hauled onto the stretcher. "Life's unfair. I finally give up smoking, and this is my reward."

O'Dea and MacCullen led the way up to the highway. Keenan walked beside the stretcher. Meagher let his hand droop out in Keenan's direction. "You there, bone digger?"

"Right here."

"If she turns up again, don't trust her," he said softly. "Two priests to hold her down, remember? The worst evil is the most subtle."

Before Keenan could reply, the sergeant was loaded into

the ambulance, which cranked up its siren noises again and sped off for Clonmel.

Rory MacCullen did not wait until the ambulance was out of sight. He turned to Brendan O'Dea and fixed a superior stare on him. "You stay with the girl until the ambulance comes back. Then follow it into Clonmel and tell them what's happened. We're needed in Carrick." O'Dea accepted the order without demur. MacCullen inflated slightly. "Come with me, Professor," he commanded. "Not a moment to lose."

On the road to the *Garda* station, MacCullen interrogated MacBreed about his involvement in the investigation, and how he knew so much about these ancient people. As tactfully as he could, Keenan steered the conversation toward what would be necessary to stop The Three. Several times, he emphasized that the borrowed bodies would have to be terminated from a distance and that the skeletons would still be deadly. MacCullen's curt, inarticulate responses worried MacBreed, but he knew the man was too proud to be lectured to. They stood inside the station within five minutes.

"Are those two lads from Special Branches still in the area?" Rory asked the guard at the desk.

"They are," came the reply.

"Then call them in. We'll be needing their weapons. And get me a good map of Counties Waterford and Cork!"

When the guard received the map, he methodically unfolded it on the counter. "Now, exactly where are they going, Professor?"

"I only know that the cave is under water," Keenan replied, "in a lake south of the Suir."

MacCullen scowled. "Let's see. There's Crotty's Lake, Coumshingaun, Coumfea, Coumduala, Sgilloge Loughs and Lough Mohra. And those are the ones within ten miles of Carrick. Could it be farther than that?"

"Maybe," Keenan granted.

"These legends you're working from," MacCullen

probed, "do they say anything about the lake's shape, depth, color?"

Keenan recalled the name The Lady used: *Loch Céo*. "They called it Foggy Lake," he said.

MacCullen dropped his forefinger onto the map. "Well, I don't know about the others, but Crotty's Lake is fogged up a lot."

"It's also the closest to Carrick," Keenan noted.

"We'll start there, then. We get our water from Crotty's Lake," MacCullen said, looking at Keenan as if there were great significance in this piece of news. Before the professor could respond, Rory turned his back and greeted the two guards walking into the station. "I hope your weapons are in order," he greeted. "You're about to use them."

Keenan did not recognize either policeman from the night before. He was grateful that they seemed fresh. "If you drop me off at my wagon, I'll follow you," he told MacCullen.

"No, thanks, Professor," Rory rejected. "This is strictly police work."

"But there are things you have to know—"

"Don't worry. We'll be most careful. I can't be responsible for a civilian in the middle of this. Sorry."

Keenan realized the wall was impenetrable. "So am I, *Garda* MacCullen."

Rory busied himself refolding the map. "We can drop you off on our way," he offered.

Keenan headed toward the front door. "Thanks. I'll walk."

The rain pelted down harder, but Keenan was oblivious. His mind boiled with conflicting emotions. On one hand he was vastly relieved about not having to face the three mad sisters again; on the other, he felt as if he were failing Dick Meagher and placing three ignorant men in mortal jeopardy. He was galled at Mary for disappearing again— probably forever, denying him the information about locations of untold buried treasures. About a hundred yards from the Bessborough, he remembered the best reason for leaving Carrick in a hurry: MacCullen had not been told about the redheaded woman and her murderous companion. Not long after Ian MacBreed's name was made public Keenan would surely have told the *Gardaí* what he knew; there would be no more purpose in their silencing him. Until then, especially without police protection, he was a marked man.

Keenan stopped at the Range Rover and opened the driver's door, to grab a sack that would help his packing. On the floor in front of the passenger's seat he saw Mary's wooden wand. He paused, contemplating it. It was surely not irreplaceable. Mary could cut another from any one of a thousand trees. The power was not in that particular length of wood but in the faith Mary focused through it and in the force that allowed her such power.

Keenan still could not name the force. "God" seemed too limiting. He still doubted that whatever it was watched the fall of sparrows or numbered the hairs on his head. But Mary's faith and her miraculous use of faith convinced him that God (or whatever) did exist, and God (or whoever) was still in this corner of the universe.

Boney fingers tightened on Keenan's shoulder. Alarmed, he whirled around, knocking the hand away.

Mary Liddy stepped back toward the center of the street. "You must help me, *Ollam,*" she said, quietly but urgently.

Keenan swallowed down the panic that had leapt out of his chest. "I thought I was supposed to stay out of your way," he replied testily. Mary was not at all cowed by his words; she held his eyes with hers, which focused as fiercely as ever. Keenan immediately regretted his words. "I'm sorry. Of course I'll help you. What can—"

"Get in the car," Mary directed, limping toward the passenger door.

Keenan climbed in and started the engine. As he did, a *Garda* van with Rory MacCullen at the wheel and the two Special Branches guards as passengers rushed past his parking space. Keenan turned the Rover as quickly as he could and followed the van down Bridge Street and onto the bridge, letting the police car keep a good lead.

"I have a plan so The T'ree will sleep wit' the *Tuat'a de Donn*," Mary volunteered.

"That's good!" Keenan enthused. "Excellent!"

"You must help," Mary reiterated. "I can not do this as old woman."

"The Three took other bodies last night," the professor said.

"Yes."

"If you took a strong man's body, you wouldn't need me. Right?"

For several seconds, Mary said nothing. "Last night, I went to take a man's body."

Keenan kept his eyes fixed on the *Garda* van ahead as they climbed through Carrick-beg, ordering himself not to shudder. "Why did you change your mind?"

"Once I believed that to kill was right for many problems. A wise man—an *ollam* so as you—taught me to t'ink of other answers first."

For once, Keenan did not need to coax the story from the Druidess. She turned momentarily quiet and then spoke.

When The Lady of the Flaming Hair was sixteen and had not yet earned her honored title, she fell in love. The object of her adoration was the *ollam* of the Tuatha de Donn. He had no woman, but he was more than ten years her senior and seemed oblivious to her timid yet persistent gestures toward him. Failure to notice her was worse than rejection, and she hid her affection with a sham of disdain for his powers and wisdom.

It was in the same summer that the *ollam*'s older brother quarreled with the champion of the clan. As was commonplace, the quarrel soon led to a challenge and the challenge to drawn swords. The *ollam*'s brother was slain. In keeping with the laws of the land, the family of the slain man demanded atonement with a fine. The fine was calculated—

as were all financial dealings—in cattle. The king and his council adjudged the mortal injury plus the "honor-price" of the victim to be six cows.

In general, the dispensing of justice was fair among the classes. By the nature of his position in the clan, however, a champion possessed some power to resist the law. The slayer ignored the judgment and directed his family to do the same.

The family of the slain man was not without its own recourse. The *ollam* was sent as the family representative, to sit before the door of the champion and fast. Among the Irish Celts, self-denial of food and drink was looked on with superstitious awe. Their law declared that any man who ignored a fasting petitioner should be considered without character and be shunned and outcast, both by his fellow man and by God. Equally effective were lyrical satires, which mocked the lawbreaker and stripped him of his good name. The *ollam* practiced both, perching resolutely on the champion's doorstep and singing out scalding verses to every passerby.

For two days, the clan's champion hid silently within his walls. On the third morning, the young redheaded Druidess took herself in front of the hut. Secretly shamed by the *ollam*'s lack of interest in her, she invented a satire of her own, mocking the *ollam* for his lack of courage. "Any man of valor," she challenged, "would not hide behind the old woman's weapons of fasting and songs. True vengeance must be a life for a life. You have muscle and sinew; take up your brother's sword and get your satisfaction as a real man and warrior!"

The *ollam* smiled gently at the girl's words, and she felt her anger grow. Then, from within the hut, came the sound of derisive laughter. The girl and the *ollam* both knew that she had given the champion the courage to continue his resistance to justice.

The same day, the *ollam* challenged the champion to battle. The next day the *ollam* was slain. Standing over the body, the slayer admitted to the witnesses that he would have paid the fine. The *ollam* had all but broken his will with the valor of his fasting and his satires. Only the foolish words of the apprentice Druidess had saved him.

"He is dead all this years," Mary said softly, "but I do not forget."

Keenan risked a quick glance at the old woman. Her eyes had lost their fierceness, and the spark that had always glowed within them now glistened within a tear hanging from her lower lash. He knew now that the difference between The Lady and The Three rose from more than a difference of age or a greater will to survive their interminable burial. The lesson of the slain *ollam* was the reason she had counseled her clan for a less rash solution to Aenghus's attack more than a millennium ago and why she had found a nonviolent solution to her problem only the night before.

Keenan knew one other thing: that he had become a part of the ancient story, another *ollam* who offered a chance to make amends. He refused to ponder the implications, reflecting instead on Mary's goodness. Since the moment of her resurrection, all her strength had focused on saving her people. At the same time she had twice disappeared to protect him from danger, willing rather to face The Three on her own and at great physical disadvantage. The Lady's nobility was humbling.

Keenan glanced at his watch; it was quarter past ten o'clock. The storm clouds made the hour look more like dusk. Honoring Mary's silence, he followed the *Garda* van down R696 at high speed. The road was straight but not even worthy of being called a highway. It was the main thoroughfare between Carrick and Dungarven on the ocean, but running through such wild, sparsely populated terrain that it had never needed more than a lane of asphalt in either direction. MacCullen's speed did not allow the guards to study the countryside on either side of the road. It was clear that he was intent on getting to Crotty's Lake. Keenan shook his head. If the three sisters had had complete confidence in their direction, they would have had enough time since crossing the bridge last night to reach the lake. What MacCullen failed to realize was that the ancients would be confused by the roads and the changes in the landscape since their burial. Only by the guidance of the sun or the stars could they have traveled fast. Since crossing the bridge, they had had benefit of neither. For all Keenan knew they might be hiding in Carrick-beg, waiting for the storm to pass before venturing on.

"Where are we now?" Mary asked.

Keenan eased slightly off the accelerator and groped in his pocket for his reading glasses. He pointed to a place about six miles south-southwest of Carrick. "Which lake is it?"

Mary hovered above the line that represented R696, hesitating.

"I am your good friend," Keenan reassured. "I swear under the most strong *geis* that I will never tell anyone of the lake or the cave. *Tu-dam?*"

"I understand." Mary smiled, showing her straight, white teeth. "Go fast!"

Thunder rumbled to the south. Mary stared in that direction. "It is a day of great *Drui* power," she said. "On such a day I could have killed Aenghus and all his warriors."

The pronouncement made Keenan shudder. He pictured a thousand heads lopped from a thousand corpses. He said a prayer to the God he finally believed in, to keep the three policemen safe until he could bring the chief Druidess to their protection.

"I am your good friend also," Mary declared, as they traveled south.

"Yes, I know," Keenan replied.

"Do the people in the red car yet wish your life?"

"Yes, I'm afraid so."

"I will help you once you help me," Mary promised.

"I don't think that will be necessary," Keenan told her. "They won't be any trouble after today."

Mary let the subject drop.

As the Rover neared the turnoff for Crotty's Lake, the *Garda* wagon burst out of the forest a little way ahead and swung south on T56. "I guess this isn't the lake," Keenan said.

Mary studied the silhouette of the local Comeragh Mountain peaks. "No. This is *Loch Céo*. Go in here."

Keenan followed the muddy road through the tall trees, up to a high wire fence. A sign declared the land on the other side to be government property, with no trespassing allowed. Beyond, across a meadow, lay the lake. Toward its northern limits, where a stream bed fed out of the lake, stretched a concrete dam and overflow spillway, a large water conduit system and a control house. Keenan hid the wagon within a dense stand of trees. He pulled out his waterproof tent as a shelter for them and then dug out his binoculars. Professor and Druidess crawled side by side to the edge of the fence. After they wriggled into the collapsed tent, Keenan showed Mary how to use the field glasses.

"Are you sure this is *Loch Céo?*"

Mary swept the panorama. "Yes. I do not see them. They will come soon."

Keenan tried to engage Mary in conversation on unemotional aspects of her distant past. The responses were terse; her attention focused instead through the binoculars. Keenan honored her silence and satisfied himself by studying the terrain. There was nothing about the little lake that suggested it held the archeological secret of the ages. In normal times, it must have been a rustic, restful spot. With storm clouds rolling above and Keenan's apprehension of doom, it did not seem at all peaceful to him.

A quarter hour later, Mary announced, "They are here."

"What'll you do?" Keenan asked.

Mary set down the binoculars. "Not'ing. I wait."

Keenan took up the glasses and focused in on the three approaching figures. They climbed the fence on the opposite side of the meadow. Keenan recognized the faces from the

French passports. Once over the barrier, the figures of the mother, father and son disappeared into the tall grasses.

"There is a man, from the house," Mary observed.

Keenan swung the binoculars toward the dam. The raincoated keeper had emerged to adjust the spillway mechanism. His yellow sou'wester cap was drawn far forward, limiting his view.

"Jesus!" Keenan gasped, struggling to his knees against the weight of the tent.

The dam keeper kept a wary eye on the slippery steps as he descended from the house, oblivious to the danger nearby. Keenan raised his hands to his mouth, to shout out a warning.

Mary grabbed him by his belt and yanked him down. "No!" she commanded. Keenan glanced at her in shock.

The Frenchwoman charged out of the grasses, closing on the keeper from his blind side.

Keenan could not let the man die without warning. Despite Mary's prohibition, he cupped his hands. Mary slapped him hard, on the cheek. A clap of thunder muffled what escaped of his outcry. When he could see again, through the tears that had flowed from the slap, he saw the woman figure sprawled on top of the struggling keeper, seeking out his thumbs. The teenage boy and father dashed out of the grasses to help.

Mary put her hand in front of Keenan's eyes. "Do not look," she said softly. "I am sorry. You could not have stopped them. And still we are hidden from them."

"But another useless death," Keenan moaned.

Mary calmly watched the sight she forbade Keenan to see. "They take this man's body because it is stronger," she reported. "They need much strongness to open the cave."

"You're going to let them open it?" Keenan asked, astonished.

"Yes. They will go inside. Then you and I close the cave. The smoke will come over them, and they will sleep also."

Keenan laughed involuntarily. Mary had no intention of

letting her clan wake. Neither was she willing to let her sister Druidesses die. The solution was ingenious—if she could carry it off.

Mary took her hand away from Keenan's face. Standing in the meadow were the father, son and dam keeper. The mother's body and the keeper's skeleton lay mercifully hidden from his view by the grasses. The Three climbed the steps to the house, then crossed over the dam, surveying the man-made barrier. The father and son stood on one side of the dam, the keeper positioned on the opposite side. From their clothing, each withdrew a slender wand. Keenan realized what was about to happen, but was no less astounded when it did.

The water behind the dam rose up like a living creature, an endless light green serpent intent on vaulting its confines. Thousands of gallons of water flowed up through the air, cleared the concrete barrier and crashed down into the bed below, hurtling wildly down and carrying away debris that had lain there for years. Minute after minute, the water twisted up from the lake like a great sea spout and vaulted the dam. The Druidesses stood like statues, concentrating their full attentions on the control of nature. At times, the thick, violent storm clouds dived within feet of their heads, but they were oblivious in their focus. Keenan watched the lake's muddy bed expose to the air with excruciating slowness, sure that at least an hour's time would be necessary to bring the water surface down to the cave entrance.

As Keenan's minute hand lapped his watch face, the center of the storm lumbered directly overhead. Lightning sizzled repeatedly through the clouds, each thunderclap volleying close behind, covering the sound of the *Gardaí*'s approach. Keenan's first awareness that Rory MacCullen and his fellow guards had returned came when their van screeched to a halt at the fence gate, less than a hundred feet from where he and Mary lay.

Rory jumped out of the wagon and stared slack jawed at the water leaping over the dam. His eyes missed the tent as he swung back into the van and rammed the shift into reverse. Keenan watched the vehicle bounce back down the road, change direction noisily and hurtle straight for the locked gate. The chain burst, and the wire gate crashed aside. The *Garda* van skidded down the muddy road and slued sideways, so that the driver's door faced the dam spillway. A lightning bolt jagged brilliantly into the trees beyond the lake.

Rory flung open the door and stepped into the rain. He looked away from the three figures on the dam, staring at something on the ground. Keenan knew he had seen the flesh of the French mother and the bones of the dam keeper. MacCullen mastered his shock and shouted to the other guards.

The funnel of water collapsed with a roar—spraying over the dam, rocking the surface of the lake. Rory jerked backward and did a sliding dance through the mud. By the time he had straightened up, the three figures on the dam walkway had faced the van and were pointing their wands, not at the vehicle but into the sky. A second guard stepped from the van, aiming his rifle at the closest of The Three.

The lightning struck in three flaming fingers, with blinding intensity. The crackle of the stroke and the boom of rent air came simultaneously. Keenan knew the van had been struck. The vehicle was on fire and the body of one guard lay on the ground, bits of his clothing blown off. Out of the van the third policeman struggled, a living, blackened torch. He took several tottering steps, then fell straight backward, sending up a puff of smoke. The flames on his front side continued to burn, finishing the immolation. Keenan had a flash memory of the car bombing in Lisburn, of the running soldier, a skeleton dipped in tar. Across fourteen hundred years, Irish enemies continued to incinerate one another.

Guard MacCullen lunged into the van, grabbed a rifle, then flung himself back out and disappeared into the high grasses. A few moments later a rifle shot exploded out of the quivering, golden weedstalks. The bullet missed its target, ricochetting whitely off the wall. The Three flexed their hands. A fireworks display of lightning crashed into the meadow, making the earth tremble with impacts.

Rory came to his feet, weaponless, and sprinted uphill toward the destroyed gate. For several moments, the storm grew ominously still. Then, as MacCullen hurtled headfirst like an Olympic runner, straining to cross the gateway, a stupendous stroke of lightning knifed out of the sky and struck the fence. Blue-white tendrils of electricity leapt across the gate opening, enveloping Rory in energy. The cleaving of the air sent his body flying forward and the lightning trailed him tenaciously. He hit the earth and planed through the mud for several feet, then lay still.

From their place under the tent, Mary and Keenan saw nothing of MacCullen's death. Only the tent's rubberized treatment and their flat positions saved them, as the lightning coursed along the nearby fence and drew inward with its energy. Keenan felt the pull on his body, smelled and tasted the odor of the ionized air.

After a few moments, when no more bolts descended, Keenan stroked down the erect hair on his scalp and dared to look out. The Three had calmly returned to the draining of the lake.

"Now you understand their power," Mary said. "If they see you, you will be killed."

Another lightning bolt hit the earth. Keenan winced. "I won't move."

Without comment, Mary returned her attention to the work of the three sisters.

Twenty minutes later the lake was greatly drained. Several feet of new shoreline showed. The Three lowered their wands. The stream of water collapsed, making the remaining lake water slosh like liquid in a tremendous teacup. The Three climbed off the dam and moved toward the mountain side of the lake.

When they were a good distance away, Keenan asked, "Should we follow them?"

"No," Mary answered. "We wait. Watch!"

Keenan focused the binoculars on the trio, who picked their way along the muddy shoreline, examining the newly exposed rocks. They seemed perplexed by their task. Mary said nothing. Only when they had rejected yet one more crop of boulders did she exclaim with exasperation.

"Ní! Isin all!" she hissed.

Keenan directed the glasses to the place they had just passed, in the cliff. Several slabs of stone seemed to rest against the cliff of rock and, a few feet out from them, like a marker, stood a finger of stone, a reddish, slime-covered tower about twice the height of a man.

The figure of the Frenchman turned back to the tower rock and regarded it thoughtfully.

"Yes, yes!" Mary encouraged, in a whisper.

The man called to his companions, who slipped and slid their way back to his position. The man pointed to one of the massive boulders lying against the cliff. Each of The Three chose a fulcrum from the wood lying in the area. With one standing on each side and the third hanging above, the three attacked the dolmenlike slab. Keenan realized why the Druidesses had chosen healthy male bodies; the straining of muscle was visible even at a distance.

Slowly, the boulder separated from the surrounding muck. The fulcrums stabbed deeper, and the three strained again. Finally, with a great concerted effort, the three figures wrestled the rock upright. It tottered for a moment, then heaved over against the stone tower in front of it. The sharp sound of stone striking stone echoed loudly across the lake.

The tower rock masked the sight beyond. Keenan crawled out of the tent and duck walked along the fence for a better perspective. A small, rectangular cave mouth lay blackly in the side of the cliff. At its bottom, wisps of white smoke slithered toward the lake surface. One by one, The Three lowered their heads and entered the cave.

Keenan sprinted back to the tent, where Mary continued

to view the scene placidly. "They're inside. Shouldn't we go now?"

"Not now," Mary answered. "They need light. Get down! Watch!"

Keenan hunkered down behind a toppled tree trunk and fixed his glasses on the area of the cave. A moment later, the son came out with an unlit torch in his hand and jogged along the lake toward the burning police wagon. With no regard for the bodies lying around the wagon, the son held the torch over the flaming engine until it caught fire. He headed back to the cave at a trot.

"Now they have fire," Mary said, crawling out of the tent and blinking at the rain that struck her wrinkled face. "Now we go."

Keenan set down the field glasses. "Do we need to bring anything?" he asked.

Mary held up her wand. "Yes. I have seen rope in your car."

"Very strong rope," Keenan amplified. "About a hundred feet of it."

"And . . ." A look of vexation swept across Mary's face at the loss of the right word. *"Scián."*

"A knife," Keenan translated. He dug out his pocket-knife. "This is all I have."

"Get the rope!" Mary ordered, hobbling toward the ruined gate. Keenan collected the nylon rope from the Range Rover and ran after the old woman. He averted his eyes as he passed Rory MacCullen's corpse, but was powerless to prevent his stomach from roiling at the smell of charred meat.

As quickly as her game leg would allow, Mary crossed the meadow and followed the old shoreline. Keenan caught up with her as she came to the shoulder of the mountain. "You can't move the rock with magic, can you?" he asked.

"No," Mary said. "I have said. The rock does not move. We must move it."

"I understand. And it took the four of you to push it shut after your clan entered."

"More than four." Mary pointed to the rectangular boulder. From where they stood, Keenan could see for the first time that a large iron ring had been secured in the center of the rock's inner side, now all but rusted away with the centuries. Evidently, the one or two men who could crowd into the opening had guided the rock into place from the inside as well.

Keenan exhaled with despair. "I don't know if—"

"We need a bigger knife," Mary said, without elaboration. "Come!"

Keenan was stunned to see Mary hobbling directly toward the cave mouth. The little wand in her hand seemed puny protection against the destructive forces of her insane sister Druidesses.

The white fog continued to drift out of the cave, around their feet and down toward the water.

"Keep your head up," Mary admonished. "If you breat'e smoke, you will sleep."

Keenan nodded and followed Mary into the cave mouth. The entranceway was not intended for a man his height. Keenan ducked as they descended for about ten paces. There the cave corridor angled up sharply and became ominously dim. A torch set in the wall ahead flickered feebly, turning to yellow the cold fog that now rose to the level of their ankles. The corridor ascended much higher than it had initially descended. Keenan understood that the passageway acted like a water trap, sealing in the supernatural fog that made his ankles tingle and which acted as both a soporific and a preservative.

Mary crouched and began to crawl, straining to keep her head above the fog. Keenan imitated her. Ahead, beyond the final rise of the passageway, other torch lights danced, backlighting what looked like the shape of a cross set in the middle of the opening.

Mary hugged one wall of the corridor and slowly stood.

Keenan moved to the opposite wall. He saw that the old woman was crying, looking across the expanse of a large cavern. No figures could be seen beneath the fog that roiled like living cotton across its bottom, but Keenan knew that her mind's eye was seeing through the vapor, envisioning her beloved people still sleeping, waiting for her return to release them.

An earthen walkway ran through the center of the cavern just above the level of the fog. It had been mounded up for the day of release, so that The Lady and The Three could safely cross the fog to reach a tower of rock and wood that vaulted upward some thirty feet, to the very top of the cavern ceiling. The Three stood at the base of the tower, staring at it with confusion. The rock of the tower had been unaffected by the centuries. The wooden staircase, however, had all but rotted away from the cave's dampness, and the Druidesses did not know how to climb to the top.

Mary tore her gaze from the cavern and regarded the shape in the floor before them. Keenan's eyes had adjusted to the darkness, so that he now recognized it not as a cross but as the hilt and upper blade of a warrior's broadsword. Keenan remembered Excalibur, King Arthur's sword, given back to the faeries of the pool, ready for his reawakening. He recalled the sword of Owen Lawgoch, still clutched in his "red hand," when he would be called awake to defend England. This sword was symbolic; it warned anyone who stumbled upon the cave not to venture farther because noble and fearsome warriors slept beyond.

Mary struggled to pull the sword from the stone floor. Keenan moved forward to help her. "No!" she forbade, in a hissed whisper. "You may not touch until it sees the sun." Mary gave another tug, and it broke free, making a slight ringing noise. Mary and Keenan flattened themselves against the corridor walls. The Three had been arguing with such vehemence that none had heard the sound.

Mary gestured for Keenan to lead the way out. He was greatly relieved to obey. The cave air could not have been

much above freezing. His teeth chattered, despite the
clenching of his jaw. Within moments, they had left the cave
and were again pelted with rain. In spite of the foul weather,
Keenan had never been so glad to see the sky.

Mary pointed up the cliff. "You see the rock there?"

A massive boulder, as big as a refrigerator and flat on its
upper side, poised at the top of the cliff. It thrust outward
about twenty feet above the cave mouth and a little to its
side.

Keenan studied the boulder. "You want to use that to help
close the cave."

"Yes," Mary said.

Keenan unshouldered the rope. "Why do we need the
sword?"

"The rock must be so to the cliff," Mary explained,
pressing her palms tightly together. "No air."

"No space in between."

"Yes."

Keenan accepted the Druidess's explanation without understanding it.

"I will cut the rope when the rock falls," Mary went on.
Her thumb ran at right angles to the length of the blade,
feeling its edge. It looked untouched by the ages, still
miraculously gleaming bright, still razor sharp. Keenan
regarded it with undisguised desire. It was definitely a
ceremonial blade, inlaid with gold and richly decorated with
Celtic lacework. The most valuable part, however, was the
wooden handle, the one part of ancient swords that never
seemed to survive down the ages.

Mary looked up. "Now you climb."

Keenan paid out enough rope for Mary to make a large
loop and secure it around the cave's stone door. Without
waiting for her to begin work, he started up. The angle was
steep, but not nearly as challenging as the climb he had
made in Carrick, to escape Fergus and Mick. His greatest
concern was keeping the rope away from the sharp rock
projections, which threatened to fray it before he had it

secured. He reached the top of the cliff without mishap and fed the rope around the trunk of the nearest sturdy tree. As he was about to secure the end of it about the overhanging boulder, he saw Mary gesturing wildly at him. Instead of securing the other end of the rope about the rock door, she had it looped around her waist. As she waved at Keenan, Mary scrambled feebly upward.

Keenan quickly knotted the rope and began pulling. Although Mary's mouth grimaced as her bad leg absorbed the jolts of a rough ascent, no sound escaped her. About halfway up, she signalled for Keenan to stop pulling. She grabbed the cliff face with both hands and squeezed her small frame into a crevice within the rain-slick surfaces.

The dam keeper came out of the cave. He walked down to the water's edge and scanned the scene. Satisfied that no threats loomed, he searched the shoreline for large pieces of wood. He gathered all his arms could hold and entered the cave without once looking up at the cliff.

Mary signalled for Keenan to let her down. He carefully fed her slack, until she stood again beside the cave mouth. Then he busied himself with tying the rope to the boulder. When he finished, he saw that Mary had skillfully tied off her end of the rope so it would yank the stone back precisely into the cave opening.

From inside the cave echoed a trio of outraged cries. Mary lunged for the broadsword and grabbed it with her boney hands. She glanced anxiously up. "They have seen the sword missing. Make the rock fall!"

Keenan got down on his knees and shoved with all his might. The rock barely budged. He tried again, with even less success.

"Hurry!" Mary called. "They come!"

She did not need to warn him; the outraged screams had clearly grown louder. "Ériu! Ériu, ní!"

Keenan quickly studied the huge rock. Balanced as it was over the edge of the cliff, it would definitely fall if he walked out on the far end and jumped on it. It would fall, but so would he. Almost thirty feet. Maybe into mud if he was lucky, onto solid rock if he was not.

"Christ, this better end it!" Keenan snapped, as he gripped the slack few feet of rope in both hands, backed onto the rock and jumped.

The rock teetered on the cliff edge, defying the laws of gravity. Then it dipped forward. As it pivoted, Keenan collapsed flat on it and threw one hand up to grasp the rope above the rock's surface. The boulder plunged half a dozen feet, then slowed, as the rope twanged tight.

Below, Mary waited with sword upraised. The rope started upward, drawing the stone door off the tower behind it and tugging it over toward the face of the cliff. As it passed the old woman, she swung the broadsword and cleaved the rope. A few nylon strands hung together for a second, until the mass of the falling boulder snapped them. The stone door toppled, slamming into the cliff and sealing it closed once more.

Groaning mightily, the boulder skidded down the cliff's steep face. With his head up and one hand gripping the rope, Keenan rode it like a bronco, expecting death if he let go. Out of the corner of his eye he had seen Mary swinging the sword and knew that his stone sled was about to crash down unrestrained. At the same time, he saw that a jump was survivable. He pushed off with all his strength, danced through the air and landed on his back in a pool of water. The boulder landed an instant later, driving itself deeply into the lake bed, spraying mud and slime and missing Keenan's feet by inches.

When Keenan opened his eyes, Mary stood over him, concern deepening the wrinkles of her old face. *"Is é slán,"* she declared.

"Yes, he is unscathed," Keenan translated sourly, moving each limb in turn, discovering that everything still functioned. "Did we close the cave?"

"Yes. But we must do more."

Keenan groaned. "More?"

"The T'ree must also sleep. We must be sure they do not open the hole." She pointed toward the top of the cliff.

Keenan struggled into a sitting position. Finally, he understood the function of the tower inside the cave. It led up to a vent, which the Druidesses were to use to clear the cave of the sleeping fog.

"There are many stones around the hole. More must be put inside, so the air does not come in," Mary explained. "Then the smoke will come up and The T'ree will sleep."

"You are *Ériu*," Keenan said.

"Yes," she answered, proudly. *"Ingen Ériu An."* Daughter of Eriu the Splendid.

"The power of your name is *ru* with me," Keenan replied, pledging the secret. He felt giddy once again, but not from his fall. *Erie*, the Old Irish word for Ireland, had been named after one of the three legendary goddess-wives of the Tuatha de Danann. The dative form of the name was Erinn. It took little imagination to suppose that the country in which he stood had been named after the very woman he now faced. The revelation tapped an unexpected reserve of energy.

Keenan stood shakily. "All right. Let's climb. This time the long way."

"I must be here," Mary said, fetching the wand from her clothing. "To make the lake come up."

Keenan's laughter rose spontaneously, as it had so frequently of late. "Okay. You do your thing; I'll do mine."

Keenan took his time working his way up into the stand of trees on the small strip of land between the cliff and the mountain shoulder. There he found an unnatural cropping of rocks. As he carried stones back from the cliff edge, he watched Mary hobbling toward the dam, the great sword resting on her left shoulder. He glanced at his watch. It was nearing two o'clock. He picked up his tenth stone. The air vent had to be fairly clogged after this, if indeed it had been open at all after fourteen hundred years. As he fitted the stone securely in place, the clouds seemed to congeal over the lake, into a mass thick enough to touch. Fierce winds blew from several directions at once, bending the trees back and forth like feather fans. Keenan stooped low and fought his way to the cliff edge. He saw Ériu on the opposite side of the lake, her wand raised once more. She made a sweeping gesture. Immediately, the clouds opened up. Rain plummeted in sheets, denser than Keenan had ever seen. He felt as if he had walked under a waterfall. He could not see beyond the edge of the cliff. He stumbled backward, tucking his chin into his chest. If he looked up openmouthed, he knew he would drown.

Keenan retreated under the branches of an evergreen and waited. The rain pelted down unabated for more than an hour. Keenan cursed the woman for leaving him on the cliff; there was no way he could descend during the brutal torrent.

Finally, a little after three o'clock, the rains lightened to a downpour. Keenan left the evergreen's shelter and slowly worked his way down to the lake shore. To his amazement, more than half the water that had been drained was replaced. Visibility was still a matter of yards. When he reached the dam and control house, he found no one. He followed the roadway past the destroyed *Garda* van and up to the gate. Still, Ériu was nowhere in sight. He walked along the fence, to where the tent had lain. It was gone, along with the binoculars. He trotted to the stand of trees where he had hidden the Range Rover. It, too, had disappeared. He reached into his pocket, found no keys, and remembered he had left them in the ignition.

"Damn you!" Keenan yelled, into the wind and the rain. There had been a purpose when she questioned him in detail about the wagon and observed his driving skills. Ériu had stolen the Rover and left him in the middle of nowhere. So much for his importance in her second life.

Keenan looked back in the direction of the dam house. He wondered if the phone still worked after the lightning barrage. Then he wondered if calling from the dam station was a smart idea. Someone would be asked to explain the skeleton, the body without a skeleton, the charred *Garda* van and the three dead policemen. He did not want to be that person. Soaked, shivering and feeling the full strain of the day's efforts, Keenan located the rough road and slogged down it toward the highway.

The lights of Carrick-beg and Carrick across the Suir glowed brightly. The clouds had lifted, and stars twinkled in a purple sky.

"I'm going to Portlaw," the farmer informed his passenger. "Can I drop you off here?"

Keenan longed to say, "Don't you see what shape I'm in, pal? Can't you tell how long I've been out in the rain? Would it be much trouble to drive a mile out of your way?" Instead, he gave the man a half-smile and said, "Sure. I can walk the rest of the way."

The antique pickup shuddered to a stop. Keenan eased out gingerly, closed the door and waved. The truck moved on, red taillight blinking as it turned right in the direction of Portlaw.

The four-mile lift had taken less than ten minutes. In that brief time, Keenan's strained muscles had cramped up on him. Every inch of his body ached, and he felt weary to the bone. Shortly after he had left the forest road from Crotty's Lake, he had seen two cars approaching. Unfortunately, both were topped with blue whirling lights. Keenan had thrown himself flat in the grasses beside the road and watched the cars speed toward the lake. For several miles after that, he was afraid to be seen by anyone on the road, afraid to be linked to the area on that day. He also expected that the Rover might be parked beside the road, just far enough from the lake to allow Ériu to make her final break from him. So he had walked on and on, avoiding the infrequently passing vehicles, stopping often to rest.

During one stretch of lonely walking, Keenan had allowed his thoughts to settle on his part in resolving the horror. He smiled grimly at his achievements. He had not been a

timorous, cowering, academic mouse. Neither his father nor
his brother had fought his battles for him. He had combined
courage, strength and wits in thwarting The Three and in
making at least a tentative friend of the redoubtable Ériu,
The Lady of the Flaming Hair.

Then Keenan thought of Dick Meagher, of how that
friend's opinion of him had lost stock during the supernatural upheaval. Meagher was right: Keenan had not given
much thought to Ireland's present problems. Just as he had
with his own personal problems, Keenan had been too
willing to submerge himself totally in learned studies, deny
that his opinions or acts had any consequence to this
country which was not his home. He loved Ireland. Eire. If
he was willing to devote his life unearthing its past, he owed
it to the land of his forebears to understand the true nature
of its suffering. Perhaps, in some small way, even to help
heal it. A cold wind whipped against his face, turning his
thoughts again to his immediate condition. His new resolu-
tion, however, burned brightly in the depths of his mind.

Finally, near dusk, he had allowed the farmer to pick him
up. The Rover had never come into view.

Keenan crossed the bridge and trudged up to Main Street.
Sitting directly across from the Bessborough Hotel was the
college's Range Rover. He looked inside and found the keys
in the ignition. As he withdrew them, he remembered the
people who wanted him dead. With Ériu's problems at last
put to rest, he needed to concentrate fully on his own
survival. He resolved to call the police from inside the hotel
and tell them that he believed the Rover had a bomb inside
it. Their questions could be explained away by a call to Dick
Meagher. If Dick was still alive. The nightmare never
seemed to end. Keenan strode across the street toward the
Bessborough, eyes shifting warily, in search of a red Ford
Granada.

Seconds after Keenan left the street, a small, black lorry
flashed its headlights on and off three times. In the alleyway
to the side of the Bessborough, a beautiful, young,

redheaded woman responded to the signal. She retreated down the alley, into deep shadow. From a pocket of her raincoat she withdrew a Beretta pistol and fitted a specially made silencer onto its nose. A group of people came into view at the top of the alleyway and paused, bantering gaily. The redhead pressed herself against the wall and waited. If by chance they came in her direction, she would have to hurry out the back of the alley and return later. At least she knew that Keenan MacBreed had returned to the hotel, unescorted. Earlier in the day, her companion had fixed the hotel's service door so that it could not lock. It would be quite simple to go in the alley door and up the back stairs to the second floor. In another five minutes, the black lorry would drive up to the bottom of the alley, and she would be waiting. They'd be long out of Carrick by the time Keenan MacBreed's body was found.

The revelers passed on. The redhead chambered a shell into the pistol and walked toward the service door. As she came nearer, she realized that an old derelict lay sleeping in a pile of garbage, next to the door. The redhead went up on tiptoes. If she could get past the drunk with no disturbance, so much the better. If not, another bullet or two didn't cost much.

Keenan's first action after entering his hotel room was to turn on the radio. The news had just begun. The reporter droned on about political events for a time but finally mentioned the name Ian MacBreed, explaining his Canadian background, terrorist activities and violent death. Keenan sighed deeply. With any luck, the people who had tried to run him down would be in hiding and no longer intent on his death.

Keenan threw his belongings into his suitcases, thought to go down to the Rover for his extra rucksack, reconsidered and stuffed the suitcases to overflowing. All that was left was Mary's bird-of-paradise flower, limp and wilted. He set it by his side as he lifted the telephone to call the police.

The door to the hallway creaked. Keenan's head jerked up. He watched the doorknob turn, staring frozen with horror as the door swung back.

The redhead stood in the hallway, wearing a gray raincoat. In her left hand was a pistol fitted with a silencer. In her right was something long, rolled up in newspaper. She smiled, showing not crooked, yellow teeth but gleaming white perfection.

"Cat'buadach," she said. Victorious in battle.

Keenan stood, dumbstruck. Ériu entered the room, handed Keenan the pistol and lay down her other burden. She unrolled the newspaper. Inside lay the broadsword. It gleamed in the artificial light.

The Lady picked up her wilted bird-of-paradise. "Now, Keenan, I leave no more."

8

Early September 1988

Dick Meagher gazed out of the hospital window in Dublin. The day was fair, but the view was not pleasing. He missed the lush greenness of southeast Tipperary. He reminded himself that he was lucky to be looking at anything. He adjusted the pillow and tried not to cough. The wire holding his chest together hurt like hell when he did.

The day nurse entered the room. "Temperature time, Sergeant," she sang. Dick obligingly opened his mouth. When she turned, he said, through clenched teeth, "Nice bum."

The nurse swung around and tried to hide her look of amusement with a stern expression. "And they want to keep you here another three days! Any man who admires such an old posterior as mine should be up and out, says I."

"Oh, to blazes with ya, Carolyn!" Dick shot back. "I already gave up smoking. The doctor says no more beer and to drop three stone. That's enough, says *I*! I'll be admiring bums on me deathbed."

The nurse took the thermometer from his hand and popped it back in his mouth. Dick retaliated by grabbing his

241

newspaper and raising a paper curtain between himself and the nurse. He *tsked* at the headlines. A lieutenant of the Royal Navy had just been incinerated in his black Capri by an I.R.A. bomb. Right in the middle of Belfast's rush-hour traffic. Three days earlier, in Ballygawley, west of Belfast, the I.R.A. had immolated an entire bus filled with British servicemen returning from furlough to duty in Northern Ireland. Eight had been killed and twenty-seven injured. The death toll of British soldiers killed by the I.R.A. totaled twenty-seven, with almost four months of the year left. To cripple the flow of fighters and weapons into Northern Ireland from the Republic, Social Democratic Party Leader David Owen was calling for the creation of a virtual no-man's-land between the Irelands, made of barbed wire and land mines.

Meagher scanned the rest of the first page and the second. To his relief, he found no articles on the murder and mayhem in Carrick-on-Suir. Less than three weeks, and most of the furor had blown over. He marveled at how quickly the inexplicable could be swept under the carpet. Much the same way as the killing in Northern Ireland could be euphemized as "The Troubles."

The nurse took the thermometer out of Meagher's mouth and studied it. "Just a wee bit high," she judged. "You'll live."

"I should hope so," Meagher returned, "after all the trouble you people have put me through."

A knock on the door interrupted the badinage. Keenan MacBreed peeked into the room.

"Professor MacBreed!" Meagher exclaimed. "Come in, come in!"

The nurse used Keenan's entrance as an excuse to leave. Keenan watched her go past, then gave the guard a sign of his approval.

"They've got to do something to make me happy," Meagher groused.

"I hear you had heart surgery," said Keenan.

"Double bypass, and may it be the last," Meagher said, swinging his legs out from under the covers. "But I'm still here, by the grace of God and the miracles of modern medicine. Speaking of miracles, exactly what was your part in the solving of our mutual problems?"

Keenan shuffled uneasily, then glanced out the window. "Have you been debriefed, Dick?"

"Tomorrow, I understand."

"Well, then, it's not wise to tell you everything until after that. Best to wait until the case is declared closed."

"But is it *truly* closed?" Meagher worried aloud.

"Closed is the perfect word," MacBreed affirmed.

Dick absorbed the words, accepted them, then adjusted his hospital gown. "Speaking of other miracles, modern or ancient . . . how is Mary Liddy?"

Keenan faced his friend. "Mary's dead. They found her body in the alley behind the Bessborough."

"Really? How did she die?"

Keenan smiled wanly. "Old age, I suppose."

"Well, add one more corpse to the count. Father Flynn, Rory MacCullen, those two Special Branches lads, that little French girl. And the rest of her family still not found."

"Nor will they be," Keenan informed. He sat on the edge of the bed, leaned forward and spoke in a low voice. "There's one more, and no one will ever find him either. This one, no one can afford to ask questions about."

"Who?"

"The fellow who tried to run me over with the red car."

Meagher scratched his leg absentmindedly. "Gone, eh? What about his lovely redheaded accomplice?"

"Funny you should mention a lovely redhead. I brought one to meet you, Dick." Keenan stood and moved to the door. "Erin?"

Meagher sat up straight with rapt attention. Through the door walked a young woman of exquisite beauty, with flashing green eyes and a wealth of red hair. She wore a white dress suit and white broad-brimmed hat. Her high-heeled shoes seemed to be giving her a bit of trouble. She smiled warmly as she handed the old *Garda* a bouquet of roses.

"Thank you, love!" Dick cooed, accepting the flowers.

Keenan stepped back in the room and took the woman's right hand in a familiar manner. "Dick, I'd like you to meet Erin Finn."

"Good afternoon, Sergeant Meagher," Erin said, with a hint of exotic accent in her very feminine voice.

Meagher laughed, then winced at his pain. "I think we've met before."

"Have we?" Erin responded.

"Erin Finn, eh?"

"Also Ellen Finnegan, also Eileen Finnerty," Keenan said. "It seems she has three sets of identities, including passports."

"How convenient. I never heard any of it. And what does Miss Finn do for a living, Professor?" Meagher asked.

"Well, until recently she hasn't been doing much of anything," Keenan said. "But now she's ready to apply herself. She thinks she wants to study psychology *and* psychiatry. It seems there are several members of her family driven insane by certain terrible events in their past."

"These members wouldn't still be at large, would they?"

"No, no!" Keenan assured. "They're . . . sedated. In a very safe place."

Meagher inhaled the scent of the roses, then held them out to the woman. "Erin, would you be so kind as to ask the nurse for a vase for these?"

The lady took the bouquet and left the room.

"This is very bizarre, Keenan," Meagher admonished.

"I know. But she's not the evil witch you suspected. She's actually the opposite—the finest person I've ever known."

"What about her body hopping?" Meagher pointed out.

"This is her last . . . for a very long time," Keenan promised. "It was done to protect me, so how can I fault her? I'm taking her back to Boston. Then, beginning next summer, I'll be here in Ireland for good. I've had a long-standing teaching offer from Trinity college, and Erin has to be here, in case the time comes for her people to awaken."

"Oh, Blessed Mother, no!"

Keenan held up his hands. "Don't give yourself another heart attack; that will mean the end of the civilized world as you and I know it, Dick. If they awaken, you can be sure that'll be the least of our troubles."

"You love her, don't you?" Meagher asked.

Keenan sat on the bed again. "Yes. And it's not just for what she can tell me about her times. Not because of the body she's assumed either. I'm convinced she's the best of what a human can be. She's also shown me sides of myself I never knew existed."

"And you've gulled her into thinking you're the golem of our age," Meagher remarked, archly.

"The word is *ollam*. I do know I'm a good teacher. Probably the best one she could have."

"You're a good teacher, all right," Dick agreed. "You're the one who convinced the people of Carrick to let the cemetery be moved. For that you deserve to have your Miss Erin!"

"Frankly, I don't care why I have her. I just thank God I do."

"God is it?" Meagher asked, surprised.

"Another thing I credit her for. She's serious about studying the human mind. Not only in case her people 'wake,' but because she eventually wants to help heal the rift between Northern Ireland and the Republic. She realizes how much of it is attitude and perception."

"A noble desire," Meagher granted.

"And a superhuman task," Keenan added. "So maybe she's exactly the answer to our prayers."

"I should say," Meagher returned, rolling his eyes upward, "with her connections."

"What is so funny?" Erin asked of the two laughing men, as she returned with the roses in a vase.

"Just two Irishmen swapping stories," Keenan answered.

"There's an old expression that sometimes you still hear," Meagher said, with a lilt in his voice. "My poor mind fails me. Perhaps you remember the old way to say 'fairy sweetheart'?"

"Fairy sweetheart?" Erin repeated. She looked at Keenan, as if for permission to translate. He nodded.

"Linnaun shee," Erin said.

"Well, my *linnaun shee,* I suppose I shall have to share you with Professor MacBreed. But you will come visit me in Carrick from time to time, won't you?"

"Forever," the lady with the red hair promised, through her perfect smile.